CHILDREN OF THE MOON

To Char,
with best wishes
from
George

Edinburgh
June 2013

D1445931

CHILDREN OF THE MOON

A Novel

George McBean

authorHOUSE®

AuthorHouse™
1663 Liberty Drive
Bloomington, IN 47403
www.authorhouse.com
Phone: 1-800-839-8640

© 2011 by George McBean. All rights reserved.

Cover Illustration: (Chameleon on a white background.) By George McBean

No part of this book may be reproduced, stored in a retrieval system, or transmitted by any means without the written permission of the author.

This is a fictional story inspired by a series of news reports on the abduction and killing of albino children that appeared during 2009/10 in the Tanzanian newspaper 'The Guardian'. No characters in the story are real and any resemblance to anyone alive or dead is purely coincidental.

First published by AuthorHouse   10/24/2011

ISBN: 978-1-4670-0108-3 (sc)
ISBN: 978-1-4670-0109-0 (ebk)

Printed in the United States of America

Any people depicted in stock imagery provided by Thinkstock are models, and such images are being used for illustrative purposes only.
Certain stock imagery © Thinkstock.

This book is printed on acid-free paper.

Because of the dynamic nature of the Internet, any web addresses or links contained in this book may have changed since publication and may no longer be valid. The views expressed in this work are solely those of the author and do not necessarily reflect the views of the publisher, and the publisher hereby disclaims any responsibility for them.

CONTENTS

A story of albinism in Tanzania

Dedicated to albino children across Eastern Africa in their struggle for equality and against ignorance and superstition

PROLOGUE

It is a brilliant day, as if the sky has been peeled open to let the full power of the sun light up the earth. One of those days that most locals in Dar es Salaam find oppressive and limiting for work, and which westerners associate with relaxing and holidays away from their jobs.

At the university campus a darkened lecture hall is full of young language students. They are all studying English and chatter to each other until a speaker enters. As the man in a wide brimmed hat and dark glasses takes centre stage he hits a small drum, smacking it hard, twice. The noise pierces the air and settles the room into silence. In the style of an **ngoma** (a story teller) the man gives a few words of introduction in Kiswahili. His story has been requested for a series of sessions over the next few weeks.

*'I'd like you to imagine that as the storyteller, I am standing on a **bridge** between thought and action. My job is to persuade people to cross in both directions. To do so, I speak of unthinkable cruelty. I speak facts buried deep in myth. I cast the seeds of progress towards this room of fertile minds. If nurtured these seeds may grow into movements of consciousness, into the taller grasses of change.'*

'Keep not your consciousness empty. Keep not these seeds dry. Confuse not, the pleasure of listening with the satisfaction of doing.'

The speaker pauses a moment from the lyrical Afro-Caribbean style of talk that the students like.

George McBean

'I've been told the topic of albinism is among the most popular choices for your essays on culture this year. As you can see, my colour qualifies me, somewhat, to talk. But before I begin, I'd like to warn you this is not a story about any particular albino. This is the story of Glen Chapman, the late Canadian researcher, who attempted to highlight this condition known as albinism and the consequences of being born with it here in Tanzania.'

Asanteni (Thank you.)

CHAPTER ONE

THE JOB

(Two years ago.)

Glen Chapman is a Canadian anthropologist living in Dar es Salaam with his wife and two children; a boy aged five and a girl, three. He is in his mid thirties and lately he's worked mostly on his tan, after his children are dropped off at school and he returns to their large house on the Msasani peninsula. Pam, his wife, works full time for the United Nations and is gone from dawn until dusk throughout the week. On weekends she often works at home. They have been in Tanzania for two years. Glen accepts an occasional consultancy to keep professionally occupied, but aside from the chores of a house husband he's rarely employed.

The Chapmans are a happy family, by most people's standards, and they make all the right comparisons to believe this happiness themselves. They feel lucky, out of the rat race of western city life and the coldness of a Montreal winter, especially at this time in their children's growth. They deal well with the brief inconveniences of power-cuts in electricity, poor public services and the lack of familiar cultural stimulation. Food is fresh and cheap and the climate is only uncomfortable for a few months a year, in the December-January hot season.

Glen is bringing up his children to appreciate the local cultures that surround them. He takes them to festivals and celebrations so they can see and enjoy these events. Glen tends to ignore the obvious poverty.

His mission is to give explanations for the quirky local customs and quaint traditional beliefs. Pam on the other hand is committed to 'Development,' which, at her level in the UN, means signing cheques over to government counterparts in the monitored-hope that funds will reach their projects.

One day Glen hosts a United Nation's spouse group meeting, and he invites a class of Tanzanian school children to sing and dance for the spouses. Helen, his house girl, is helping with arrangements, since her son attends the school who have been invited. Glen's children are keen to watch so they sit on the grass facing the group. The spouses are seated behind on rows of white plastic chairs, hired for the event.

Four lines of children appear in an orderly way and sing in Kiswahili, while a troupe of six young girls come out in front. They begin to gyrate their hips in separate rhythms from their upper bodies. The choir sings, the troupe dances and the spouses clap.

At the end of the performance Glen's daughter takes to her feet and runs back towards him. She points to the single white face in the school choir and asks,

'Daddy, look its Emanuel, he looks like he comes from the moon, doesn't he?' Glen smiles as he sees the child's point of view. There is one radiant white face, in a sky of singing black children.

'No,' Glen says, 'Emanuel is from Tanzania, just like the other children!'

It is a sunny February day, and while sparrows storm a cluster of bamboo and crows chase a kingfisher from the swimming pool, Glen serves the spouses coffee and cold drinks. A money collection is organised to help the school as the troupe disperses for some refreshments of their own.

A sizable group of nationalities attend these meetings. They plan their month of parenting and leisure responsibilities with the same efficiency as their spouses do their work. A feast of different shaped cookies, made from the same local dough and sugar mix, are offered as national delicacies from several countries. As a large group of members mingle and munch, Glen is taken aside by Martin Bryan from the Canadian High Commission.

'Hey Glen, are you working on anything at the moment?'

'Nothing. Except this.' Glen gestures towards the event that is occupying his time.

'No jobs on the side? No writing assignments?'

No, honestly, cross my heart and hope to die!'

'We are looking for someone to do some research and wondered if you might be interested.'

Glen rubs his index finger and thumb together, enquiring if money is involved.

'Yes, it's a paid assignment. We need some background information on the recent killings of albino children in Shinyanga!'

In an instant, Glen's pleasant day and his idle lifestyle are put on hold. He considers this proposal and its effect on his leisure time. Coincidentally, and Glen is a great believer in coincidences, he watches the albino boy Emanuel walk across his garden to greet his mother Helen.

'Tell me more Martin.'

'We have an interest in finding out about this terrible spate of abductions and mutilations of albinos up-country, especially the role of witchcraft in all this. There is also some concern among diplomats that there may be international links to these crimes.'

'International links?'

'What I mean is the demand for body parts across borders from countries like Burundi, Rwanda, Uganda and Kenya.'

9

'Let's talk more, somewhere away from all these cookies.'

Glen is no stranger to the superstitions of rural faith healers. He has already published a book of his research on the Inuit in Northern Canada. He has spent months living and talking with Shamans in different parts of the world about their practices and beliefs. He's noted an increase in appreciation of ancient myths and practices in modern literature and cinema, where there was once only ridicule. Ethnic groups are now regularly credited with abilities to talk to spirits and to live in harmony with nature. Glen however is no expert on belief systems. He is more a social scientist at heart. His curiosity is spiked by this offer simply because he has never studied anything as brutal as human sacrifices before.

'Ok, you have aroused my interest. When would I start?'

'Tomorrow. We can draw up the contract then.'

'OK, this is a bit of well timed good luck!'

Glen spontaneously agrees to take on the Canadian research assignment. Little does he suspect that this decision will change his life forever!

In a lush quarter of Bariadi District in Western Tanzania, where *matoke* bananas grow and baboons roam free, like citizens, Kaka Damu is a popular faith healer. He has learned his trade from his father and is considered by many to be a witch doctor. Witchcraft is outlawed in Tanzania but there are hundreds of thousands of faith healers operating with government licences.

Kaka's father has helped him translate some of his older tribal remedies into meaningful health solutions. He has helped in curing a variety of local ills with medicine derived from aloe vera and other tropical plants. He still invokes ancestral spirits at his local shrine but he keeps a low profile from the authorities when he does this.

Kaka is secretive, although he openly conducts 'special' faith meetings, once a year and has a large cult following for these events. In this part of the country, health posts are scattered, often under-staffed and poorly equipped. Many are too far for villagers with serious or immediate health problems to reach, so traditional healers are the first port of call.

Kaka Damu (Brother Blood) was given his name by his father after he joined in ritual blood sacrifices at a tender young age. It all began with chickens, under his father's supervision, but once he reached his teens he moved up the food chain to goats and occasionally cows.

Nearly every sacrifice that is performed in public is surrounded by colourful ceremony and ritual. In recent times, some of the ceremonies have been made safe and theatrical under the guise of cultural identity, with dancing and dressing up taking precedence over the slaughter.

Kaka has never been to school or to Dar es Salaam but he knows from experience that sickness is not the only thing that bothers his clientele. A bout of misfortune can also be a source of income for him. It is the risky side of his business, since people who have fallen on hard times have no money to pay, but he gets round this with some creative thinking. He demands that a portion of what people earn in the future is given to him, if he initiates a turn of luck. In the day to day workings of villages, there are always a number of people facing hard times. It is during Kaka's 'special-good-luck ceremonies' that his creative skills are most profitable. The more superstitious and desperate the client is for a change of luck, the more elaborate Kaka makes the ceremony. Kaka knows the importance of mystery and surprise in his trade. If he can shock or amaze a client with inventive or outrageous displays, the rewards are greater. With no public participation, these private sessions don't cost him anything to set up and it is always kept secret by his clients and performers.

There are also seasonal aspects to Kaka's trade. When the rains come, children suffer from diarrhoea and shortly afterwards contract malaria from the increase in the mosquito population. Fathers and mothers search desperately to find a convenient healer during these busy seasons.

Sometimes in the rainy season Kaka will see five to ten families in a day. When the wet season ends, there is a long dry spell and Kaka is then approached by farmers who are desperate to bring rain. In the village Kaka's powers are both revered and feared.

————◦◉◦————

Pam Chapman walks naked through her marble floored house when her children are asleep. She loves the feel of marble on her bare feet. The tease of a cool breeze is refreshing through Dar's sauna-like nights. Once her house help, Helen, has finished work and gone to her quarters and the curtains are drawn, Pam feels liberated. She regularly takes an evening swim to cool down, washes her body with local aloe-vera soap and rinses her hair with sea-weed shampoo. She feels in good shape, despite the extra weight she gained during pregnancy. She feels lucky to have quickly regained her figure after the children were born. Pam believes she can maintain her shape more through her genetic French Canadian ancestry than any serious efforts with exercise. If her mother is anything to go by, she believes she will keep in shape well into her fifties.

Pam has taught Helen to keep the Chapman's marble floor clean with a mixture of vinegar and water. This instruction on cleaning and washing is the nearest Pam gets to frequenting with the locals. Pam likes Helen because she is neat in her work. She likes to have beautiful things surrounding her, so it helps that Helen is young and attractive. She is Maasai and has the long slender figure of a Nilo-Hamitic woman.

In her bathroom Pam lights candles mainly because the neon strip light is not flattering. In the mirror she makes a ritual of cream applications, believing it will slow down the appearance of wrinkles, one of her major concerns. She monitors the aging process each evening with the efficiency of a United Nation's Planning Officer. She grumbles at the appearance of blemishes and shines moisturiser on like polish. She superstitiously closes all bottle tops and caps on her cosmetics, as if the healing spirits may fly away if she does not. She regularly argues with Glen about leaving toothpaste tops off the tube. She insists he keep his untidy habits to the part of the house she has designated as his.

Recently Pam's intimate moments with Glen have been endured more than enjoyed. For almost a year she has been sexually reserved. She has replaced the abandon of their early years with a limited and more orchestrated response. Because her career barely survived two pregnancies, she does not want to become pregnant again. She waves packets of condoms at Glen when he makes advances because although she loves both her children she is no longer willing to let another child interfere with her career prospects.

Pam also senses Glen is pre-occupied and distant as soon as they finish making love. It has become such a well practiced, twice a week, routine that Pam knows what to expect. Lately she has questioned the frequency and cut down their sexual liaisons by half. She believes this might make Glen more appreciative of their times together.

At work Pam flirts shamelessly with her fellow workers. This openness with others is a trait she shares with Glen. They are both outgoing and flirtatious people. Both seem to understand that marriage is not about submission to one person alone. Pam knows that in reality there are hundreds of potential partners out there whom they could both easily live with. They have discussed this point. It is a poor relationship where people only have each other. Their relationship is made richer with the intellectual kinship and support of many other people. It is this basic mutual understanding and its consequent freedom that keeps them together.

—————⊙—————

After further discussion at the Canadian High Commission, Glen finalises the details of his contract and makes plans for a field visit to the district where most albino abductions have been reported. He is provided with a set of contacts living in the worst affected areas, to help him gather information. Before leaving, he is advised to look at several short films on albinism posted on YouTube and to read a collection of newspaper and magazine articles.

Back at his house Glen sits on the porch listening to The Killers at full volume, drinking fresh mango juice and shuffling handfuls of roasted cashew nuts into his mouth while he studies. His children jump in and out of the swimming pool, screaming and splashing in an excited frenzy. Glen calls out to them above the music.

'Remember, keep your sun cream on, otherwise you're both grounded.'

They pretend not to hear through the blare of Mr Brightside.

Glen repeats his demand for sun cream coverage more menacingly.

This is the one threat that the children take seriously from Glen. They have already experienced his dreadful bans on watching TV cartoons, imposed after they forgot to protect themselves from the sun. They skip across the sandstone tiles, too hot for walking on, to where Glen is reading. They present their bodies, like baby baboons for grooming. Glen holds their hands and paints the underside of their arms. They laugh as he tickles them and slaps on the lotion. He leaves a thick coat of white cream on the tops of their feet and shoulders. He lathers the rest of them in this screen of Sun Factor Fifty, applied with well-practiced hands. The children run off once more to splash and play. Glen returns to his canvas chair and reads.

In the last few years some thirty-one albino children have been reported abducted and murdered for their body parts in Tanzania. Even more children have had their limbs amputated and survived. Sometimes children's arms and legs have been hacked off in front of their parents. The illicit trade in body parts has been going on secretly for some time but this recent increase in reports is unprecedented. It is a gruesome story filled with misfortune, bad luck, and hard times, along with curses, cures, witchcraft and basic criminal brutality disguised as custom. Glen thinks there is little one can do to exaggerate such a story since the facts themselves are so extreme.

The plight of those born with albinism, has recently gained International attention with the publication of some photos taken during an attack on a seven-year-old albino girl. She lost both her arms. Another story tells of a boy the same age, taken and killed.

Glen finds all this hard to read and returns to his cluttered work room. In the midst of this chaos of books and artefacts he has set up space for himself. He prints out a few images and pins them to a cork wall board. He spreads the reports across his desk, and tries to make some sense of this absurd cruelty. Glen decides the images are too graphic for home display. He does not want his children to see these on his project wall. He returns the images to a work folder and sits again, within sight of his children, reading more background information.

Tanzania, with a population of some 40 million, has a comparatively high number of children born with the condition known as albinism. Estimates range from ten thousand to some one hundred and seventy thousand individuals scattered across the country. It becomes clear that attacks have not taken place in every district. However, as a result of the publicity given to these attacks, most albinos throughout the country are now living in a state of fear for their lives.

That night after the children have gone to bed, Glen pours Pam an extra large glass of Merlot, and begins to explain his plans.

'I have to visit at least one of the regions where albino children have been gathered for their protection.'

'How long will you be gone?'

'Two or three weeks! I am going to drive myself there.'

'Why so long?'

'I need to conduct interviews with albino children as well as with some local faith-healers and witch doctors if I can find them.'

'Don't forget the St Patricks Day Ball, at the Kempinski. We have tickets and they cost eighty dollars each.'

'No I won't forget. To be sure!' Glen says with a brogue.

Glen drives for three days to the Shinyanga Region, near Tanzania's western border and is met by Crystal Mpira, a Doctor stationed there by the Ministry of Health. Glen begins to speak enough Kiswahili to get through the pleasantries of an official introduction. Although there may be some initial suspicions of Glen, he is confident he can raise Dr Mpira's interest in his assignment. She is a woman in her early thirties from Arusha who speaks far better English than Glen speaks Swahili. She did a Masters in Public Health at the London School of Hygiene and Tropical Medicine and spent a year in the United Kingdom before becoming a doctor. She is posted to a remote area, and seems to welcome the conversation.

Crystal takes Glen into the Dawakubwa clinic where she has assembled a few families with albino children. One mother has twin albinos, Doto and Kunwa along with their black baby brother. They have come seeking refuge after hearing reports of a killing near-by. There are also two other albino children that Crystal describes as having been dumped on her doorstep by their families.

Glen spends the next few days interviewing all family members at the clinic. He then takes off with a guide into the remote bush areas to speak to local faith healers.

Glen collects information on local beliefs and superstitions. He gauges that the current efforts to prevent more killings are somewhat lax. Away from the glare of publicity, sitting in villages, talking to people, Glen finds no urgency on the part of local villagers to do anything about the situation. There is some concern, but there is also, he feels, a disturbing fatalistic acceptance of things as they are. This is in great contrast to the view of the families who have gathered in Crystal's health post and who are desperate for help.

'There is nothing different about these children, except they are born with a skin condition that is far more noticeable than in other parts of the world.' Crystal gives Glen an explanation. 'The fierceness of our African sun along with an out-door lifestyle puts these children at greater risk of contracting skin cancers and is one of the main reasons they have a life expectancy as low as thirty five. They obviously have the same potential for growth and happiness as all newborn children, but because of their skin colour, they are treated as different. And through being treated different many actually become different. Many find it difficult to make relationships and parents seldom encourage these children to go to school. As a result, very few in the past progressed beyond primary school.'

Glen also interviews the local police chief who shows some genuine outrage at the killings. He says he is prepared to hunt these killers down but doesn't know where they come from. The local healers in his district are docile and harmless old men and he believes their practice will die out in one generation. Glen realises his work is becoming more complex and interesting by the day, but he also recognises he will need more time to complete his report.

He arranges a return visit with Dr. Crystal so he can continue his research and says he will contact her soon with more details.

During his stay in Shinyanga there are no reported incidents of killings from anywhere in the country.

—————————⟨⟨○⟩⟩—————————

Kaka Damu's quiet home is disrupted by the wailing of a solitary man. There has been heavy overnight rain and as the sun rises and the frogs rejoice, the man kneels outside Kaka's unfinished concrete home and beats himself across the chest. He is a simple but rich local farmer that Kaka has helped many times in the past. This time the farmer is beside himself with grief. His wife is missing, along with his only son. Kaka tries to calm him down enough to hear his story.

'Rest yourself Mafabi. Everything will be fine. Tell me what has happened and how I can help you.'

Kaka kneels beside the man and continues. 'What is wrong?'

'My house, my land, my wife, my son, they are all gone!' The farmer speaks through sobbing breaths.

'Don't worry, I can help you, things will be OK.' Kaka says.

Kaka stands, as if to accept this consultation, and also as if to affirm his confidence and power. He then takes a lion-skin headband from the rafters of his roof and places it on his head for the rest of the conversation.

The farmer tells Kaka that a freak rainstorm has taken his house. The whole building has been swept away during a river flood which also submerged half of his farm land. Traces of his wood and mud-brick home have been found three miles down-stream, but there is no sign of his son or his wife.

'*Pole-sana*' (very sorry) Kaka says.

'I missed the flood by moments, after going outside at night to secure my cows. I left my family sleeping and when I returned I was cut off. Water forced its way through the bend in the river and my farm disappeared. Help me Kaka. Speak to the spirits. I cannot cope with this much bad luck at one time. You have helped me in the past. I have money in the bank. You know I can pay you well.'

Kaka then makes the quiet suggestion that only a sacrifice of special significance will change Mafabi's luck. The farmer stops sobbing as his mind clutches to this ray of hope. He believes passionately that Kaka's powers can return things to normal.

'I will summon friends who are well placed to obtain strong medicine.' Kaka then warns, 'this offering does not come cheap. It is dangerous to obtain. It will cost 260,000 shillings.' ($200)

Moses Mafabi asks no more questions. He nods understanding. He has realised immediately from the price that the sacrifice will involve the body part of an albino child and he is willing to pay.

Glen calls Pam on his mobile phone as he approaches Dar es Salaam. He has driven his beat-up Land Rover almost non-stop for two days. It is a Saturday, Pam is at the Yacht Club and the children play in the sea. After parking his car Glen races into the ocean fully clothed. He splashes his children, causing squeals of delight. He is always surprising them, playing jokes and generally exciting them, too much for Pam's liking. He lifts his daughter out of the water and places a large raspberry sound on her tummy. He does the same with his son and warns both of them he cannot taste their sun cream. He chases them up the short beach into the shade to be sprayed and covered with protective cream once more. They protest, pointing to the African children still frolicking in the ocean.

Glen sits, in his wet clothes, next to Pam in her bikini and tells her briefly about his trip. The sun is so hot; his clothes are almost dry before he finishes talking.

'It was a very emotional trip. I had several meetings with some pretty terrified families. There is a doctor there who is very clued into the situation. She was great, very helpful and hospitable.'

Pam looks over at Glen, trying to interpret his use of the word hospitable.

'The drive and the scenery are spectacular. I need to go back there and I thought we could all go together?'

'Together?'

'Yes. Us, and the children.'

'When?'

'Don't you have some holidays you can take? Soon.'

'Yes, but we usually save these for Canada, our parents and the in-laws.'

'Look at this as a chance to see the country you are helping to develop. We can stop off and see Kilimanjaro and the Serengeti on the way back. Come on, the children will love it.'

After two years in an air conditioned room at the UN offices in Dar, Pam knows she needs to see more of the country, so she agrees on one condition. She insists they drive her more luxurious but less hardy Land Rover Freelander, because it has air conditioning. Glen texts a message to Dr. Crystal at the clinic, informing her of his return visit. He will arrive with his wife and two children in a few weeks time.

———◆———

Kaka Damu summons a group of helpers he calls the 'Tatu J's' (Three J's), since their three names are Juma, Joseph and John. They are all local men Kaka has known since he was a boy. John is a landless labourer always desperate to find work and will do just about anything he is asked. Juma and Joseph are older and are the local circumcision specialists. They are also short on work because of the government's moves to professionalise the practice. Kaka disagrees with the government policy. He knows the circumcision business is still flourishing in most parts of the country. But, recently after a boy died of complications in Nzega, the authorities asserted pressure to put more control on the practice. It now costs half of what Kaka makes on a ceremony to keep a few local officials turning a blind eye to his traditional antics. Kaka believes it is wrong of the government to interfere—what do they know, except to impose rules that others exploit, or how to siphon taxes! It was the Nzega boy's time and the spirits took him. What a sad loss for the community to outlaw the ancient ways of an important festivity. Much is learned by youth about life, duty and pain if they go through a proper Kaka circumcision.

Juma and Joshua are the best at their trade; they are great ritual performers, good at scaring audiences into belief and customers into cures. They are all round entertainers. Kaka keeps all his special jobs for them. He tells the Tatu Js of Mafabi's plight and how they can all benefit from helping him.

After several days, the river level drops from an all time high and a good part of Mafabi's land is recovered. He thanks Kaka for this outcome, believing even more in Kaka's powers. He also asks Kaka if he has made any progress with efforts to help him find his wife and son.

Kaka is reluctant to talk. He tells Mafabi only that there will soon be a new offering for the spirits, a fresh 'cut' for good luck. Kaka keeps it to himself that he has sent his helpers out across the bush to a Health clinic where he knows albino children have gathered.

———————⊪⊙⊪———————

Glen's children are well behaved on the road west passed Dodoma. As they drive Glen tells more of his local folklore stories. He explains how it is believed that Baobab trees were planted upside down by a great God, and that local healers regard them as a special house for good spirits. They see whirlwinds of dust rising up into the clear blue sky and then disappearing. Glen tells the children that these whirl winds are named 'Ladies tempers,' by local Maasai, on account of their quick appearance and their short life-span.

Pam gives Glen a look of sexist disapproval.

'There, see what I mean kids?' Glen says, pointing to Pam's reaction.

When Glen announces that they will not see the animals of Serengeti until the way back, his boy becomes annoyed; he wants to see animals now. He's not interested in visiting a village. He unclips his seat belt to protest loudly into Glen's ear. Pam quickly tells him to get back into his seat, and in the struggle to secure him catches his finger in the seat belt clip. The boy cries as his finger bleeds and Pam tells him to suck his finger and it will heal. This is an acceptable family custom and the boy obeys, sucking his own blood, until Glen stops the car to administer a more efficient Mediplast.

Pam assures her son that the journey will all be worth the wait, that the village will be 'cool,' and she promises she will try and take the boy to meet a witch doctor!

When they arrive at Dawakubwa, Crystal meets them with friendly handshakes. She squats down and brushes her hand through the small girl's blonde hair. She then shows the family into a makeshift room at her clinic. It is the same room where Glen conducted his interviews with the albino children. Crystal has set up beds with mosquito nets.

'Where have the albino children gone?' Glen asks.

'The whole group left unexpectedly, a few days ago, without any warning or explanation.' Crystal says.

The Chapman family bed down for the night, with Pam reading the children a passage from their favourite book 'Maasai and I.'

————◉————

Juma knows exactly where to find the children he is looking for. He's been told they are gathered in Dawakubwa Health clinic. The Tatu Js stay off the main road and make their own trail with the help of a full moon. Juma tells the others what he wants them to do when they reach the clinic and he supplies them with a *panga* (local cutlasses) and some bottled *pombi* (local beer) to make the job easier. As the village comes in sight, he insists they should not arouse suspicion as to what they are doing here. There are some people from their own village living in this area but they must avoid contact. If approached, they will act as if they are undertaking a regular circumcision tour. They need to be quick and careful when bringing the *ku chinga* (sacrifice) back to Kaka Damu.

Juma sees them first, through the window of the clinic, it's a whole albino family, he thinks. He is surprised but climbs quietly into the room beside them. Joseph and John enter through the front door.

The albino man wakens at their noise. As he moves to get up, he is struck on the head with a wooden *rungu* (knobkerrie club). It is not a heavy blow, which could easily have cracked his skull. Juma strikes with just enough power to render the man unconscious.

The Tatu J's are so silent, the woman is not disturbed; she sleeps through the abduction. The men leave the parents and 'albino' daughter and take the boy.

Later, when the girl notices her brother has gone, she crawls into her mother's bed and falls asleep between her parents.

Along with the dawn and the morning songbirds comes the commotion.

Pam notices there is blood on the pillowcase next to Glen's head. She is confused and concerned and shakes him as she calls out his name.

Glen responds slowly and begins swearing as he recovers consciousness. He is so loud with his shouting he startles his daughter. 'Men were here.' he calls as he jumps from under his mosquito net. He looks around the room. Pam follows his gaze to the empty bed and they both realise at the same time, their son is gone.

Glen runs outside calling Douglas's name and screaming in limited Swahili. '*Ulishu wahii kumuona mwangu.*' (Have you seen my son?) People begin to gather in response to the sight of Glen's panic rather than his words. Some children run off to bring Dr Crystal. Glen scrambles for his cell phone and calls Martin Bryan at the Canadian High Commission, because he realises immediately what danger his son might be in.

Pam is still inside the house holding her daughter tightly and gripped by fear. But somehow she follows the procedures she has been taught in security training. She is desperate not to display any of her fears to her daughter. People are now running in and out of the clinic. No one can find the boy. She calls the UN security number on her speed dial to report the incident. She hesitates to use the word 'kidnapped' but knows it will spark an almost immediate response. She begs for urgent help as her legs buckle under her. She squats on the floor answering predetermined questions that are fired at her by the UN Security Officer.

'Yes, we are isolated but in no immediate danger ourselves. No, they don't know where the boy has been taken. Yes, we will remain where we are until help arrives.'

Glen recovers some control of his emotions after Crystal arrives with the village police chief. She has heard the commotion and has begged the officer to form a search party immediately. She also takes a moment to clean Glen's head wound and tells him the cut is not serious.

Pam refuses to believe all is lost and questions Glen as to the purpose of such a kidnapping. Why Douglas? What sense? Is a ransom needed?

Glen knows only too well what the consequences could be if the kidnappers are searching for an albino child. He keeps this thought to himself.

'Kuna tofauti gani' (What's the difference?) he keeps saying to himself. If the kidnappers are looking for albino body parts, who, in such unthinkable circumstances, will be able to tell the difference? The thought overwhelms him and he runs outside to throw-up in a bush outside the clinic. His insides are churning with emotion. When he returns, he reassures Pam they will get their boy back. His brief studies of the rituals surrounding such abductions tell him he does not have much time. *This is what it must be like for all the families that fall victim of this practice.* Glen's research suddenly takes a very personal turn.

Pam resists being overcome by the full realisation of what has just happened. Glen realises he has little idea of what to do next. Despite all his knowledge, which should help him, he can do nothing.

Crystal also knows the consequences and tries to comfort Pam. As she holds onto her daughter, Pam keeps asking Crystal if she thinks the kidnapping is racially or financially motivated.

'Crystal, will a ransom help?'

'No Pam. Don't worry, we'll find your boy. This is a mistake. I'm sure of it. No one here will harm him.' Crystal tries to sound positive.

Pam continues to convince herself that all this is related to an increase is kidnappings for ransom. Across the country, new statistics show that the ease with which mobile phone users can transfer money has resulted in kidnappings, a completely new phenomenon in Tanzania. The money is virtually untraceable. Pam knows the statistics are small but that such incidents are on the rise. She searches the clinic once more, in the hope of finding a ransom note. She does not dare think her son has been captured for ritualistic sacrifice. This is all too horrific—all too 'boil-the-white-man-in-a-pot' Africa.

———◄(◦)►———

The main difference between an albino child being abducted and a young white boy is in the response to the kidnapping. Within hours, the UN has dispatched several vehicles from a security firm they employ in Mwanza, the nearest large town. The main UN security advisor is alerted in Dar es Salaam and UN Headquarters in New York is brought into the communication loop. People in Manhattan are being woken from their sleep with this news before the story has fully circulated in the village surrounding the clinic. Glen's call to the Canadian High Commission also prompts them to hire a helicopter and dispatch their military advisor to help coordinate the search. Within hours, both will be on site at the clinic.

A local farmer comes forward to the police chief with some information that he has found fresh tracks across his land. These tracks clearly leave the area of the clinic and appear to be made by three adults and a child. He leads the police chief and Glen to the scene. Glen is pleased to see the footprints of his son; it means the boy is walking and therefore still alive. He is unsure how many hours ahead the kidnappers are and he has no idea where their final destination might be. The local farmer also identifies a separate set of three footprints coming into the village on the same route. They look like the same people. If they are strangers to this area they will likely follow their own route back out.

Glen digs out his detailed road map and offers to drive the police chief and two other men to a road that crosses the direction of the kidnapper's trail. He draws a pencil line on the map in the direction of the footsteps

25

and the police chief instructs a group of volunteers to carefully follow the trail by foot. Glen then drives the chief and two men as fast as he can to the point on the map where the dirt road crosses his pencil line. It is very difficult to gauge an exact crossing point but as they approach the area Glen drives slowly looking for any disturbance in the bush. His windows are open and they all look for signs. Fresh cattle tracks make it difficult until suddenly the police chief calls for him to stop.

Glen thinks the police chief has spotted something, but in fact he has smelt something . . . something human. Glen follows him cautiously into some long grass, remembering the damage a *rungu* can make on a skull. The police chief has his revolver drawn although he has forgotten to sign out ammunition for it and it is empty. A few meters from the road, the police chief points out a twist of fresh human faeces. Flies are swarming around and it gives off a pungent smell. At the side of the stool are a set of only three adult footprints. The police chief quickly finds the continuation of these on the other side of the road and tells Glen to leave the car and follow them.

Glen is visibly troubled. He tries hard to interpret the signs. Three sets of footprints but no fourth. It could mean the boy is now being carried or has been abandoned. It could also mean the worst; that the kidnappers have removed what they came for and are now less restricted in their escape.

Glen wants to head back on the trail; at least to find the spot where the four sets of footprints become three, but the police chief disagrees with splitting up the group.

'We should all stick together,' says the police chief. 'Greater numbers and my revolver will make the abductors give up if captured. Once caught, they will tell us where the boy is, if he's not in fact still with them. To go back when the criminals are moving ahead could mean that they escape.'

Glen insists he wants to go back. He gives his mobile phone with its link numbers to Pam, the High Commission and also the helicopter pilot to the police chief. He tells the police chief to use it as he moves forward following the kidnappers. He also shows the chief how to use the mobile phone's sat-nav to identify his actual location. Glen then sets off back on the trail, while the police chief and the two others follow the footprints of the kidnappers.

Glen's bush skills keep him on the trail for half an hour but then after taking a couple of wrong turns he reaches a large piece of open savannah where a young herdsman is grazing his cows. The trail is completely obliterated by now. He manages to ask the herdsman in broken Swahili if he has seen any men with a young boy. The young man replies he saw three men at dawn, but there was no child with them. Glen's only alternative is to return to the car. Once there he waits, feeling lost without his phone and overcome to the point of tears. He bangs the steering wheel with his hands and cries so loudly he almost misses the sound of a helicopter overhead. Glen jumps out of the Freelander and waves into the air just in time to see it bank and fly back lower over the road.

Glen can see there is no place for it to land but he runs into the widest stretch of clearing in the hope that he might see a signal from the cockpit. He prays it will be his son in the arms of someone on board. The helicopter slows and hovers overhead before lowering an empty water bottle with a message inside. Glen braves the hail of dust and spray to grab the bottle. Once delivered, the helicopter flies off. Glen catches a glimpse of the police chief and his men on board, but no child.

The note instructs Glen to drive back to the clinic. The police chief has followed the trail as far as he could, and then the helicopter picked him up. They are now going to continuing the search from the air. There has been no sign of the kidnappers. In an effort to be positive, the police chief has written that one set of footprints had seemed deeper indicating that someone was carrying the boy and that he was therefore still alive. Glen takes little consolation from this news, since he knows that the remains of his son might weigh a killer down as much as a live child.

Glen drives back into the clinic alone and despondent until he approaches the gate. He sees people running and waving at him joyously. As he parks the car Pam comes running out with a smile on her face. The boy is safe. He has wandered back into the clinic on his own after being abandoned at first light. He is inside, playing with his hand held Nintendo game.

Pam has notified the helicopter pilot and the police chief. Dramatic as this has been, the incident is concluded in a matter of hours. It's not enough time to have a lasting impact on those involved, or is it?

The helicopter pilot offers to give Pam and the children a ride back to Dar but she declines. She wants to keep the family together and to act as normally as they can for the sake of the children. In fact at this stage she refuses to accept any link of the abduction with ritualistic killers. She keeps talking of the failed kidnapping attempt. The alternative is just too horrible to imagine. They prepare to drive back to Dar together immediately. They will save the game parks, the wild animals and the natural beauty of Africa for another family safari.

———◉———

As news of the kidnapping leaks out of the UN community in Dar es Salaam, there is some international interest in the story. On their arrival home Glen's house is visited by a group of reporters and he's asked questions by the western journalists. First, does he feel the response from the local authorities was adequate? Glen heaps praise on the local police chief for his help; he also mentions the swift response from the UN and the Canadian High Commission, but he laments that the kidnappers have not yet been identified or caught.

The second question asked is whether Glen feels the kidnapping was racially motivated or whether the abductors were looking for an albino boy.

'No, I don't think this crime has any racial motive.' Then in a calculated way Glen dares to speak his thoughts aloud. 'I do not think this was an isolated attack against a white child. I believe this was yet another attempt to abduct an albino child for the purpose of sacrifice.'

'Do you have any proof of this Mr Chapman?'

'No, but I do have a list of confirmed reports of albino abductions in this area. It is too much of a coincidence not to link these events. In a peace loving country like this, no citizen should live in fear. There are superstitious criminal motivations at work here not racial. And it will only be when they are met with a stronger motivation by the authorities and general public to stamp these out that albino citizens and their human rights will be honoured.'

Glen's story and statement runs in the local newspapers the next day on page three as "Kidnappers plot foiled by authorities.' And in a Canadian tabloid newspaper with the front-page headline, 'White Canadian child survives albino kidnapping scare in Africa.'

A few days later, buried on page six of the Citizen Newspaper in Tanzania, there is a one-inch column story of another young albino boy being found in a river in Shinyango. His throat had been cut and his left leg removed. The story sits between a paragraph on the rise in local road deaths, and a short article on Kenya's 2.5 million registered orphans.

───────

As the floods completely recede on Mafabi's farm, the bodies of his wife and son are found. Mafabi is grief stricken but thanks Kaka Damu for his work and he sees the recovery of his family's remains as a consolation. The secret sacrifice he contracted was not strong enough to find his family alive, but at least now Mafabi knows the truth of their fate. He need search no more. It is a small indication that his luck has changed.

CHAPTER TWO

THE EXPERTS

Over a period of weeks Douglas tells his mother and father only small parts of his ordeal. He says that after he was taken, he was dragged by the arm and carried until first light, when one of the men suddenly stopped. They looked at him and ruffled his hair before arguing with each other. They then suddenly let him go. He ran all the way back to the clinic without stopping. He ran fast, he was not afraid.

Douglas does not elaborate on his story and Pam does not press for any more details than he is willing to provide in his own time. Pam decides she wants Douglas's haircut short as if to erase any trace of her son's abductors touch. Since their return home Gail, her daughter, has also not said much about their ordeal. Although Gail still cries on occasion, mostly when Douglas creeps up on her pretending to be a witch doctor.

Outside the local hairdresser is a display of wall paintings of David Beckham next to the hip-hop star Fifty Cents. Both celebrities are painted the same colour of grey-white, rendered in a flat amateur style on the bright yellow wall. Pam has always found the hairdressers and painted mini-buses in Tanzania amusing. It's a reflection of the ever-increasing influences from abroad on some ways of life here. Western hip hop and football teams being the most influential. Douglas picks this hairdresser, since he plays soccer and he relates to the image of Beckham. Pam sits both children down on stools in the salon.

'Shave it like Beckham,' she says in front of Douglas. She's consciously positive around the boy at every moment. She has already convinced her son to go for the shaved-head style but she is also doing this for more practical reasons; to rid him of the lice he's gathered on their trip up country. Pam has already re-dyed her own blonde hair after her return, believing that the bleach will kill anything she might have picked up. Gail is a natural blonde and Pam gives her a gender reprieve from completely shaving her head. She chooses instead to have Gail's hair treated with lotion then trimmed.

After they leave the salon, the local hairdresser picks up the cuttings of Gail's hair. It is beautiful unusual and bright coloured hair, so fine and thin. The hairdresser puts the strands of hair into a small plastic bag and keeps it for good luck.

Douglas settles back into his morning school in Dar without showing any negative signs from his experience. In all, it was a six-hour ordeal and although Glen knows time is not a factor to measure the effects of trauma he, Pam and his teachers are amazed at Douglas's composure.

Pam does not yet realise that Douglas's method of accepting the witch doctor, who came in the night, covered his mouth with cloth and dragged him outside, making him pee himself, forcing him to walk for miles, has been the belief that the man was a friend of his Dad's. There is no other explanation. He believes he did well, that he did not scream or talk; that he did not cry and he got back to the clinic on his own. These men must have laughed with his Dad over this. At least he showed them he was not frightened.

Douglas has interpreted the abduction as something his father staged as a joke, to give him a fright. The worst scares he has ever had were on two occasions when his Dad played tricks on him. Although his mother talks to him regularly and he has the opportunity to tell her the truth of how frightened he was, he makes no effort to do so. He sees no point. He sees his mother shake her head often with his father's jokes and she berates naughty Glen and brave Douglas. Glen is the familiar villain for the boy. Douglas does not want to dwell on this subject but his mother does.

'You did well Douglas. Many boys would not have been as brave as you.' Pam tells him. He is too young for any attempt at a real explanation.

Since the incident his mum and dad have been with him all the time and spoken about his 'adventure'. Douglas doesn't really understand why his father pulled such an elaborate trick, but one thing he knows for sure, he never wants to see these men again.

'I know what these men look like Daddy, I can recognise them.' Douglas says this often, as if to ward off another prank.

———=(()=———

Two weeks after his son's abduction Glen is still having difficulty sleeping. His academic confidence in the value of maintaining man's ancient traditions is badly shaken. He increases his fitness regime, running nearly every morning for at least four miles. He has always had a lean physic and kept in shape. Nowadays with his hair thinning, he also keeps it shaved off in the look of a serious athlete. He is so disturbed by what happened to his family, no matter how much he occupies himself with his work, he feels bothered. He wants to return to Shinyanga and find the culprits. He considers it as necessary; as justice. He never interprets it as revenge, but he recognises that justice is the civilised version of the same emotion.

The Canadian High Commission extends Glen's contract to include some compassionate leave. They also encourage him to complete his research. Glen knows he possesses a unique set of skills that will help him shed light on this issue and he is driven by recent reports that another albino killing has taken place. He calculates that this death happened around the same time as Glen left Dawakubwa. The body of a mutilated young albino boy was found in a near-by river. Glen thinks it could be the same abductors!

The Canadians give Glen the names of two people he is encouraged to interview in Dar es Salaam, before he heads back up country. One is an active church leader named Reverend Albert Mosha who is at the forefront of local efforts to stop all ritualistic sacrifices and killings. The other is Professor Michael Graham, a retired UN development specialist with forty years of experience in Central America and East Africa. Glen sets appointments to meet both of these men.

Kaka Damu strolls to the edge of his compound where his father donated some land and he is in the process of building a house for his wife and first child. He wears his lion-skin head band. He takes his cow-tail stick and swats the flies on his shoulder with cow tail precision. Parrots fly from tree to tree squawking. The recent rains have brought out sprigs of grass, even on the well trodden pathways. He walks to the shade of a large Baobab tree at the end of his compound where Juma and the other two J's are seated. Kaka has called a meeting so they can explain the difficulties they had on their last mission and why it took so long to find a proper sacrifice.

In the partial shade of the Baobab tree, seated on four, three-legged stools, the four men engage in conversation. There is a large pot of freshly brewed beer, positioned in the middle of the stools to encourage their talk. They take four long straws and place one end in their mouths while the other end drifts at the strategic heart of the brew. Just above the thick mixture is perfect, not too high to be weak and watery. They talk of human sacrifice in their own dialect, as if they are discussing a seasonal harvest, which for them, it often is.

'Greetings, what's the news?' asks Kaka.

'Good. Things are good.' Juma replies.

'So things went well?'

'Yes, but you did not warn us of what we would find on reaching the clinic.'

'White chickens in a basket!' Kaka jokes.

'In the darkness we saw an albino man, a woman and two children asleep, an entire albino family. The woman and daughter had yellow hair, the man was bald.'

'The man moved almost as soon as we entered.' Joseph elaborates.

Juma begins to speak in a more respectful Swahili but Kaka detects a concern in his voice over this encounter and urges him to continue in the village dialect. The village has many new Swahili-speaking ears he does not trust.

'We entered the clinic prepared to cut, right there in front of the parents.'

After an exceptionally long draw on his straw Juma continues, 'I decided the spirits would not be pleased if we cut, there in front of this albino family. So we struck the father . . . and took one child.'

'We gagged him with a kanga and marched him back on the trail. In the late night, with the moon ebbing, it was too dark and difficult to see him properly.' Joseph continues, detailing their professionalism.

Kaka nods with aroused curiosity.

'At first light, I saw the boy did not have the look of an albino,' says Juma. 'The child had dark hair and blue eyes. He had the look of a Mzungu (European) child.' Juma continues and looks deliberately at Kaka, questioning him.

'We had found a white family at the clinic! What were they doing at the clinic?'

Kaka does not answer.

'On realising the boy was white, we talked and I felt uncomfortable. I let the child go.'

Kaka Damu takes a long deliberate suck of his beer then continues his questioning. 'Where then did you obtain the actual sacrifice we used?'

'As if by fate, a *zero* (a derogatory name for an albino) was there washing at a riverside on the way back. We bound him tightly to a tree. We cut both arms at the elbow.'

There's a long pause while all four men hold their straws and look at each other as if toasting their success. Kaka adjusts his lion headband and with it reasserts his control of the group. *Who can possibly interfere with the way of the lion? The lion kills a zebra and before the carcass is cold the zebra are back grazing around the lion, living in peace, together. What the lion kills or why, is never questioned.*

'The boy was alone and bleeding badly. He fainted and looked unlikely to live, so we gave him to the river.'

Kaka thinks long and hard about what Juma is telling him. They sit in silence a little longer. There is nothing that Kaka is afraid of, except the wrath of the spirits, he serves. He stands and walks to the surrounding bush, breaks a branch from the tooth-brush tree and polishes the banana and millet residue from his teeth. Finally he responds.

'Did the white child return to the clinic unharmed?' Kaka asks.

'I do not know for certain, but we saw a 'helikopta' circle in the sky and then disappear. I think the boy was found safe.'

'Yes a 'helikopta'. I'm sure the boy was found,' repeats John smiling.

'Yes,' Joseph agrees.

'Then the spirits have been satisfied. But you both should not have discarded the boy into the river in this way. It is the same river, in which Mafabi's family were later found dead.'

Juma does not react to Kaka's words but Joseph groans as if anticipating a future punishment from the spirits.

'What do we do now?' Juma asks.

'The ways of the spirits are unpredictable. We have had a small success. We have done our best. Do not fear. Everything will work out well.'

Kaka Damu doesn't mention the white boy's abduction any more but, it has entered his mind. Kaka knows that any visiting thought, at some point, demands more attention. He knows that talking about it now will confuse his friends and turn this troubling thought into a permanent unwelcome guest in all of them. Kaka knows how disruptive an unwelcome thought can be and he is not about to confront one, just yet.

———◦❮◉❯◦———

As much as Pam is neat and tidy, Glen is not. Helen is instructed to leave Glen's office space as he leaves it. His filing system is time based. He knows where everything is, because in time he uses up all the available space and he remembers how far back in time he placed things, rather than where he placed things. The obvious flat surfaces, tables and shelves were the first to be filled and therefore older in his filing system. Books and papers balancing on the arms of chairs, or left on the top of the cistern and in room corners, are his latest acquisitions. If Helen ever enters Glen's space to dust or clean, she is chased, as he does with the children, until she leaves. Helen is not allowed to remove a sheet of paper even if it is crumpled on the floor.

Not only papers and books are stored in this way but also aboriginal artefacts and a variety of indigenous weapons. Glen has a collection of animal bones used by Maasai laibon and other pastoral tribes for their healing rituals. Two Giraffe thighbones carved and polished along with some skulls of small animals fashioned into musical instruments and charms. Short fishing spears from Inuit Canada sit next to wrist knives from Southern Ethiopia and daggers from Sudan. In amongst his mad Indiana Jones collection, Glen knows where everything is and what everything is for. He sees order where others see chaos. Pam prefers to have the doors to Glen's spaces closed, but with this latest assignment she is beginning to see newly printed papers and reports creep into her clean and tidy living room. Pam is not happy about Glen's obsession with this latest assignment.

One day when a friend comes for dinner the visitor compliments Pam on her décor and attention to detail. She has visited the toilet and found a bar of soap with little petals.

'Your soap looks so nice in your toilet sink,' she remarks.

'But that's Glens toilet,' says Pam, mystified at this compliment.

Later, after the guest leaves, Pam calls Glen out of his study and mockingly asks for permission to visit his toilet. On one side of the sink she finds a large bar of soap with five small petals stuck in a flower shape on one side. Pam realises it is the remnants of five other bars of soap that Glen has not cleared away which have stuck to the new bar in a flower-like formation.

'Typical,' says Pam.

'Unconscious creativity!' Glen replies.

Then from the corner of his eye, Glen sees a new addition to his filing system. It's an article on albinism written by Professor Michael Graham sitting face up on a pile of papers perched on his toilet cistern. He lifts the article and reads a footnote.

'Let's hear it for coincidence.' Glen says.

———◦((•))◦———

Glen Google's Professor Michael Graham and discovers from Wikipedia that he was born in Trinidad, moved to England at the age of twelve and is a British citizen. He is a respected education specialist and has written several academic publications and a couple of semi-successful novels. Glen knows from the UN Spouse Group that Michael lives not far from him, near the Yacht Club on Msasani. Glen puts a fresh note-pad into his backpack. He is now much more prepared for his appointment to meet Prof Graham.

After knocking on the gate fruitlessly, Glen calls the Professor's mobile number and within a few moments Michael himself opens the gate, a rare occurrence in these parts. He is wearing a large Panama hat, thin white overalls and dark glasses.

'I won't pay good money for a guard to sleep on the job,' he says, by way of an explanation.

Glen is ushered into the small Colonial house in the centre of a lush tropical garden. Glen laughs out loud as he enters the house since it has the look of every well-travelled UN employee.

'Yes, my decor is my CV!' says Michael.

On the wall are three Ethiopian crosses, positioned like flying ducks. There is a painted cartoon of Solomon and Sheba. A large Makonde sculpture sits beside some African fabrics. Nepalese rugs lie on the floor beside a Zanzibar chest in the hallway, alongside a collection of Ethnic art from every duty station that Michael has worked.

'I heard what happened to your son. You are very lucky . . . man.' Michael moves straight to serious discussion. Glen notes Michael's mild Caribbean accent with his use of the word, 'man' as if it's an exclamation mark.

They sit down facing each other across a coffee table. There is a pot of tea on a special holder with a burning candle beneath. Michael takes off his hat and glasses and pours two cups.

'Yes, things could have turned out very differently. I am a lucky man.' Glen says.

'I'd say your boy has more luck than you . . . if luck played any part.'

As Glen takes a sip of his too hot tea, he looks across and examines Michael Graham's face closely. Glen knows from Google his host is sixty-eight but he looks older. Michael's realises he has rarely seen albino men of this age. He could not find any photos of Michael on line.

His face, hands and arms are freckled. He has the strong features of a black man yet he is a pale white. He is bald with shaved eyebrows. Glen looks straight into his eyes, and sees strong grey pupils surrounded by a tell tale glow of pink. Glen realises that not many men like Michael live to such an age, with the skin condition called albinism.

'Are you surprised?'

'At what?'

'The fact that I'm an albino . . . man?'

'Yes a little surprised, I found no reference to your condition in the articles you wrote. I'm more surprised I heard nothing about it in from others here. Even your article on Albinism in Scientific American did not mention it either.'

'Anyone who knows me, knows it's been part of my life's mission, not to become known for something I had no part in creating. I'd much rather be known for what I produce.'

'Which is impressive.'

'Thanks. My skin condition is irrelevant to what I do, yes?'

'I agree.'

'So why have you come to see me?'

'I came to hear what you think can be done to change perceptions on matters related to ritualistic killings. I'm here to tap into your background experience in education and human rights. But if you are uncomfortable talking about this subject then just say so.'

'Ah ha! The cure-all legal solution we call 'Human rights!' Did you know in most of the local languages here there is no equivalent word for 'rights,' no historical concept of what that word really means. In fact in many countries, all over the world in minority languages there is no word for 'rights'. That's why it's wrong to assume any universal understanding of the law, even if there is universal ratification. We are not there yet, there's still much explaining to be done.'

'So you don't mind talking about albinos in Tanzania?'

'Mr Chapman, I'm a retired educator and international civil servant. I'll talk all night about anything. I may well be remembered for my talking. When I die you can remember me as the albino, who talked a lot.'

There is a silence as Michael chuckles to himself. 'Actually I'd like to be remembered as the Trini-born writer, brought up in Peckham London who wrote twelve books on education and won a regional Commonwealth prize for Literature before joining the UN. But my recent babbling on albinism keeps creeping into my obituary credits.'

Michael Graham spills out thoughts on a number of subjects. It's as if he has rehearsed and given these talks numerous times. Black crows, sitting in mass on the trees outside, squawk before they fly off to annoy another expatriate. A dark storm cloud seems to rumble in the distance. Michael talks of a lifetime's dedication to the United Nations and how in the days when he joined he was given great respect across Africa because of his skin condition. He tells Glen he has given lectures on numerous subjects but never on albinism.

'In most countries people thought I was one of their own, in a position of responsibility.' Michael says. 'And strangely enough I have very few albino friends. My experience with this skin condition is personal, not social. All my life I moved in circles where there was no need to herd together for protection.'

Michael talks of several countries with great affection and describes his early work contributions to Africa, just after independence as historic and important.

Glen curses the fact he does not have a recording device and finds himself with a full notepad long before Michael has stopped talking. He asks Michael some specific questions about the spate of killings in

Tanzania and laments about how little the United Nations seem to be doing about it. Jokingly Glen accuses the United Nations of priority overload and some indifference to this issue. Glen can tell instantly he has upset Michael with this statement. After another moment of silence, Michael appears to change roles from orator to defence attorney.

'How dare you suggest that the UN are not doing enough! After independence Tanzania had virtually no social statistics on record. They had no records at all on the number of albinos born here. They had poor census data on everything local. They did not even know how many people actually lived in this country. It was the same all over Africa, a continent, only recorded through the eyes and priorities of its European colonial powers. There are a few historical footnotes and references in Islam and Christianity to albinism but virtually nothing remains from a wealth of oral traditions and un-notated languages across this continent. Even today, communications and trade routes go north and south to these old colonial centres more than across the continent.'

'So what are you saying?'

'Newly independent African countries were born handicapped compared with the developed systems of governance and social data gathering of long established countries. Africa had no accurate population figures for all their differing tribal regions. They had the chance to collect it, but some chose not to. They had very poor registrations of birth or death; they did not know how many mothers gave birth every year or how their birthing practices differed, or how many mothers died in childbirth. They had no way of knowing how many children reached their fifth birthday or how many went to school. They had a poor statistical picture of the society they referred to as a country. They had no idea of the gender balance; potential natural resources or indeed the extent of the nutrition, health and medical challenges the country faced. There was also a very naive understanding of 'politics' and if you ask me, these naïve political systems have lasted because most young people have in turn remained politically naïve. If people really understood the power of democracies they lived under, there would be much less corruption and nepotism.'

'It's hard to know if you are criticising present politicians or colonial powers.'

'A country just given the status of a Nation and a place at the UN needs help to understand itself. It was the UN,' Michael raises his voice, 'the UN, who helped train and fund and introduce the very notion of development, the essential nature of a bureau of statistics, so that Africa's people could see themselves in the context of a country as well as a tribe.'

'Point taken.'

'Good.'

'I am in fact married into the United Nations, so I do have some sense of its history.'

There is another embarrassing silence but Glen senses Michael's hackles retreat. He keeps his head bowed as if submitting to a superior gorilla's strength in a bush encounter.

When he looks up he sees a vacancy in Michael's eyes that disguise his obvious intelligence.

'Can you smell that?' Michael asks, twisting a delighted face towards some fresh drops of rain falling outside.

'Yes . . . I know. It's a powerful aroma.'

'The smell of soil and seed rejoicing! Our first rain in three months.'

The birds in Michael's garden are also in celebration, chirping wildly across his bamboo and bougainvilleas.

'I hear people say that 'development' has failed; there simply would not be as many people alive today on this continent if it had failed. It's like saying politics has failed! It's always failing. It moves forward on our perceptions of failure. We have to understand both politics and development are linked. The tax bases of newly independent governments were simply too small to sustain nation-wide government programmes back then. They needed the International Community's help and in some cases they still do.'

There is a quiet spell before Michael pours himself another cup of tea. He ignores filling Glen's cup, indicating some inner demons are still occupying his mind. Glens tries to change the mood by looking into his empty cup and reading the tea leafs. 'I still see some difficulties ahead, even for the UN.' Glen says. Michael's hand covered in freckles; pale and as wrinkled as a cow's udder, stretches over and fills his cup. 'I can change that.' Michael says pouring fresh tea into Glen's cup.

'Tell me more about how you think the past relates to the situation today?'

'Thirty years ago I met people whose opinion of Africa was based on their own personal experience of the place. Whether they were Africans or visitors they would tell you what Africa was like, because they had seen it with their own eyes. They had lived it. That's how naive and unscientific descriptions of Africa were, even from Africans themselves. The smaller the village an African came from, the more they spoke for the whole continent when addressing a European. It was the same naivety for Europeans who visited here. Either it's a continent of extreme beauty and wildlife, of friendly people with warm hearts or a place of deep-rooted poverty and starvation, of brutal oppressive leaders and exploitative foreign business investors. Some visitors will say just leave them be, while others want to give everyone charitable help.'

'What do you say?'

'I start with the internationally acceptable premise that no matter where you are in the world . . . no pregnant mother to be wants to loose a child! It is hard to find a more humanly agreed on principle. If I see that children are dying needlessly it's only right to help any way possible. Whether it's through giving to charity or designing and lobbying government intervention.'

'So saving children should be a political goal in a country?'

'Until there is a collective human decision on an even better goal yes!

'We're back to the UN.'

'Well, at least we're back to the principals of the UN. You have to see how all-inclusive they actually are compared to the priorities of our varied religions or the national interests of individual countries. Today there's at least enough information available, that even a pop star like Bono can take a look at a country's social data and give a fairly accurate picture of what is going on. That's what the UN has brought to the world of politics. An internationally accepted standard on which to judge a nation's progress or lack of it. So don't tell me the UN is not doing enough on the subject of albinism. This country already has enough laws in existence to deal with this sad situation if there was enough political will to do so. It is pathetic to give them excuses. It's not for the United Nations to be putting policemen in villages to enforce laws. This country has to deal with this itself. It has all the tools of statistics and laws to do so and it should enforce them . . . mercilessly man!' Michael finishes then sucks air through his teeth.

'It's getting late but I'd like to talk to you more, perhaps after I have finished the next phase of my research.

'OK.'

'I'll look forward to Round Two.'

'You might have to go the full twelve rounds with me on this. You take care now!'

'Yeah I know. I must go now before it's too dark,' says Glen.

'Come any time you like. I may be old and *kali* (fierce) but I'm willing to help you. If the Canadians are willing to fund good research on this, then it's only a matter of time before the Europeans get jealous and join in. They all might do something further as a result of your research. We have to exploit them, don't we? Remember, the UN is nothing more than it's member states and in fact the UN has less staff than the Disney

Corporation to cover the whole world's problems. Just give them a break, Glen.'

'If only we could get Disney on board, eh?'

'Yep . . . an albino Mickey Mouse could do the trick for publicity.'

——◦《◦》◦——

Pam wears a loose fitting cotton top over her bikini and ties her Monday *kanga* (cloth) around her waist. It is dusk, she is outside and this is her compromise to the nudity she prefers. Seated in her favourite spot, she scrolls through a seemingly endless list of email on her Blackberry. She remembers when this device was given to her as a tool to make her work easier. Now she is a slave to its relentless capacity to inform her.

Glen joins her in silence and sits next to her on his favourite canvas lounge chair. He drinks a half glass of cold Kilimanjaro beer in one gulp. He doesn't like the beer to go cold on him. He proceeds to transcribe the notes of his meeting with Michael Graham onto his lap top.

'What do you plan to do now?' Pam says.

'I think Michael can be helpful once I reach the end of my research. I have another interview to conduct, with this Reverend in Dar, then I plan to set off back to the Dawakubwa clinic.'

'Why do you have to go back there so soon?'

'I'm preparing to expand the interview circuit with faith healers. I called a photographic shop and ordered some cheap disposable cameras to use in my research.'

'Why cameras?'

'I want to distribute them to faith healers and ask them to photograph the work they do and people they meet. You know, the things they feel are part of their business. I've arranged a few thousand shillings stipend for them. I used this method in previous research, remember?'

'Not with such a gruesome subject matter.'

'We're talking headless chickens, mostly from the area I'm researching and anyway I'm not interested in photos of actual sacrifices. I'm more interested in photos of the people who conduct them.'

'Why?

'When I collect the cameras, I can review the content and make a video diary. It will provide useful visual material I can use in the final report.'

'Glen, I know you. You are not answering me.'

'It will also give me the chance to look closely at the faces of those helping the faith healers. And maybe Douglas can recognise the men who took him.'

'Glen!'

'What? You don't want me to help catch the men who took Douglas?'

'You are a researcher . . . not a detective.'

'Pam, these are men who actually kill albino children; the longer they are left to their ways the more children will die. It's as simple as that.'

'Do not,' Pam shouts, then lets her emotions drain from her voice, 'do not put this family in any danger. Do you hear?'

'Pam, this is a unique chance to help, to make a direct impact on this issue. Not just by writing research, which then goes onto bookshelves in Embassies, then it's the agenda for some meeting; which is then considered for resource allocation; which then prompts a small grant to be paid to the government to help deal with it. Pam, this is a chance to catch the abductors who took Douglas . . . and stop them from killing any more children.'

'Glen, anywhere else I would support you. But I don't feel safe here, not from these types of people. They could easily target us. Think of Emanuel, think of Helen.'

When Glen sees Pam's eyes swelling he moves around the table and hugs her. He understands her concerns, but this insecurity also gives him a rush of determination. He feels he has to work this project through to the end for both their sakes.

'I'll be as cautious as I can be, but I have to do this Pam. Don't worry. Everything will be OK.'

———◈———

The Reverend Albert Mosha is based in Mwanza and travels the countryside extensively. He knows the trade in albino body parts is not limited to areas outside where Christianity is the dominant religion, and the Reverend has been invited to talk in Mosques and Hindu Temples to inspire the same social outrage as he generates in churches. The trade spans the country, wherever this strange and, in the Reverend's mind, foreign superstition is reinforced and supported.

It is a problem that needs to be tackled in the Islamic coastal areas as much as the Christian countryside. The Reverend knows it is very often funded by respected businessmen and community leaders from all religious backgrounds—by everyone naive enough to believe their luck is influenced by something other than the Lord. In the Reverend's mind it is only true religious faith that will stamp out sponsorship of this human slaughter.

Reverend Mosha also knows that a great number of albino victims do come from areas he is yet to spread his message.

For the past four years the Reverend has led public demonstrations in Moshi and Arusha against the killing and mutilations of albino children.

In addition he has been present to give comfort wherever they have occurred. He runs branches of the Anglican Church in both Mwanza and Dar es Salam but the majority of his faithful are based up country.

The Reverend's name has been on the top of Glen's interview list from the beginning. He is a hard man to pin down. He finally receives an invite to meet the Reverend for lunch at the Movenpick hotel. There is an air conditioned cafe overlooking the garden and the Reverend can only spare an hour or so to eat and talk.

Glen is already seated when the Reverend arrives shortly after him. He is a well built mid-size man, soft spoken, in his mid forties and seems keen to move straight to the subject of albinos after introductions. They sit opposite each other.

'I saw your story on CNN . . . an excellent point about protecting human rights. But, may I say, long before man had human rights, there was God's laws.' The Reverend roars with laughter as if he has cracked a joke. 'Yes,' he continues through his chuckles, 'there are some very important commandments that have still not been given the serious attention they deserve.'

The Reverend speaks good English, and gestures for a waiter to bring the menu for lunch.

'I know the service here, put in your order quickly.' he says.

A flamboyant service waiter seems to dance around the table with the menu, and takes the Reverend's order. After Glen gives his, the Reverend begins talking again.

'On a recent visit to a game park in Mukumi, I saw an albino buffalo. There in the midst of a huge herd of black Cape buffalo was a young male whose skin was white and his eyes almost clear. I have never seen such a thing in nature before. Behold it is part of God's work to give us such diversity in his creations. I have since heard from fellow Tanzanians that they have seen albino giraffe and even elephant. But, as you know very few Tanzanians ever go into game parks so many don't know how creative the Lord can be.' The Reverend laughs out loud again, in short bursts of laughter, at his own words.

'I knew then,' the Reverend continues, 'that God has given me his permission to march ahead with my efforts to protect the weak and the disabled; to speak out against these terrible crimes and to seek financial help from every quarter. What,' he says quietly, 'do you have to offer me in terms of funding?' A smile again appears on the jovial Reverend's face but there's no more laughter.

'I apologise for not explaining my research more to you. I have nothing financial to offer you Reverend except a *mandazi* (doughnut) and coffee. If my research is done well it could be of some help to your initiative, perhaps help bring more funding for the cause.'

Reverend Albert smiles again, 'I never refuse a *mandazi.*'

He then talks about himself and his mission through lunch. He seems to Glen to be level headed and dedicated. He fishes for any type of financial commitment that Glen can make, including some help to travel abroad on fund raising trips. He talks with some authority about both albinos and the work of the church to stamp out all cults of sacrifice.

'The albinos in this country were never a target in the past. With the socialist government of independent Tanzania, there was a clampdown on many of the old traditions and beliefs. We have one hundred and twenty different ethnic groups in this country who have all been united through the one language of Kiswahili. There are now many attempts to educate parents of albino children to better cope with their condition.'

'How would you say witch doctors come into this?'

'I would not say 'Witch Doctor.' It is a colonial, expression. It's a name given by the white man. We have always had traditional healers in our communities . . . they are not witch doctors.'

'I agree it's an English name but don't you think that witch doctor is a reasonable translation of the way some of these healers perform their trade. We had witches in Europe for centuries who used fear, superstition and sacrifice in their rituals according to the church.'

'Witches, yes! I'm a man of the church so there is no need to tell me of the hatred of witches. They were burned at the stake. The history of my church is full of such stories. Anyone even suspected of being a witch was killed. And you know it is the same here today, some three hundred people have been killed in the last two years, stoned and beaten because people believed they were witches. In some circles this is a more pressing problem than the plight of albinos. Seven times the number of albinos killed, simply for being suspected of being a witch. But my point is that many of these faith healers you might call witchdoctors are respected. People are queuing to become registered healers. You can be enrolled in a Government organisation which gives you qualifications in traditional healing. There is a waiting list for such applications. There are more people who want to become traditional healers here than there are places for them.'

Glen ponders for a moment on these figures for the killing of suspected witches. He knows that this issue is an extension of the deeply superstitious beliefs that are common in many across the country, including albinos; that if misfortune befalls someone, then people are quick to believe they have been cursed. The power of suspicion and superstition to unleash mob justice tends to go unpunished if the authorities believe justice has been served. Widows and older women in families who suffer the brunt of these accusations are basically murdered, but Glen needs to stick to his brief and keep this conversation on albinos.

'Who then, is responsible for traditional healers who, let's say, turn bad?' Glen asks.

'What do you mean?'

'Who is it in your old traditional society that will hold those who perform ritual human sacrifices accountable?'

'Mr Glen, you talk as if this is an ancient problem for Tanzania. It is not. It is a recent problem, and of course the proper modern authorities are responsible.'

'What makes you say it's recent?'

'When a transition from the socialist government took place some fifteen years ago, we adopted capitalism. Our markets are now free. We are in competition for a better life rather than cooperating for a better life. Your neighbours no longer need to play a part in your business success.' The Reverend takes his *mandazi* doughnut, smears in with ketchup and takes time to chew it before continuing.

'There has been a lot of dissatisfaction since this transition. Confusion over why some people are rich while others remain poor. There is also a lot of interest in how one can influence 'luck'. It happens all over the capitalist world. Gambling casinos, bingo, and lottery tickets, so that with luck you can become rich overnight. In the West you have a rabbit's foot for good luck, no? Here there is a more God-less business surrounding ones luck and how to change it.'

'You make it sound common and horribly acceptable.'

'Not me Mr Glen. It's portrayed like this daily on hundreds of thousands of TV's across Africa. There are hundreds of movies from West Africa, showing semi-naked village healers, practicing all sorts of devil worship and witchcraft. I believe one major contributor to the increase in sacrificial rituals here, has been these stereotypical African movies. They are set in villages that resemble places and peoples from all over the continent. They regularly show these bizarre rituals as our African culture. Make no mistake this sort of behaviour had died out. It is only in the last ten years it has grown in scale.'

'It's very common in the West to blame media for promoting social violence, but I've not heard this argument here.'

'Come on, Mr Glen, be real. Ten days after a TV is introduced into a village, the children are Kung-fu-ing each other. Where does that come from?'

'It's just children's play though.'

'It's play until they grow up. Mr Glen, I would like to invite you to my church in Mwanza to see for yourself the work that we are doing to end a whole set of imported barbaric practices.'

The Reverend pulls out a folder from his brief case. 'Take this. It explains the scale of our efforts so far.'

'Thank you. I'd especially like to see how you tie in your community work with law enforcement in the rural areas.'

'Certainly, that's also a part of our effort. We invite local police to attend service and community meetings. They are all aware of our message.'

'One last question, Sir, do you encourage your followers to pass on information to the police . . . that could help arrest some of the culprits?'

'It is not the job of my flock to pass judgement, Mr Glen.'

'I'm not talking about passing judgement, only information.'

'When necessary, yes! Make no mistake the evil men who do this will definitely suffer in the fires of hell. This is our message. They are sinners. Judgement will be done by the Lord himself.'

'I think the law states they should be punished in this life.'

'I have no doubt they will be, somehow. I make the call for the practice of sacrifice to be stamped out, it is un-Christian; the Bible tells me this. I condemn everyone involved. I am a Minister of God; we are people of the church. All we want is to live in peace.'

Glen pays for the bill and gives a generous tip to the flamboyant male waiter. As the Reverend stands to leave, he sees the waiter bow in a girlish response to Glen's tip. The Reverend shakes his head in disapproval. As they head for the door the Reverend turns to Glen and says, 'You must be careful not to encourage them Mr Glen! They too must face the judgement of the Lord one day.' He then bellows out a boisterous laugh and continues laughing all the way out of the hotel.

⸺◉⸺

At home, Glen reviews his laptop notes. He edits and fills in more observations from his interview with the Reverend. He highlights the Reverend's calendar of activities, thinking they may be useful for his field visit. He also realises the full scale of the Reverend's community awareness efforts from the folder he was given. The Reverend has thousands of people mobilised and teaching the wrongs of any sacrifice. Glen transfers the Reverend's travel plans to his own calendar and then sits back in his canvas bush chair on his porch with a beer.

Pam is practicing her butterfly stroke and splashes loudly on a warm cloudless night. The children are asleep in bed. Glen shakes his head in amusement as he remembers the last thing that Reverend said to him. After two hours of talking social justice and acceptance for albinos, Glen heard a distinctly homophobic comment from the Reverend. He is still not sure if it was all a joke. He knows the ongoing quarrels within the African church about homosexuality and the exclusion of gay preachers into their hierarchy. In Uganda there is a movement dedicated to making homosexuality illegal. This is another issue of human rights versus entrenched beliefs, but hardly comparable. At least in Glen's mind it seems incomparable.

The more Glen drinks, the more he is disturbed that he has not yet found anyone who sees the albino issue in its full complexity. Despite the government response and the newly formed albino organisations; the football teams, the hostels that offer protection and the awareness building campaigns, Glen sees a failure to bring the organisers of this illicit trade to justice. He is sure there must be champions out there somewhere, but he's not come across any yet. Everyone he has talked to tends to be defensive of his or her own limited role and that is not a good sign.

Glen watches Pam step out of the water in the moonlight. He notices her tan lines are more pronounced than usual.

'Have you been sunbathing again?'

'I need the vitamin D.'

Glen wants to return to their comfortable life together. He wants so much to hand over responsibility for his new found knowledge, to someone else. He feels trapped in this unique role he finds himself in. He knows that at least during this next stage, making progress will be up to him.

CHAPTER THREE

ULTERIOR MOTIVES

Some of Kaka Damu's most regular clients are miners. Numerous riverbeds and mountain ranges across Tanzania are known to contain precious minerals and stones as well as gold. Ever since the spread of the mobile phone into rural Africa, the locations where these riches can be found are no longer secret. There has been an abundance of local information shared in local languages across stretches of countryside on a scale never before experienced. As a result, it is not only the large mining corporations that pour in money and workers to exploit the wealth of the land, there are thousands of free-lance miners coming to small anonymous sites to do the same. In these nomadic mining communities luck plays a large, if not the largest, part in finding these riches.

Juma awakens Kaka Damu, in the middle of the night. There is a mother some four miles away who has given birth to an albino boy and the father has called on Kaka Damu to remove the child from the family. Kaka Damu is annoyed. Why does he have to go now in the middle of his sleep!

'The father wants the child taken before daylight. He does not want to touch the child, he thinks it is 'zero-zero'!'(Worthless)

'Are you sure this can't wait?'

'I would not be waking you if this were not true. The father is outside waiting for us to go with him.'

Kaka Damu sits up in his wooden bed and stretches. He flips aside the mosquito net that swings from the wooden beams of his house. He walks over to a single tap located high on the wall in his adjacent washroom. This is a new addition to the house he is still in the process of constructing. He turns on the tap and tepid water rushes out. He shakes his head and his naked body underneath. Kaka is in his early forties and is beginning to show a belly as a result of his wealth and affluence. The regularity of his feastings and the lack of real physical work are beginning to shape him.

He dries himself quickly and pulls on a patterned square shirt with a keyhole-embroidered neck. He slips into long light grey trousers, rolled up at the bottom. He also has a selection of football shirts from England that he now wears for such occasions. It is only rarely that he puts on the old tribal outfits of his father. He hears Juma call '*Harakisha*,' for Kaka to hurry up and he groans a complaint in reply. As the three men leave the compound, Kaka stops suddenly. He curses his forgetfulness and tells the others to wait for him. Kaka jogs back to his house. He has forgotten his lion headband, along with his charms and good luck attachments. He also gathers his leather pouch of human knucklebones from a beaded basket hanging in his living room. He then goes to his kitchen, searches around for his butcher's cleaver, scrapes it up and down his sharpening stone a few times then leaves.

Everything is silent in the house of the newborn albino child. The teenage mother sobs noiselessly, muting her shock and pain. She is delusional and distraught at the discovery of her unusual child and the conduct of her husband. It is her first born and the village mid-wife, a woman in her fifties, accompanies her. The mid-wife tries to assure the mother that what is about to happen is for the best. That this child will not have a normal life; that she can have other children, proper black children. That if she gives the child away without touching it, her luck will change.

The mid-wife has already buried the umbilical cord and the placenta outside. She has wrapped the child tightly in a white cloth and placed it onto the rush matting on the floor, exactly where it was born. The child is constrained like the bound roots of a banana plant, ready for re-planting. It is making all the facial movements of a baby seeking its mother's breast, but it is silent.

When Kaka Damu arrives he enters the house chanting softly. He circles the sobbing mother as the quiet baby lies sedately on the floor. The mother has little strength to argue with her husband. He is adamant that the child is taken away immediately. He does not seek any payment for the child although he knows its value. Kaka Damu also knows its value. He instructs the parents to follow his instructions carefully.

In order not to arouse suspicion in the village, the couple must conduct a mock funeral the next day. Their story to neighbours and their families must be that their child was still born. They can say that Kaka Damu was called in to help save the mother but unfortunately the child passed away. Kaku Damu repeats this story in the local language of the mid-wife and gives her a threatening glance to see if she understands. She nods a confirmation, and recoils slightly. She'd thought the husband was simply giving the child away. On seeing Kaka Damu, the full severity of what will now happen is slowly dawning on her.

Kaka Damu leaves, carefully carrying the newborn in his arms. Juma is at his side with a shoulder bag inside which he's pre-packed some plastic bags. A few hundred yards from the village Kaka looks around, to make sure no one is looking. When he sees they are alone, he lies the silent child down on a fallen tree trunk and with no thought of human rights and little respect for life itself, he hacks it into pieces, valuable pieces. Kaka Damu knows that he will now, at last, be able to finish building his house.

———————

This time Glen flies to Mwanza instead of driving. The flight seems remarkably short and hardly enough time for Glen to work on his questionnaire for faith healers. Crystal has agreed to meet him at the airport with a taxi, before they drive together to Shinyanga. As he exits the arrivals gate, Glen cannot see Crystal. He looks around a theatre of faces waiting for passengers. He realises he has rarely seen Crystal without her white medical jacket, or the ever practical kanga she seems to live in at home. As he is approached by a pack of men offering taxi services, he notices an attractive woman who is staring at him. It is not until she steps forward that he recognises her walk and her smile. She is wearing western clothes, a red cotton blouse and three quarter length light blue jeans. She has freshly braided hair and looks sophisticated and completely different to the Dr. Crystal he remembers from Dawakubwa. Crystal has dressed up for the big city.

As Glen moves excitedly to meet her, they clasp each other's hands and speak a chorus of Swahili greetings. He feels her hand in his, lingering affectionately.

Crystal directs Glen towards the parking lot and is surprised to see how much luggage Glen has brought. A porter helps Glen load four large but light boxes into the boot of the battered Peugeot 504 taxi.

'What is in the boxes?' Crystal inquires, shouting above the noise of honking horns and traffic chaos at the airport exit.

'Mostly it is disposable cameras. And a few research papers and books.'

'What do you mean 'disposable' cameras?'

'Oh . . . they're small plastic cameras that only have one roll of film in them. After you use them, you throw them away. Dispose of them. You are teasing me aren't you?'

Crystal laughs at Glen's description.

'What are they for?'

'I'm going to distribute them to the faith healers and ask them to take photos of themselves; their home; family and work; the things important to them.'

'You should not encourage them.' Crystal replies. It reminds Glen of the Reverend's advice in Dar. 'My clinic is full of young boys who suffer at the hands of these people during the circumcision season. Accidents with knives, happen frequently.'

'I hadn't thought of that. But I need to supplement my writing with at least some visuals.'

'Be prepared for some explicit photos.'

'Oh, I hope not!'

'What are the research papers?' Crystal changes the subject.

'There is one book that you would find interesting. I've carried it around since my Master's research. It's called 'The Dissemination of Innovation,' by a communication specialist called Everett Rogers.'

'What's it about?'

'It's about how new ideas gradually spread though societies.'

'Good ideas or bad ideas?'

'Both really, it's much the same process. It's the definition of good and bad that's more debatable, isn't it? But that's too long and complicated to get into right now.'

'We have a long and complicated road ahead Glen. Try me.'

Glen can hardly stretch his legs in the back of the taxi. The seat in front is locked in place. He has to move his legs over into Crystal's side. She accommodates and their legs rest lightly against each other. The driver is alone in the front with both windows open. This brings in a pleasant supply of cool air on the open dirt road, until another vehicle passes and the taxi fills up with dust. Crystal takes out her ever-practical kanga and wraps it around her head and shoulders to protect her eyes and mouth.

Glen explains more about Ev Roger's theory of disseminating innovation. He tells Crystal he often uses the book for inspiration. He also mentions Michael Shermer's research into over interpreting random acts. The fact that many people wrongly link cause and effect, where it does not exist, and ignore it where it does exist. He tells her that somewhere in the work of these two researchers is the scientific key to solving the problem of dangerous superstitions. He finds it easy to talk to her. She is intelligent and responsive and much more relaxed in his company than when they first met. Glen knows little about her, but he has no time for small talk. He keeps the conversation on global issues. It's what Glen is like when he is interested in someone. He talks shop. Glen shows Crystal some papers he has downloaded from the Internet that deal with research into gambling addictions, and cultural concepts of luck.

Crystal looks at photos of packed casinos in Las Vegas and shakes her head unable to understand the connection that Glen is suggesting between life in Shinyanga and Caesar's Palace.

'I feel I understand the role of the faith healer,' Glen continues. 'What I need now is to better understand the clients. It's the clients that seem to pass through a temporary state of weakness. They call for help because they feel helpless. This feeling of helplessness is at the heart of so many social addictions, to gambling as well as the misuse of drugs. It requires two different problem-solving approaches doesn't it? Either address this problem of the clients or use the strength of the law to deal with the excesses and abuses of faith healers?'

'Or in this case maybe a third, use our existing laws to protect the albino population? Don't forget them.' Crystal adds.

'Yes you're right. There are actually three solutions to the problem.'

'There is still a lot of fear and ignorance among families with albino children to overcome.'

'Do the albino families still come to the clinic?'

'Yes, and a lot of my time is spent dealing with skin condition and their disabilities with sight. The albino population is one group among many that are stigmatized. They have difficulties with the community's perception of them because they look so different. If parents better understood the condition of albinism, they'd better help their children.'

'What do you mean?'

'Some parents try and treat their albino children the same as their brothers and sisters.'

'Is that not a good thing?'

'Yes, up to a point. But there is ignorance among some parents as to the dangers of light skin in this climate. Some parents send their albino children out into the sun to work on their farms, or else make them walk long hours to school without protection. This can lead to fatal consequences. I'd say there are more albinos at risk from the ignorance of their parents than there are from ritual sacrifices.'

'Is this a nation-wide problem, or just here?'

'Not just a country wide problem, but every neighbouring country to Tanzania has this problem, especially those around the central lakes.'

'That's interesting . . . so how many albinos do you think are out there.'

'I believe the official figure is that one child in every four thousand is born albino here . . . four times the figure from Europe where its only one in every twenty thousand.'

'That would give us some ten thousand albinos in a population of forty million.'

'That's a low figure.'

'How?'

'Around here we estimate the number is much higher, and in some areas one in every fourteen hundred is born albino. This is unofficial but there could be as many as a hundred and seventy thousand albinos in Tanzania.'

Glen digests this new information. He can see Crystal is tired of talking. She must have been awake for hours, driving to the airport. He stops asking questions and studies the passing countryside, deep in thought. There is silence in the car and Crystal drifts off to sleep at Glen's side.

Glen's studies taught him to be curious and tolerant of native and ethnic cultures. Even more so in recent years as the consequences of modern human activity have come under serious scrutiny. Rural populations, long seen as the majority, are quickly becoming the minority. As a result of consumerism and industrial lifestyles, the cities are expanding at an alarming rate, with possible negative consequences for the planet. On a long stretch of smooth road, Glen makes notes on his writing pad. This is how he passes time. For him this is as good as a crossword. This is his Sudoku, a way to contemplate worldly thoughts in his head and ponder conclusions. Glen loves this type of mental stimulation. He can put himself to sleep at night with such thoughts. He looks across at Crystal who is now sleeping with her head leaning away from him. He examines the light on the side of her face, the smooth beauty of her skin and the strong jaw line. Her lips curl in the suggestion of a smile and they protrude further than her nose. It is such a distinctive and elegant profile.

Glen looks out his window as a cluster of mud huts with thatched roofs drift by his rattling taxi. Population growth rates are slowing down according to the UN but again this does not change the fact that in the next fifty years the world's population will double for the last time from its current six billion people, to an expected 10-12 billion. To Glen this is not just another six billion births in his lifetime but another 6 billion job seekers; house owners; car buying aspiring consumers. There will be 6 billion more mouths to feed, with fish and food and water already in short supply. These 6 billion, the fruit of man's loins could be the most serious single contributor to the destruction of the planet. Why, because they will be young ignorant and ambitious, in massive numbers, with little appreciation of the history and knowledge of man's cultural struggles. Man has intervened with nature to assist more humans to live. But Nature is equally capable of striking back to reduce our numbers. If only we could change the reproduction and lifestyle habits of our species to have less but more cherished children, Glen thinks philosophically with the ease of someone playing Nintendo to pass the time. He looks back at Crystal. She is still asleep. Her kanga has fallen off her shoulder and her blouse is open at the top revealing the clear plastic strap of her bra. She is breathing lightly, unaware of Glen's stare. Glen once more looks out the window and ponders the futility of controlling man's reproductive urges. No way man, he thinks. It's not in our nature.

They are welcomed at the clinic by a number of people Glen recognises from his previous visit. Crystal is once again alert and energetic. She organises some waiting patients and fixes the dislocated finger of a young boy before she has even entered the clinic. Glen is very impressed by Crystal's instant provision of medical care. He realises again how attractive she is. It's partly because of the extra effort she has put into her appearance that day. He wonders if the effort was for him. Glen knows she has two children, boys, just a few years older than Douglas. That she is in her late twenties, and that there has never been talk of a husband.

Crystal offers Glen the use of a spare bedroom in her house and he accepts. She arranges that her sons move in with her and for a mattress to be placed on the floor. She explains it will be more private and comfortable than the waiting room at the clinic.

Once settled, Glen takes a walk around the village so he can familiarise himself once more with this area and to stretch his cramped legs. He acts like a dog marking his territory and walks around the familiar spots that hold such bad memories. He is reminded also of the easy pace and the beauty of the village. In a way it's a crime, he thinks, that this lifestyle is under threat from the environmental side effects of industrialisation. These villagers have done nothing to contribute to the current global climate crisis, yet they may be the first to suffer as a result. They have a culture and economy that is given little value in Western economic terms. Their togetherness is overlooked in preference to their natural mineral and agricultural resources.

The value of villages, Glen thinks, must surely become recognised, especially by the young who are born here. These places have a wealth value for the planet that is ignored in the aspirations of their own young. As he strides back to Crystal's compound Glen turns his mind to the immediate challenge. He pushes open the large wooden gate, surrounded by a broken fence of bougainvillea. Now, he thinks, I must find some faith healers who can help me.

—————=•(I)•=—————

The day after Glen arrives, Crystal introduces him to Azaad Velji who walks into her living room covered in red dust and holding a crash helmet. Azaad is the youngest son of a prominent Ismaili businessman in Mwanza. Crystal has known Azaad from medical school and has asked him in advance if he would help Glen with his research. Azaad is around the same age as Crystal. Crystal explains to Glen that Azad has travelled to Vancouver, worked in London on several occasions and visited the village of his parent's birth in Gujarat, India. He's also spent a gap year living with the Maasai, hence his love of red dirt. He is qualified as a chemist but recently has been helping his aging father with the family grocery business. Azaad speaks fluent English, Kiswahili and a little Maasai. More importantly Azaad is also an accomplished dirt bike rider.

Glen is very pleased that Crystal has found him such a helper. Azaad's skills fit in very well with Glen's needs for the next few weeks.

As they sit around the diner table in Crystal's living room Azaad recalls some of the memorable ice hockey games he witnessed in Canada. He and Glen hit it off immediately. Azaad proudly shows off his custom 500cc Yamaha single cylinder motorcycle. He confesses that he does not know the district where Glen wants to travel very well, but if they spend enough time together they can carefully plan their route on Glen's map.

Glen wants to maximize the number of places they visit without staying overnight too often. All supplies cannot be carried at the same time, but if they fan in and out of the countryside and use Crystal's as their base, he believes they can manage.

Azaad moves into the same room with Glen, also sleeping on a floor mattress, in what they nickname Hotel Crystal. Crystal's children have some of their drawings and paintings pinned to a corkboard on the wall. Otherwise there are no pictures. The room is sparse with the most obvious investment of the household placed in their TV and DVD player. Sadly for the boys the TV is moved into a cupboard in the bedroom to make space.

On the second morning the two men find Crystal grooming her sons in their school uniforms before sending them off. She then turns her attention to her guests and serves them coffee as they draw more lines and dates on Glen's map.

'There's a limit to the hotel services in this place,' she says 'I ask only that you let me know when you want dinner in the evenings. You must take care of yourself during the day. OK?'

'Hakuna matata,' Glen answers in Disney Swahili.

'Don't drive this man too fast' she says to Azaad, 'no flips or three sixties over bumps . . . or helicopters or whatever they're called.'

'I don't do that now . . . unless I'm angry or overworked.' Azaad replies.

'I don't have the surgical experience to put you back together again if you fall off.'

Crystal puts on her white jacket, lifts her medical bag and heads for the clinic. Before leaving she smiles at both men and blows them each a kiss. 'See you later. *Tutaonana* and good luck.'

From Crystal's dining table the two men wave her goodbye and continue to draw up their plans.

The first village Glen schedules is one he spent most time in during his first visit to the district. He remembers the old faith healer there as one of the most reasonable of those he interviewed.

'Tabibu Willie is definitely a faith healer in transition,' Glen reads aloud to Azaad from the notes of his previous interview. 'This means he is a faith healer open to new ideas. The ultimate aim of his work is to cure the sick, to stop people dying, and we can help him do this.'

———— ◉ ————

Glen and Azaad arrive in the Tabibu's village, and they remove their helmets. Azaad brought the necessary headgear for Glen more for protection against the dust than any accident. They step up to the faith-healers house and are met by the grinning toothless healer in his sixties, known as Tabibu Willie.

With Azaad's help translating, Glen explains that he wants to leave a camera with Tabibu so he can photograph any patients he treats; what he does for them and anything that Tabibu regards as important in his life and work. Azaad shows Tabibu Willie how to hold and use the camera by taking his photo and then how to wind it on for the next shot. He explains that there are only 36 shots in each camera, so healer Willie will have to use the camera sparingly. They will return in two weeks time to take back the camera and reward Tabibu Willie for his help. Before departing Glen asks Azaad to explain that they are hoping for group shots of everyone involved in any ceremonies or rituals. Lastly Glen slips Willie a few shillings, the equivalent of a normal consultation with the healer, to show his good faith in their agreement. Albinos are not mentioned during their conversation.

Glen and Azaad proceed to deliver the cameras and instructions to three or four faith healers per day over the next ten days. They cover a wide section of the countryside, and on route see several albinos in and around villages. These sightings give credibility to Crystal's theory that the incidence of albino births in this area is much higher than the national average. After ten days on the back of a motor cycle Glen is ready for four days of rest before he and Azaad have to do it all again, to retrieve the cameras in the same order they were distributed.

At Crystal's house Glen rearranges an old wooden chair in a comfortable position facing the garden. It is quite a large compound surrounded by a hedge-fence, broken in several places. There are a few well-established fruit trees and flowering bushes. Mango and avocado trees shelter a clump of banana and lemon, with bougainvillea stretching across some of the fence gaps. The lawn is kept short and is slash-cut by a gardener with the golf swing of Tiger Woods. The entrance has double wooden gates, large and grand. They open inward on big metal hinges mounted on two concrete pillars.

Glen plans to head out later for a run to shake off the tiredness in his legs. He is sitting reading when Crystal comes home early. She looks tired and a little concerned. She has barely seen the two men since they started their distribution and interview circuit. They've been arriving back at sunset and leaving before she's awake in the morning.

As soon as she sees Glen, she begins to talk.

'A man came into the clinic this morning after you left with a very dehydrated child. He told my assistant that he felt the child had been cursed. The interesting thing was he said the child had been cursed by an albino family.'

'Really,' says Glen.

Azaad overhears this conversation and comes out from the house to join them.

'How is the child?' Azaad says.

'He is very sick indeed. He's about five years old, but has the body weight of a three year old. His skin is slack, his features are skull like, and he has the classic look of a starved, thirsty child. He can't keep down any food we give him. We have him on a drip but there seems to be other complications. Someone is with him now, but I don't think the child will last through the night.'

'Is the father here?'

'Yes.'

'What exactly did he say?'

'It's strange. He spoke of this child being cursed by an albino family. People here know there is no such thing as a whole albino family. He also told us the child had been sick for exactly five weeks.'

'So what?'

'That is exactly the time since you were here with your family, Glen.'

'Goodness me!'

'I don't know, but it's too much of a coincidence. Perhaps this man was involved in some way in the kidnapping of Douglas, and his son took ill. I know how these folks think Glen. If this is what happened it is likely that he'll return to the source of the curse to try and have it removed.'

'This is wild!'

'Where is this man now?' Azaad asks.

'He is staying at a compound along with a few other families who have children under our care.'

'Can I see him?'

'I don't think you should see him, at least not now. If he recognises you, he might just run away. I can find out more details tomorrow. His name is Joseph Kawanga. We can find out where he has come from. I think we should then let the police and the authorities deal with this.'

'What if he just disappears?'

'Glen we have no proof he is involved. This is just a hunch I have. Trust me, we don't want this to interfere with your research, do we?'

Glen's mind is racing. What is the purpose of his research if not to put an end to these butchers of children? That is his secret goal. He steadies himself against the wall. 'I need to go for a run, to sort out my head Crystal.'

'Well, don't go running north of the village in case you are seen. There is a path heading south for as far as you want to go, and please come back before dark. There's a good clear trail that starts at the break in my fence, near the bananas.'

'Did this Joseph say why or what he thought caused the curse?'

'No he didn't say anything to me. He just mumbled to my assistant as his child was being taken away.'

Glen changes into his Asics Kayano running shoes; pulls on his running shorts and vest, and takes off at a sprint through Crystal's broken fence into the bush. He powers through the first mile in an attempt to clear his head. What should his next move be? He has to go through with his research. He has to collect as much historic as well as current information as possible; yet the situation is changing all the time.

He sidesteps an ant infested log. There is a new sense of urgency to his task. He needs to consolidate all this information, and prepare the key points in a write up that will clearly state some of the civic actions required. He jumps over an ant-bear hole. He will illustrate these with the photos he collects from his camera distribution. But now, perhaps a little bit of luck has fallen his way.

This man Joseph needs to be photographed so he can show the photo to Douglas. If there is a confirmation that he is indeed one of the three abductors, the authorities can be informed and apprehend him and his accomplices. Crystal can help him do this. If Douglas does recognise this man then at least they will have information on where he is from and will be able to follow up on who else might be involved.

Glen runs solidly for three miles. On a particularly fast steep downward slope he scratches his arm on some thorn bushes. In an open piece of ground he disturbs three warthogs who trot off into the distance with their tails in the air. He reminds himself that he is in the African bush, not a Canadian suburb. Here, there is a food chain at which he is not tops.

Glen realises the sunlight is fading and turns back; its approaching feeding time for a few animals that would consider him worth tackling. He looks at his watch. It's nineteen minutes since he started, not a bad speed for this terrain. He heads back on the same trail at a slightly slower pace.

Glen slows walks the last fifty yards up towards Crystal's house. As he ducks through the broken fence he hears the noise of a scuffle come from a back room. There is a movement of the curtains on the south-facing window. As he draws closer the muffled noises grow louder. He hears a scream and sees a hand grab at the open window ledge then disappear.

Glen is stunned and crouches down to assess the situation. He approaches quietly, considering his limited options. He's unarmed, and untrained in any way to encounter an intruder. But there's no time to loose he has to do something. He bends down and picks up a large stone as a weapon. He considers barging in through the door, but he needs to first see how many people are involved. He creeps up towards the window just as Crystal's face is being forced upwards violently. He steps out from the house wall to attract her attention. She looks terrified, frightened. He sees someone immediately behind her, but in that same instant realises it is Azaad. Crystal's terror look turns to embarrassment. She is still rocking forward as Glen realises he is peering into Crystal's bedroom. He has interrupted something special, something very personal that only appeared violent for a moment. He retreats. He had never considered such a partnership.

At dinner that night Crystal is extremely giggly. Azaad is aware of Glen's discovery at the finish of his run and is apologetic.

'I thought you would be longer.' Azaad says to Glen.

'I thought **you'd** be longer,' chimes in Crystal, laughing at Azaad.

'Yes, sorry I didn't realise you were a couple.'

'Most people outside this village don't know we are a couple . . . certainly Azaad's parents don't know, do they?' says Crystal, casting an angrier look at Azaad.

'They'll be told in time,' says Azaad.

'So what's next for the research team?'

'We have to collect all the cameras and number all the locations and people in the images.'

'I reckon we could collect these cameras in half the time it took us to distribute them.' Azaad suggests.

'I'm afraid that's not possible since I would like everyone to have the same two weeks with the cameras and we only distributed our last set yesterday. We're better to take the same time collecting them as we took to hand them out. I'd also like to get a photo of this man Joseph Kawanga. Crystal, do you think that's possible?'

'Let's see.'

'Two more weeks in the saddle,' Azaad says then looks at Crystal and laughs.

'It's a good job you are financially supported by your family, Azaad Velji,' Crystal says.

'Oh, and any time you want a little privacy, just let me know,' offers Glen.

'Any time you see Crystal's kids are not around, Glen.'

'Stop it Azaad.'

'Seriously,' says Glen, 'I'm not paying Azaad enough expenses to deny him anything.'

Crystal turns and glares at Glen, who seems to immediately realise his stupidity and wishes he could take back his words.

'You're offering something that's not yours to give,' says Azaad.

'Please let's move on, there's far too much testosterone in here.' Crystal concludes.

⟨◦⟩

Early next morning Crystal is awakened by one of her staff. The child on the drip has passed away peacefully overnight. Crystal instructs her helper to inform the father and summon him to the clinic. She then enters Glen's bedroom and speaks quietly to him.

'The child has died. I'm going now to meet the father. I have a few formalities to complete for the death certificate. I want you to stay here, but give me one of your disposable cameras and I'll try and get Kawanga's photograph.'

Glen gets up in his boxers. The ceiling fan rotates lazily, distributing the smell of sweating male bodies. He fumbles in a box and gives Crystal a camera.

'Good luck.' Glens says before returning to his bed relaxing, but not sleeping.

———◦《◦》◦———

Crystal is cautious when she confronts the father. She greets him outside the clinic just as the sun is rising, and gives her condolences on news of his son. The father seems completely un-emotional and as Crystal asks him some questions he looks at her with suspicion.

'God be with you. I need to have a few details for the death certificate, if you don't mind,' she says in Swahili. 'We have your son's name as Daniel Kawanga, is that right?'

'*Ndio*,' (Yes) Joseph replies in a quiet voice.

'How many years did your son have?'

'*Tano*' (Five) Kawanga says.

'And what is his home village?'

Kawanga answers and Crystal writes down the details. But then Kawanga continues to talk, mumbling something about his hope that the curse will now end.

'Is there anything you would like to ask me?' Crystal adds.

'*Hapana!*' *(No)*

'Do you have any other children Mr Kawanga?'

'*Mbili*' (Two)

'There is no need to think that your son's condition is contagious if that's what you are worried about.' Crystal says this despite not having confirmed the reason for the child's death. She doesn't want to raise the father's suspicions or let him know that she understood exactly what he said about the curse. She then has a moment of inspiration.

'We will need your signature or finger print for the death certificate also. Can you just hold up your finger for me and I'll photograph it. We have no ink pad in the office.' Crystal then takes out the camera and flashes a photograph of the finger and the face of Joseph Kawanga. It is a portrait, as close as the camera will allow. She then suggests that the father can remove the child's body from the clinic.

At breakfast Glen is very pleased with Crystal's detective work. He is not only optimistic over his research he believes also that Crystal's photo may help identify one of the abductors.

For the next fourteen days Glen and Azaad revisit all the sites where they have left the cameras with the faith healers, and they record the names and locations accurately. He also conducts an interview with the local police chief whom he remembers fondly from his first visit. Crystal is the perfect hostess and becomes more and more relaxed as the days go on. There seems to be no further developments from the death of the Kawanga child.

Azaad and Glen have regular discussions about worldly things as a way of passing their time together. Glen voices once again his concern that not enough interest is being taken by local people as to the violent events that are surrounding them. Azaad dismisses this concern as being unreasonable and tells Glen that it is a sort of privacy and not indifference that people have and that it is not unique to this countryside.

'When I did some of my pharmacy studies in an emergency unit in the UK, there were victims coming in every weekend with serious wounds from violent crimes. None of the ER staff or general public went out hunting for the culprits on their days off. Most people know these things happen around them but don't do anything themselves to prevent them. They treat it as c'est la vie.'

Glen knows people have statistics piled up against them, that they can't make sense of, both here and abroad. More young people committing suicide in Korea and Japan than anywhere else and the full power and sophistication of the authorities there have not been able to stop the trend. Some three and a half thousand people killed on Tanzanian roads every year, but does that affect a bus driver's urge to over-take? Perhaps it's not indifference on the part of the general public to help correct these behaviours, but Glen cannot deny there's a desire to hunt culprits down, when something happens to you.

As this part of his research comes to an end, Glen packs up his notes and his boxes of cameras. Remembering how untidy he can normally be, he makes an effort to tidy up his room. He sticks one of his business cards onto Crystal's son's corkboard in their room and writes a thank you message on it. He then orders a local taxi ride back into Mwanza.

'Your flight is not for another two days?' asks Azaad.

'Yes, but I have an appointment to meet up with the Reverend Mosha at his Sunday church service in Mwanza. And I thought I could save time and space once I'm in town by handing in the rolls of film for processing onto CDs.'

'There would not have been room on the back of my bike with all these cameras and papers,' Azaad points to the packed boot of the taxi.

'Thanks a lot for all your help, Azaad. I'll put you on the credits page.'

'No problem, Bwana Glen! If you need anything else once you're back, just give me a call.'

'I'd like to read your research before you hand it in, Glen, especially the bits from here.' Crystal says. She then moves closer to him and takes his hand.

'For sure I'll get it to you . . . also let's keep in touch with the follow-up on Joseph Kawanga. Let me know if you see or hear anything more about him.'

Glen leans forward to kiss Crystal on each cheek, but she turns her cheek to his chest and gives him a strong hug instead.

'I won't forget you Glen, or your very brief running shorts.'

'I won't forget you Crystal . . . or your face at that window. I wished I'd had a disposable camera!'

CHAPTER FOUR

THE RESPONSE

Mrs Kawanga ties her mourning kanga tightly across her chest. She is wailing inconsolably even before she sees her husband returning home with her dead son. News reaches her as soon as the bus rolls into her village and the boy's wrapped body is handed down from the roof, along with a bag of charcoal and a bunch of bananas.

The noise echoes around the circular walls of her hut and she sways forward and back in grief. She has three children, but her last born Daniel is now gone. A few friends come in and try to comfort her. She grieves that her husband took the boy so far away. She could see he was in no shape to travel, but Joseph insisted. Kaka Damu's attempts to remove the boy's bad spirits had not helped. His advice to stop giving liquids only worked for a few days. The boy grew increasingly weak. Whether it was a curse, like Joseph said, she did not know. Now she knows he is being taken to Kaka's for preparation for burial in accordance with their traditions

Joseph carries Daniel's body under one arm, like a rolled up rush matt. The smell is not noticeable outside but once inside Kaka's preparation room, it is overpowering. He unwraps the frail, stiff corpse while Kaka composes himself to strip and clean the child one last time. He has scented water brought to him by neighbours. Later the body will be taken to Joseph's house for a short ceremony and burial.

Joseph hardly knew his youngest son. Like so many others in the village, the boy had been brought up by his older siblings. Before he could walk, he was carried on the hip of his sister, only a few years older than himself. She took the boy everywhere. When she was given household chores he was placed on the ground and watched carefully. She amused him with twigs and seeds, teaching him his earliest hand-eye coordination. She'd make noises with spoons and metal cups. She taught him how to roll round things around, from pushing and throwing oranges or limes. He'd realise that things were soft or hard from pressing his fingers into bananas or pineapples. He found out what was rough and what was smooth from a variety of vegetables that his sister gave him to hold.

As he grew older, Daniel's language skills were built, not from books with photographs of ducks or chickens, but from seeing these live creatures walk in and out of his house. As soon as he could walk he followed his sister and her friends around, finding other young boys to explore with. From dawn until dusk he had access to a play-world created by nature. By the time he could run, his legs took him unsupervised to the edge of his world and beyond into an exciting wild environment, where small creatures could be scared off by shouts or chased with sticks. He'd reached an age where he would soon be made responsible for looking after goats. The boy had never seen a city, never seen a television and until the day he died, never seen a doctor. Daniel Kawanga's life was as natural as nature itself, which here meant he never felt alone.

Kaka Damu is anxious to find out what happened at the clinic.

Joseph meantime, expects some formalities to be conducted and wants to make sure there is no leakage of the curse from this boy's body.

Kaka takes charge of this and tells Joseph everything will be well. He assures Joseph that in the next seven days there will be a dramatic change of fortunes for him; that the spirits will now look more favourably on the rest of his family. If he believes this sincerely, and the key is this submission to belief, it will happen. Kaka's powers can only help to facilitate this change up to a point. It will depend on Joseph to commit whole heartedly and do what Kaka says.

'But what of this white man?' Joseph asks.

'What white man?' Kaka replies, obviously startled by the question.

'The one whose child we took from the clinic.'

Kaka Damu has been dreading this moment. He is reluctant to take this conversation any further, but knows he must. The knowledge that a white child was involved has been locked away in the back of his mind since the Tatu Js returned and told him of their mistake. It sits like a mystery threat in his mind. It's about to become a released prisoner, this thought, and it's now threatening to take over the whole prison.

The very idea that a white family have become involved in Kaka's world does not rest well with him. They do not understand what they are dealing with. They are well known to be a threatening and predatory race. Who do they think they are? He must do something substantial about this continual thought that they 'might' interfere.

'Is the white father still there, at the clinic?'

'I did not see him, but some people from our neighbourhood living there told me the white man had come back and he's visiting faith healers.'

Kaka Damu is even more disturbed by this news. He knows how relentless and troublesome these people can be, especially among the locals who speak English, whether it's the headmaster, the government officials or doctors. He'd sent Joseph back to the clinic because he believed a curse could be removed from its own source. The spirits had indeed acted by taking a sacrifice of their own, Joseph's son. On one hand this could be deeply cleansing to Joseph's family, on the other hand he finds himself listening to something more sinister. He detects a fear in Joseph's voice, fear from a source other than himself.

'Is this white man alone?'

Joseph answers, using an unfortunate word in his description of what he has heard. He uses the word, *'kutafuta'* (hunting). He says that the white man has returned alone but that he is hunting Kaka Damu!

This news puts a rare flash of fear into the heart of Kaka Damu. He is not afraid, but he knows exactly how to act if indeed he is being hunted. He must now take the hunt to the hunter

---

Glen lies on a raised bed for the first time in almost four weeks. He is watching television in the Champion Hotel, Mwanza. He flips channels on the DSTV satellite network. All around him on the bed, the floor and across a small table are stacks of photographs he's just picked up from the photo-processing lab. Glen stops flipping at one channel where a white man with a heavy South African English accent is talking about his personal weight loss program.

'In seven days,' he says, 'you can dramatically lose weight and change your life. If you drink my tested mixture of fruit juice, you will regain your fitness and health. Guaranteed! Don't just take my word for it. Listen to some of the people who have followed my diet plan.' The advert then cuts to a series of once overweight people. The split screen shows bad posture and large bellies on the left and suntanned toned images of the same people on the right.

'In just seven days I lost twenty pounds. I've never felt better.'

'This recipe (Glen hears potion) is the best thing that has ever come into my life. I feel ten years younger.'

'I can now fit into a dress I wore in my twenties.'

Glen flips channels, away from these satellite faith healer's claims and onto the local news.

Here the newsreader is covering a violent outbreak among pastoral tribes across the border in Kenya. It's described as cattle rustling, but

Glen knows that these pastoral tribes are finding it hard to meet the very high bride prices needed for marriage. Local families are demanding larger numbers of cows in marriage deals, so young men feel forced to go out and raid herds from their neighbours in order to buy a decent wife. In the local Tanzanian news, a young presenter mentions how a mob has beaten a thief to death after he was caught stealing a bicycle. It's a mention of public participation in the by-the-way section of the news, next to the cost of Lake fish rising.

Glen switches off the television. Bizarre but wonderful he thinks. Under the footprint of this satellite there are thousands of different ethnic worlds vying for survival. The ancient and the modern are alive and kicking at the same time. They all need their customs and beliefs to endure; there is no mystery in this. What is scary is how much both are guided by their gullibility and how much both seem to be depending on luck for their future.

Glen begins to shuffle through the photographs taken by the faith healers. His instructions to take photos of anything they feel precious or special has provided interesting results. He is shocked at just how many photos there are of livestock. The response from most faith healers has been to snap photos of their favourite cows, goats and chickens. There are some shots of people standing alongside the animals smiling, but mostly the photos show the animals most clearly. In terms of importance, very little value seems placed on women. There are only two incidental shots containing wives and children. There are no happy family shots. It may exist but it's not a photographic priority for a village-working mind. Glen is surprised to see a few scenic views until he realises there are actually small herds of animals far in the distance.

Perhaps Glen's brief was misunderstood. He realises that the faith healers have an intimacy with the life and death of animals above all else—that their priorities revolve around what they obtain from animals, not only in terms of food, but also of wealth. There's also the power that animals offer in terms of changing negative mindsets at festivals, celebrations and at appropriate sacrificial occasions.

Glen is not too disappointed. There are certainly enough visuals to illustrate a power point presentation and for his final research paper. He has in addition one gem of a photograph he has enlarged and kept separate in an envelope. He digs it out and looks at a man in perfect focus presenting his finger to the camera. Glen writes on the envelope Joseph Kawanga.

Glen checks his watch and, realises he is late. He grabs his oversized notepad and backpack and heads out from the hotel. He is rushing for an appointment with Reverend Mosha at the house of someone who, in the Reverend's eyes, made the ultimate **sacrifice** for mankind.

———⋙◉⋘———

At the Church of Our Lord Jesus Christ, the service is already in progress, and the rafters are vibrating with the sound of full voice singing. The Reverend Mosha stands at the pulpit, robed and collared, with his experienced auditory voice instructing his congregation to sit, once the hymn singing stops. Glen creeps into the back row and takes a seat. He realises quickly that he is the only white person in the church. The Reverend spots him immediately and nods recognition.

Glen sits through a sermon which is spoken in a spontaneous mix of Swahili and English. Glen is not sure if it's for his benefit but somehow the English is used to stress meaning and give authority to the biblical passages. It's like, if it's said twice, in two languages, who can doubt the wisdom. Glen listens to words that are familiar to him, but that he's long believed are dated and sometimes divisive in today's multi-cultural world. He listens to the words 'faith' tied to the story of a healer from Galilee. He feels, for the first time, these words trying to draw in the people around him to a slightly better and more organised belief system. He considers what it must be like to hear this story having come from a village where animist or ancestral worship is predominant. It is a compelling tale. It is a fantastic story. On one level the structure and power of the church must impress, but also the freedom to give up endless worry and costly sacrifices is also being offered. To upgrade one's faith a notch and take on a better model, to trade in cruel traditions for a message of love and support, it must be appealing. This is virgin-mind territory for an evangelist from any one of the mainstream religions. The enthusiasm that the Reverend stirs up is self-evident.

After the service Glen remains seated as the congregation leaves. He is greeted by nearly everyone as they leave, smiling and comfortable with their hour of faith re-enforcement therapy. Their Christian handshakes are enthusiastic and gentle. After some time, the solitary voice of the Reverend echoes through the church.

'*Karibuni* Bwana Glen.'

Glen stands and shakes the Reverend's hand heartily before they sit down together in the now quiet church.

'An impressive sermon Reverend.'

'Yes? But something tells me you're from the Darwinian school of thinking. Am I right?'

'What makes you think that?'

'Your attitude of course.'

'Really.' Glen says.

'The trouble with science as an object of faith Mr Glen, is that it gives us so little time to place our faith on things before they are debunked. There's never enough time for faith itself to grow and become strong.'

'Well we have such little time here anyway. Its more a choice of what societies should pass on is it not? A never changing story from a Religion is OK but so too must be the intelligent reasoning of the facts we discover about ourselves and our existence.'

'Yes, maybe! But we are creatures of faith. And where as our existence might change, our selves do not. The very notion of passing on implies someone else will get the benefit . . . and you ignore the tremendous strengths that come from an individual's submission to an ever-lasting faith.'

'If only submission did not also breed all sorts of religious extremism.'

'You have to know your enemy.'

'I'm not your enemy, Reverend. I just have some specific questions to ask you.'

'Go ahead, sorry. You're in the house of the Lord and I don't let people off when they are in here. How is your research going anyway?'

'It's fine despite the lack of accurate overall national numbers. I've been sent a list of areas in the country where albinos are most at risk. I also have some good samples of knowledge and practices from one particular site in Shinyango. But it's not my research I want to talk to you about. I want to ask you what I should do with some information that could possibly lead to the arrest of the gang that abducted my son.'

'You know who they are?'

'Not exactly, but I believe I may soon get a confirmation on the identity of one of the men and if I do, what next? Pass it onto the police in Dar es Salaam or deliver it to the local police here?'

The Reverend sits silent for a moment, looking up to the figure nailed to the cross, before talking.

'It is up to you. If you would like this to be a high profile arrest and conviction, you are in a privileged position to make this happen. The politicians and police in Dar will no doubt make international headlines over such an arrest. The full weight of Tanzanian law will fall on these men, and you will be surprised how heavy that weight can be. They will be made an example of and there will be shock waves up and down the country. The fact that a white man's family has been threatened and you've been able to track and capture a local faith healer will be very big news.'

'Not a faith healer, Reverend . . . a gang of possible murderers.'

'Granted.'

'What's the alternative?'

'You can pass on the information you have to the local police chief here and have him initiate the arrests and the convictions. This will make it a local breakthrough for the justice system.'

'Is there an advantage in doing it this way?'

'Not an advantage, but strategically the more success the local police have with this, the more competition there is for greater local success. If local police are able to apprehend such criminals, then other districts will believe they can do it also, even with their meagre resources. It could also drum up support for community groups to take local action.'

'So that's what you advise.'

'It's entirely up to you Glen. I've no doubt if you choose the first option you will become famous and your research ground breaking, leading to another wave of international effort and pressure to be put on our government on this issue. If you choose the second option you could help begin more grass roots action to stamp it out. Choose your move wisely. You have the choice to bully the police here into action or strategically help them.'

Glen considers the Reverend's advice on his way back to the hotel. He cannot decide if the Reverend is fishing for some local publicity for himself by bringing in the Mwanza police. It would certainly be easier to hand information over to the police in Dar, especially if he gets a positive identification of Joseph Kawanga's photo from his son Douglas. Glen is wary of the media and what sort of a circus could surround his family in the light of fresh arrests. He gets on the plane to Dar es Salaam undecided.

Kaka Damu shouts instruction to some of the workmen he has recently hired, making sure they get the right mix of cement and sand to finish the construction of his house. He has already recovered two stolen bags of cement that were only brought back when he threatened the thieves with the curse of a slow painful death. Now he suspects the workers are diluting the mixture. He doesn't want his house falling down when they add the new corrugated iron roof he has bought. He points his ju-ju stick at the suspected workers in a last ditch attempt to keep them in line.

'You'll suffer if this building is not finished properly.'

Kaka is adding an extra large room at the back of his house where he hopes to perform some more personal treatment and consultations. He has tolerated the inconvenience of the builders, but more troubling to him at the moment is Joseph's state of mind.

Kaka decides to call an emergency meeting of the Tatu J's to discuss the circumstances surrounding the death of Joseph's son.

The four men assemble in the shade of their familiar Baobab tree. It is full of pins and ribbons of cloth from people seeking the tree's help to change their luck. Kaka moves away the three legged stools and sits on a section of roots that look designed for a conference of elders. They stretch out in two quarter circles, each a foot or so above ground, to make two rounded benches. The tree is well worn by bottoms from previous discussions, and it's now comfortably shaped. The men sit facing each other.

'Things turned bad after we returned from the Dawakubwa clinic.' Joseph speaks with a shaky stress in his voice.

'It is not all bad, Joseph. We have had some good fortune since you returned,' says Kaka, looking at the other two and thinking of his new consulting room.

'Joseph, we understand how hard this has been for you but the bad luck has now passed,' adds Juma.

'Why can I not sleep at night then?'

'We can give you something to make you sleep.' Kaka offers.

'I have already tried your medicine, but all I see is the flash of that doctor's camera in my eyes.'

Both Juma and Kaka react simultaneously to this statement. They grunt and spit to their side, as if to put an end to words that might bother them. They rub their mouths and scratch their thighs sharply with their nails in an attempt to ward off more impending bad luck. After a moment Kaka continues the conversation.

'You said there was a doctor who took a photograph of you?'

'Yes the Chagaa, at the clinic.'

'Why did she take your photograph?'

'She took a photograph of my finger for Daniel's death papers.'

Kaka seems satisfied for a moment, until Juma asks, 'Why do you see the flash in front of your eyes?'

'Because she held my finger up and pointed the camera straight at my face like this.'

A sheep herder passes the four men and whacks a stray lamb that has drifted into the centre of the conference. The group sing out an exchange of greetings with the herder before returning to their business.

'Did you see any sign of the white man or his family there?' asks Juma.

'I already asked that,' says Kaka.

'No, I heard that he was there, but his family were all back in Dar es Salaam.'

'Did the white man see you?'

'No, I told Kaka I did not see him, and I'm sure he did not see me.'

'How do you know he was hunting for Kaka Damu?'

'Each day he would go out with an Asian on the back of a motor cycle visiting faith healers and asking questions. Why else would the white man do this if he was not looking for Kaka?'

'*Mzungu, mzungu, mzungu.*' (European.) Kaka repeats like a curse.

'He should consider himself lucky that we let his son go free.' Juma adds.

'He is not likely to see it that way. He must have been afraid.'

Although Kaka has never spoken to a white man before, he has seen a few from a distance. He thinks he knows them. He believes he can sense what a white man may be thinking from the behaviour he has been told about. He has seen both men and women in the streets of Mwanza, mostly in vehicles. He has some knowledge of their busy world and their creations. He has seen them on television and movies that are made by the *Wazungu* storytellers. Kaka makes his decision.

'Juma we need to find out what this doctor has done with your photograph.'

———◉———

'What did you think of Glen?' Crystal asks Azaad.

'I'm glad he's gone,' Azaad says, putting his arms around Crystal's waist and pulling her towards him. 'I thought he would never leave.'

Crystal looks disapprovingly at Azaad. 'Leave, so you can molest me, you mean.' Crystal offers some resistance and backs away from Azaad smiling. 'Tell me what you think. You have spent over a month with him.'

'He's so serious. You know what they can be like? Every lunch he would go on about some global problem that needed to be addressed before we all destroyed the planet.'

'But that's cool.'

'One day he went on about Africa's population and how it will double before we have a chance to save the eco-systems here.'

'Did you say anything?'

'Yes, I told him there were other ways of looking at it; that it was not the behaviour of people here that was screwing up the planet. And he agreed. I told him that any stop-fornication message would not go down well here.'

'Yes. Especially with you.'

'No. That after years of being denied every type of freedom . . . Africans should now be denied sex?'

'Yes exactly that sort of thing. Heaven forbid.'

Azaad stretches his arms out to Crystal who slaps his hands.

'And what was your other way of looking at it?'

'I told him basically that the earth was not at risk from the poorest people even if we are all breeding like rabbits. It was in danger from carbon emitting industrialists who are sucking up the earth's resources to promote an unattainable as well as an unsustainable lifestyle.'

'Very intellectual Azaad, that's cool too.'

'I know I got it from a book.'

'What did he say to that?'

'He agreed again. He still thinks there's danger in having too many people with . . . as he put it 'the same aspirations . . . at the same time.'

'Yes, let's slap a ban on African aspirations too while we're at it.'

'It wasn't so much Africa he was talking about. He mentioned India and China and their current growth rates.'

'So you liked him?'

'Yes . . . intense though he is. He's definitely makes you think you know less about everything than you thought you did.'

'He's a researcher at heart.'

'Yes. He knows all about the Ismaili community here, their history and habits. He was talking about the Aga Khan's roots, the split in Islam, things I hardly know anything about myself. Shit, he even spoke about the Maasai and their customs like he had lived with them.'

'Oh I see. You mean he spoke to the great Maasai historian and blood-brother to the tribe, Azaad Velji, about his favourite topic . . . the mighty Maasai?'

'Don't underestimate the value of a gap year summer holiday living in a Maasai *boma*.'

'And you've talked about it for ten years, as if you are a complete authority on Maasai culture.'

'And I made one good friend in the process. But Glen knows the rituals of the Maasai Laibon and all their tools and bones and stuff and what they are for. A whole lot of customs and beliefs I've no knowledge of.'

'Well learn a little and you can elaborate your own Maasai stories.' Crystal laughs at the irony of Azaad's confession.

'Stop it. You don't know how hard it was for me to get away from my parents that year. I just took off on my bike and hung out on the slopes of Dionyo L'engai. I was basically adopted by the Big O's family.'

'The Big O!' Crystal laughs as she recalls Azaad's knick-name for his Maasai friend. 'He is such a stereo-type Maasai.'

'He deserves to be. He earned his credentials. The Big O explored all of the Maasai lands across three countries before I met him.'

Azaad crouches and creeps up towards Crystal, like a warrior hunting, 'Did I ever tell you about the time he walked from Mount Meru up through Kenya into Southern Sudan staying with people he called, his relatives?'

'Only a gazillion times,' says Crystal pretending to recoil.

'Did I ever tell you about the time my friend Big O spent with the Dinka, outside of Juba,' Azaad continues his story telling voice, chasing Crystal and putting his mouth close to her ear. He whispers 'The time the Dinka gave him one of their long bladed spears?' Azaad pushes his pelvis closer to Crystal, 'about the time he single handed killed a lion with one thrust?' He nudges her once with his hips on the word thrust.

Crystal starts laughing uncontrollably and Azaad barely stops himself from joining her in hysterics.

'I met his wife and she seemed very nice. Not so intense.' Crystal recovers.

'Who, the wife of Oli-siye Tip-bad?'

'No . . . Glen's wife.' Crystal laughs once. 'Where did you get that name?'

'The Big O's full name is Oli Siye Tip-tip, but I call him all sorts of nicknames. Tip-bad stuck after we met in Nairobi. He refused to give a Kikuyu waiter a tip at the Thorn Tree restaurant. It was funny. Big O was dressed in his red and purple robe, wearing all his Maasai bling with his white plastic sandals. They almost didn't let him in. He couldn't believe what they were charging for a glass of milk. He kept asking the waiter in Swahili, is this cow's milk? You charge how much for cow's milk? He refused to drink it. The waiter got so angry he grabbed a bottle of tomato sauce and plopped a shot of it into O's milk, like cow blood. He was shouting 'is that better?' I had to keep the two from fighting right there in the restaurant. Anyway he became Oli Siye Tip-bad from then on. He's back living near L'Engai tending his cattle. I recently gave him a cell phone, a small Samsung which he occasionally wears in the lobe of his left ear, when he's peeing.'

'What?' Crystal gives Azaad a disbelieving look.

'I'm serious. He's no where else to carry it. We're still in touch.'

'You should give his number to some Hollywood director.'

'I know. Dial a Maasai. He's an impressive looking man for sure. There are no spindly legs on that one. He had too much bull blood when he was young.'

Crystal, heads off to the kitchen to fix up the evening meal. Her eyes are still soaked with laughter. She has not laughed that much in years. One serious break-up after another has left her cautious of the local men in her life. She finds it extremely difficult to maintain the basic levels of equality she feels she needs in a relationship. Up until now her men have all pushed their superior gender credentials at times when she was most vulnerable. Her first love left her when she was pregnant with their first child. She left the second after he took her pregnancy to mean he was free to move and play with other women. Luckily her salary and her status in Dawakubwa allows Crystal to employ as much help as she needs to bring up her two boys. She finds she is respected and supported by the community, but she likes it most when Azaad comes to visit.

This is certainly not the life Azaad envisaged after studying pharmacy, but he still feels too wild to settle down in a single occupation. He has toyed with plans to open a pharmacy, but keeps them on hold. He believes that experience running the family grocery chain is a secure way to train him self to open a local chemist shop.

On the third night after Glen leaves Dawakubwa, Azaad receives a call from his mother saying that his father has taken sick. He tells Crystal he has to return to Mwanza to see his Dad and put time into the family business. As Azaad starts up his orange Yamaha, he blows a kiss to Crystal. She stands at the open gate of her compound with her two boys. Azaad revs the motor cycle and powers out of the gate. Crystal pushes shut the heavy wooden gates but it does not close properly. She leaves the gate slightly ajar and returns to the house.

The boy's room has been reclaimed by them. They bring out the TV and DVD player that was put in a cupboard for the duration of Glen's stay. For the time being they leave the cork board with Glen's card, maps and charts still pinned to it behind the TV. Crystal relaxes once more in her own space, alone.

CHAPTER FIVE

THE DECISION

Glen returns home after almost six weeks away. He crouches beside his children and passes his hand through Douglas's re-grown hair. He feels the boy must have stretched inches during his absence since he seems taller. He chases both children out of the house around the pool and the garden and eventually, after taking off his shoes, lets them push him into the pool.

Pam sits smiling at this familiar chase-and-capture game. She is wearing her Tuesday kanga, tied around her chest the way she has learned from Helen. She sits on her porch with a glass of red wine and a folder full of newspaper reports she's downloaded off the Internet. All of it is coverage of Douglas's abduction.

Three local newspapers run the story as a mistaken kidnapping, while two respectable international papers plunge into the issue of Albinism in Africa.

Pam is glad Glen's back safely; she's missed him. She has only heard nuggets of news from his trip but she is pleased that Glen is putting his energy towards the children first, now he's back. They will soon tire and go to bed, and she will then find out more of his story.

The light rains of the afternoon have brought out the annual armada of ants seeking new colonies. As if some underground industrial whistle has blown and all ants are released from work, they stream out from openings all over the Chapman's garden. They have been preparing for this since birth. Millions of worker ants feverishly clear a path for those among them who have grown wings. As darkness descends, these queens are carried out through the deep dirt troughs like rock stars through a mosh-pit. They're then launched into the air with the precision of a full military air assault.

Wave after wave of flying ants take off, struggling for distance like miniature De Vinci flying machines. It is dusk but still light enough to see the sky full of them drifting in every direction, upwards, over fences, over trees, high on the wind of exploration. As darkness falls and the house lights are illuminated, the remainder take off and head for the lights. These outside lights are death stars and attract the creatures in their thousands. They fly senselessly towards anything bright, lit windows, in some ambitious cases, the moon. It becomes too much for Pam to bear as they swarm around annoyingly above her head. The whole family then move inside the house to avoid a battering from the blinded aeronauts.

Glen sees Helen, the house girl, collecting the fallen queens in a jar. He knows she will use these to fry up a nutritious snack for her children. It's a seasonal delicacy.

Glen takes his children for a bath and then coats them in after-sun cream before putting them to bed. Glen then pours Pam another glass of wine and tells her of his time with Azaad and his motorbike; with the cameras and the faith healers; with Crystal and the clinic and his audience with Reverend Mosha. Because of his movements and poor mobile coverage around Dawakubwa he has not managed to fully update Pam over the past five weeks.

'What was he like?'

'Who?'

'Azaad.'

'He was nice, very helpful. Very different from a lot of the Asian lads I've met here in Dar.'

'What do you mean?'

'Well Azaad doesn't seem to have an ounce of prejudice in him!'

'It's not just Asian lads who are racist here.'

'I know. I know, too many people don't even realise when they're being racist. A lot of it is just language problems with English, talking people down all the time.'

'*Sahihi.*' (Exactly)

Azaad is well travelled and he speaks kindly about people living in the countryside. He has lived with the Maasai for a time, and he's sensitive to their culture. We had some good chats.'

'And Crystal, how is she?'

'She sends her greetings to you. She is good. She's in a relationship with Azaad . . . a romantic relationship I mean.'

'Is that not unusual?'

'Not really, she's an attractive woman. She's much more switched on than I thought when we last saw her.'

'So was the research successful?'

'More than I imagined.'

'Good, so you have now given up your detective work?'

'On the contrary, I have a photo I want to show Douglas. I believe it's one of the men that took him.'

Pam's facial expression changes immediately.

'God Glen, we're just getting over this. What do you think this will do to Douglas? What will it do to us? Have you thought this through?'

'Yes, I have.'

'And?'

'Who will do this if we don't?'

'Will Douglas have to give evidence in a court? I'm not having our boy put through more traumas for this . . . ' Pam stands up and walks to the curtain before she shouts an explosive 'Bullshit!'

'Trust me. Douglas won't have to go through anything traumatic. We have a chance to ensure that no other children will be taken by this gang. If Douglas recognises the person in the photo, these people can be found and stopped.'

Glen takes Pam in his arms. She resists for a moment then relaxes in his embrace.

'Everything will be fine,' Glen says, stretching his arms around Pam's shoulders. He looks into her eyes. 'We have been apart too long to mark our first night with an argument.'

Glen kisses Pam and she responds. They kiss so little these days and Glen feels it like a jump-start of electricity. He pushes Pam till her back is against the window. They become lost in passion. Outside a thousand queen ants are responding to their need to procreate, by bashing their heads against the windows.

———◎———

There are very few plans in Kaka Damu's life but there is routine. Each morning he wakes when the cockerel crows and after a leisurely breakfast, he moves from one friend's house to another. He helps if he can, not only cult members, but people whom he trusts and who put their faith in him during times of trouble.

Top of his list for consultations are matters of the heart. Most people that come to see Kaka are scorned men or smitten women. Kaka has a remedy for them both; a potion which makes men's words irresistible to women and a scent which weakens men's resistance to women. Next in the ranks of good business come those suffering from infertility, then infidelity, then infinite bad luck and illness. Kaka can move effortlessly from being the faith healer; the soothsayer; the diviner, priest, shaman or out-right witch doctor. Each of these roles he oversees, as if they are branches of government under his control.

Kaka's keeps his potions in a dug out ant hill behind his home. There he uses the remarkably efficient air-cooling system of tunnels and hallways to keep his ingredients dry and fresh. He has the assistance of an eleven-year-old apprentice priestess, Nyanzu, to whom he is teaching the ways passed down by his forefathers.

Nyanzu was a gift to the shrine from a woman who pleaded help from Kaka for infertility. Kaka's price for her treatment was the voluntary donation of her first child to help him in the shrine. Kaka's treatment for any woman's infertility is to mix an appropriate potion, which often puts the woman to sleep. Nyanzu's mother came for treatment several times, and on each visit, Kaka had intercourse with her. This was his way to discover if it was a problem with her husband's fertility, or hers.

Within a few months the woman was overjoyed with news of her pregnancy, and after giving birth, she nurtured the child for five years. During that time she failed to conceive another child with her husband. Kaka kept up his considerable pressure on the mother by hinting that she was failing getting pregnant again because she had not honoured the spirit-law promise she made to Kaka. She was convinced she needed to donate her daughter to the shrine in order to please her ancestors, the deities and local spirits she believed in.

That was six years ago. Now the girl has become an excellent young priestess for Kaka's business. He has shown her how to pick herbs and plants and how to store and mix them. Kaka has also marketed a healthy respect for her power by using her at festivals and displays. There with the right mix of exposure, theatrics and dread, he's grooming his illegitimate daughter for stardom.

One of Nyanzu's special tricks is to help Kaka in a performance that he prepares when he detects bad spirits in a village. Also on occasions when Kaka feels threatened by the authorities or the evangelical religions that constantly intrude into his realm, he organises a special sacrifice. Kaka knows his authority is continually being challenged, by people returning from the city with messages of Islam or Christianity. He believes he must reassert his power by staging these grand traditional displays of drumming and dancing that usually last well into the night.

Typically Kaka waits until the crowd is gathered and sufficiently plied with alcohol or special drinks. When everyone is near exhaustion Nyanzu enters the centre of a crowd of frenzied drummers carrying a live chicken on her head. Kaka then appears dressed in his father's animal horn headdress, with a lion's mane cape and a hippo tooth around his neck. Kaka dances in circles stamping his feet in time to the drums as he finally approaches the girl.

Nyanzu is innocence personified with her long sleeved dress, her doe eyes and the terrified large chicken on her head. Kaka walks away from the girl then suddenly turns to point his knife in the direction of the chicken. As the drums stop on a loud thump, the chicken collapses and dies. Kaka is several feet away from his victim. The chicken has died as a result of Kaka pointing his knife at it from a distance. People scream with surprise. They praise his powers. The sceptics are dismayed and a few are even converted back to Animism.

What the audience cannot see is the girl Nyanzu puncturing the heart of the chicken with a long steel needle she has slipped from her sleeve. She does this with such dexterity the chicken slumps in silence into her hands. No one sees her put the spike back into her clothing.

Kaka is aware that the threat from 'Religions' and 'Educators' and the 'Government' is real. It is either the law or one of these imported faiths that threatens to take away his customers. He is concerned they will team up. His survival, he believes, depends on the spread of his influence in an equally evangelical way. After such performances some un-educated young people, who want to travel to other parts of the country, come to Kaka for advice. He has had some success giving away his knowledge and supplies to those seeking luck to find work. If all else fails, he tells them, they too might be able to sell potions and the power of the spirits to make a living.

Kaka knows many people living in Mwanza, Moshi and Arusha who are basic extensions of his practice. One of his longest serving disciples is a man known as Cheetah, living under the Selander Bridge in Dar es Salaam. He has been among his customers for herbs for years and retails them through a fleet of beggars and street sellers. Cheetah is one of Kaka's oldest friends.

In a few years Nyanzu's fertile eggs will be singing for attention and Kaka is considering whom he will allow to answer their song. He has considered Cheetah, but in current times he thinks that Juma will appreciate the girl most. He can think of no one who has been more loyal, no one he trusts more than Juma. He also understands that Juma is naive enough not to question why he himself is not taking the virgin. Under normal circumstances Kaka would reserve the girl for himself, but she is his daughter. He is not about to anger the ancestors with incestuous behaviour. There are some lines he will not cross.

Before the Tatu J's set off to Dawakubwa, Kaka Damu takes Juma aside and offers Nyanzu to him as a reward from the shrine. He tells him that he must now do whatever is necessary to make things right. Juma is surprised both at this reward and the implications to Kaka's suggestion. Juma knows that he is trusted and that he has given long service, but this is a gift he never imagined. He is very pleased and vows to Kaka he will do whatever is necessary in Dawakubwa.

'Go and remove this curse once and for all. Seek out any information that can help Joseph. It is not only he who is suffering through this, but it is our whole clan. If you find out who is the cause of this threat, they must be buried.'

Juma nods his understanding.

'All of them! Understand?'

Juma nods once more.

(TWO DAYS LATER)

Azaad is working in his fathers store when he receives a panic call from Crystal, six days after leaving her in Dawakubwa. He immediately recognises a level of concern in her voice.

'There are three men back in the village Azaad. It could be the same three who took Glen's son. They are asking questions around the clinic. I'm worried.'

'Slow down Crystal! What have you heard?'

'Friends here told me it's the same man whose son died, but I don't know about the others. He is asking staff at the clinic what I did with his photograph.'

'Have you said anything to the police chief?'

'No, he's travelling. I've only just heard this minute, and that's why I'm calling you.'

'What do you want me to do? You and the boys are welcome to come here for a while.'

'I thought about that and I'm tempted.' Crystal pauses for a moment. She controls herself a little more. 'I'd especially like to see you explain me to your folks.'

'The timing of this is very bad.'

'Dah! *Ndio* (Yes) bwana.'

'No. I mean my father's still not well. He got sick when I was travelling with Glen. I've been doing a lot of catch up work at the family business.'

'I also have a clinic to run. I can't just leave here, Azaad. Can't you come here for a little while? I don't know why, but I'm concerned more for my boys.'

'OK Crystal. I'll try and come next week-end.'

'That's five days away.'

'Hold on a minute. I'll call you back.'

Crystal is left holding her silent mobile. She wonders if she is being paranoid or not. The villagers are her friends and she has never felt afraid in their company. But, there is definitely something sinister about this dead boy's father. She goes over the security precautions she can take with her home. Her garden fence is not good, she has no guard and even her front gate does not close properly. She walks back to her house from the clinic and makes plans to fix up her property and to hire a guard. This is all she really needs. Then her phone rings once more, she is startled and she smiles at her own insecurities.

'Hello.'

'It's Azaad. I've fixed up some security for you.'

'Goodness, are you a mind reader? What do you mean you've fixed up security?'

'I've just come off the phone with Big O. He's going to take the overnight bus to Mwanza, then a taxi for Dawakubwa tomorrow. By tomorrow afternoon he'll be at your house to protect you and the boys. I've explained everything to him. He already knows of you. Trust me, once these men see Big O, they won't be messing with you or the boys. I'm planning to come at the week-end.'

'Are you sure about this Azaad?'

'Definitely. It's the best plan under the circumstances. I'll come on Saturday and we can assess things then.'

'You don't really need to come if the Big O's here protecting me.' Crystal teases.

'I think I will. If I don't come and pay him by the weekend, he'll be out rustling cattle to make ends meet. He believes that all cows were given by God to the Maasai.'

'Ok . . . how will I recognise him?' Crystal again teases Azaad.

'Take care, keep safe and give me up-dates on what you hear. Do you want me to tell Glen about this?'

'No. I thought about it, but until we have something definite to tie these men to the crime, let's leave him out of this.'

———•(•)•———

At first light Pam walks out to the pool for her morning swim. There are piles of dead and exhausted ants under each security light and along the length of each window. They are in heaps where they have fallen, as if they've been swept there. Some are still wriggling, lured from their genetic task by Thomas Edison's brightest product. Pam splashes handfuls of the amphibious astronauts from the pool.

Glen watches Pam from the bedroom window. He can lose track of time when he's in a sensual daze, usually when he returns from a long absence from Pam. Recently he finds his work engrossing, but when he is in the presence of this woman, he changes. He hopes that their escapades last night become more frequent than they have been recently. Sex is no longer the lynch pin in their relationship, but it is a spectacular confirmation that they are still supportive of each other.

Helen approaches Pam at the side of pool. The house girl is carrying a large brush and dust pan and after a moment of conversation, she continues sweeping up ants. Glen notices how naturally athletic Helen is and how smooth and rhythmic her sweeping movements are. He admires how straight her back is when she bends forward to gather up the ant corpses. Glen also thinks of another girlfriend in Canada who looked good in a bikini, the same colour as Pam's wearing. He then thinks again of Crystal and when he might see her again. These are all flashes that Glen gets from his sensual daze.

Glen watches as Helen stops sweeping for a moment and adjusts her skirt. It's a routine she has, like a nervous tic. The long dark cotton skirt is too tight for her. She unzips the back and swings the zip around to the front so that the skirt is looser and she can bend forward more easily. Helen's back is even straighter now, as if she is planting rice in a field. She has a forward bend that leaves her legs straight and slightly apart. Glen drags his thoughts, full circle back to last night with Pam. He still has to decide whether to deliver any relevant evidence about his son's abductors to the police here in Dar, or to pass it on up-country.

After breakfast, Glen drives his children to school. He passes the crossroads where every other day an old muscular man digs holes in the road and stops vehicles to ask motorists for money for the repair he's doing. At first Glen paid a small fee, but recently he ignores the man. He weaves in and out of the packed *dala dalas* (Minibus taxis) taking people to work. Glen's blue United Nations car number plates allow him to bypass the police that regularly stop traffic asking for insurance and licence details as well as occasional money for sodas.

When Glen drops off the children at the International Nursery School, he takes Douglas to one side and tells him he'd like to show him something after school; something that will help with Daddy's work. The boy enthusiastically agrees, before running ahead of his sister to play with his friends. This is Douglas's last few months at nursery school. He and his friends are the oldest and therefore the rulers of this playground. In a few months he will begin his proper primary education and move onto the lower rungs of playground power, for the second time in many that are likely over his life.

After passing on his herding responsibilities to his younger brother. Big O walks eight miles to the nearest township. Once there he makes a quick deal with another relative to borrow the bus fare to Mwanza. Overnight he travels in the back of the bus with his Dinka spear and short Roman style sword wrapped tightly in cloth. He is in fact dressed as in ancient Rome but he draws little attention on route to Mwanza and exchanges several greetings with fellow Maasai he sees standing guard around shops and garages on the way.

Big O reaches Mwanza early morning. Azaad, who thanks him profusely for coming and explains the situation, meets him. Azaad does not believe Crystal to be in any real danger, but he senses the concern in her voice, and wants Big O to assure her that she will be looked after. Azaad suggests that Big O's first priority should be to fix up the fence around Crystal's house, like a *borran*. (Maasai compound.)

'Make it as protected as your *boma*, (house)' he tells Big O 'then fix the gate so that it closes. Only follow Daktari Crystal if she wants you too. She has two sons that need your protection also. Watch out for the people that may have taken albino children and killed them.' This last piece of information affirms the suspicions that Big O has of all settled Bantus. He's heard of their soothsayers and priests with their shrines and sacrifices and cult followings. He takes a sharp piece of metal from his necklace and scratches himself across the stomach to help him absorb this information and remember how repulsed he has just felt on hearing this news.

Big O and his Maasai brothers carry with them the talisman they need to communicate with their spiritual ancestors. The tools and artefacts of his belief system are much more portable than other tribes. That's why the Maasai are so often adorned with ornaments and jewellery. They are pastoralists, nomadic but also evolving spiritual beings. Azaad and Glen know this although they have come to this knowledge from different directions. Big O carries one special talisman necklace—a large tooth from the lion he killed, and that Azaad had prepared and paid for to be clasped and chained in gold.

'I don't expect trouble once they see you. Who is going to mess with the Big O, anyway?' Azaad tries to joke.

Big O takes this assignment very seriously and he does not reply.

Azaad jumps like a Maasai and chests against the Big O in the way basketball players do. O's feet never leave the ground but he smiles and responds with a punched fist against Azaad fist, as he's been taught in return. Big O then opens the taxi door and places his spear, still wrapped in cloth, diagonally across the taxi's seats as it will not stand vertically nor fit into the boot. It's around five feet long and one third of it is thick metal spearhead. It's the deadly Dinka spear he was give on his travels north into South Sudan. He climbs in and arranges his robe to cover his upper legs.

'Try and sleep in the day time.' Azaad calls through the taxi window. 'Guard the Daktari's house at night. I'll come in a few days time. *Safari njema.*' (Good journey)

The Big O sits in the back seat of the taxi and relaxes. The journey has been long, but he has great experience in settling his mind and passing time. The road throws up occasional clouds of dust as other cars and buses pass by. Big O recalls walking for mile upon mile over endless landscapes with nothing but bush and wild animals between him and his destinations. He has some sleepy visions of his cattle and the good cows that he's lost recently to drought. All his life he has been able to instantly recognise his herd. One time he took them to a watering hole where there were hundreds of other cows. After an hour or so he walked away with every single one of his herd. He could identify them down to a calf.

When he passed into adulthood he walked from his place of birth, under the sacred volcano of Dionyo L'Engai to the coast of Tanzania at Saadani. Then he set out on an epic journey that took him three years to complete. He walked all the lands that the greater Maasai people inhabit. Colonial and National borders have separated these lands into artificial districts, but their size and history are enough to impress any young Maasai. As he grew up he heard many tales of places and events lost in the weakening of traditions, stories that are still passed on orally through generations of Maasai.

Azaad believes that Big O' has a special gift. That his memories are stored as an overall experience rather than filed as thoughts to be revisited or reinterpreted again and again. Big O in other words does not busy his brain unnecessarily. His mind and body react instinctively. As he looks out the window of the taxi, he's in a state of deep meditation, with no thought-activity taking place. His senses are alert enough to bring him out of this state instantly, but when one has 'time' on ones hands, why spoil it with thought.

There is a saying, which O's father taught him. Translated from Maasai it means '*Peace exists . . . until it is disturbed.*' He has found only a few people who understand the wisdom in this statement as much as he does. For most people, peace, is something that is declared, after a time of war. Big O knows that before, during and after any conflict there exists a deeply felt quiet. Understanding how to use this quiet can help one in the confusion of battle, when peace is indeed, disturbed.

———⟫◍⟪———

Glen sets out a number of the portraits he has brought back from Dawakubwa on the dining room table. He has watched enough episodes of CSI, the TV crime series, to know that you do not show a witness just one photograph of a suspect. You have to set out several and let the witness pick the one they believe they saw. Glen sits with another cup of coffee and feels apprehensive. He will soon have to pick up his star witness from nursery school.

Helen's boys Emanuel and his younger brother Thomas come running into the compound from their school and head straight for their quarters at the back of the house. It is an unwritten rule that they do not go into the Chapman's garden even if there is no one around. They squash their school books into a storage shelf then change out of their school uniforms. This is a daily procedure since these uniforms are precious; it's their passport to an education. Both boys are slightly older than Douglas but smaller in stature. They also take off their shoes and within minutes are once more like the bare-topped street urchins they'd prefer to be. Emanuel enjoys these brief topless moments in the day, since he is under strict rules to keep his pale white skin covered with a shirt.

The two boys run passed the kitchen door to see their mother and in the process kick a half empty plastic bottle of sun cream. Glen halts them in their tracks and instinctively spreads the remaining cream over Emanuel's body. He feels the sensitivity of the boy skin as he rubs his shoulders. He sees large freckles in the shape of Africa's great lakes across Emanuel's back. Before he's fully finished the boy runs off at the first sound of the local ice cream man approaching

In the leafy tree covered lane outside Glen's gate the *Barasa* (ice-cream man) is playing 'O solo mio' on his bicycle cart. Emanuel's brother Thomas begs his mother for ice cream money. She reluctantly hands over a thousand shilling note she keeps stored in her bra and the boys run off passed the house guard to buy some. When they return a few minutes later, Helen notices Emanuel is covered in cream. He is laughing and jumping around. Helen thinks he has smeared himself all over with ice cream and scolds him loudly. The younger of the two is laughing so much he collapses onto the ground. Emanuel shows his mother the bottle of sun cream and she realises Glen has rubbed the protection on her boy. She laughs also. These boys can be so naughty. How has she managed without a father's help to bring them up?

Glen drives to pick up Douglas and Gail. On route he passes the hole-digger once more. This time he slows down and shouts some uncharacteristic abuse at the man. Then he drives off, leaving the man stunned. A moment later, Glen sees him in his mirror stopping another vehicle and asking for money to fix the road that he's just dug up.

When Glen returns to the house with his children, he feels nervous. He intentionally takes his daughter aside and mixes her a chocolate drink. He tells her that he wants to talk to Douglas alone, and that she can watch her favourite Sponge Bob episodes on DVD. He puts her in front of their TV, the size of a bay window, in their living room.

Glen then leads Douglas to his study. As soon as the boy enters the room, he becomes suspicious and scared. Glen's room is a dark den of old bones, tools and scattered papers. Glen manoeuvres Douglas over to his desk and talks to him gently. 'Douglas, I have some photographs that I want you to look at.'

'What kind of photographs?'

'Photos of some men . . .' then Glen adds the word 'friends,' to help Douglas relate to the situation. He continues, 'Some friends that I've been working with. Tell me if you recognise any of them?'

Glen might just as easily have pushed a pin through a voodoo doll of his boy. The reaction is instant. Douglas is faced with a table full of pictures he recognises as witch doctors, some dressed with beads and skins, nearly all of whom would be intimidating to a normal adult. However, there is one photo he identifies instantly as one of the men who took him. One of his father's friends! He looks around the room terrified, then runs out, screaming at the top of his voice. Douglas does not stop running until he is in the arms of Helen and begging her to hide him from his father's friends. He is inconsolable and begins stamping his feet as well as screaming.

Glen is shocked at Douglas's response. He was standing right there beside the boy up until the examination of the photographs. He admits to himself he almost willed Douglas to pick up this man Joseph's photo. He was so keen to identify the man from Dawakubwa, he completely lost sense of the young boy's fear.

'Douglas, son, come here. I'm so sorry.' Douglas is embracing Helen with genuine terror in his eyes. As he walks towards him, Douglas shouts. 'No, daddy, no, I don't want to play this game anymore.'

Glen has to peel the boy off Helen. Neither of them have ever seen Douglas act like this, and almost as soon as she is separated from him, Helen does what she has been trained to do when the children are disturbed. She calls Pam on her mobile phone and tells her of the boy's hysterics.

Glen is both frustrated and annoyed at his own foolishness. He carries the boy around the garden attempting to distract him from the scene of his crime. He is concerned for his boy, and the picking of a lemon from the tree, seems to calm him a little. As the boy appears to settle even more Glen also experiences the satisfaction that he finally has proof of identity. Pam and himself can easily help Douglas over this short trauma, and Glen will finally be able to use this information to send the Tanzanian police in the right direction. Joseph Kawanga has been well and truly busted.

⬛◉⬛

Juma makes enquires shortly after the Tatu J's reach Dawakubwa. They establish a base in the home of one of Juma's distant relatives. They are curious about this Doctor Mpira, but they are even more curious about the white man who had been staying with her. They decide to keep their presence a secret and for most of the daylight hours remain indoors. Juma asks his relatives to see if they can find out what the doctor has done with the photo she has taken of Joseph Kawanga.

Big O arrives at Dawakubwa and hands over payment to the taxi driver before making his way into the clinic. As soon as Big O enters the waiting room, a noticeable silence spreads through the building, and children run to their mothers. Crystal comes out to see what the silence is all about and greets Big O with some familiarity. She feels she knows this man from Azaad's stories. They exchange pleasantries in Swahili and as several small children begin to cry at the sight of him, Crystal suggests that Big O goes on to her house. She will follow him soon.

Big O walks through the village following Crystal's direction to her compound. Once there he walks around the exterior of the fence, assessing the gaps and how the low bush could easily let an intruder enter. He examines the gate and notes that the hinges have rusted. He adjusts one side so the centre of gravity is improved and the wooden gate closes properly. Big O then looks around the outside of the house and finds the best vantage spot where he can see the front gate and the back door of the house at the same time. It is here that he sets up camp.

He takes out his small head-stool from its cloth wrappings and sits in the shade. He unwraps his spear and waits.

When the heat leaves the sun, just one hour before sunset, Big O goes out in search of thorn bushes. He has to walk quite a distance to find some. When he finally finds a decent thorn tree he identifies three branches which will be enough to secure the gaps in Crystal's compound fence. Big O takes his spear and expertly hacks three strategic cuts into each branch and then bends the branches to break them off. As he binds the three branches together, a large thorn stabs into his finger. Away from anyone who can hear him, Big O shouts a curse loud enough for all the Gods to hear. He bleats in pain, like a wounded warthog, knowing there is no mortal around to see or hear him.

———⚬———

When Pam arrives home late in the afternoon she needs all her skills as a soothing mother to calm Douglas down. As soon as Douglas sees her, he returns to crying again. Glen has to shift his attention to Gail who is now also on the verge of hysterics also. She doesn't understand why Douglas is so upset, but a brother's tears are infectious. Neither parent has ever seen both their children like this at the same time. It is as if they are possessed.

Pam finally mixes some cough syrup into a glass of milk, knowing its drowsy effect will calm the boy down. As soon as he is safely asleep, she confronts Glen.

'What possessed you to show him these pictures?'

'I thought it was the only way to find out if he recognised this man.'

'Just showing him the one picture would have been enough. Why not wait till I'm here to do it . . . what were you thinking?'

'I'm sorry I didn't know what to expect. Have you ever seen him like this?'

'No, and I never want to again and what are you going to do now?'

'I don't know. I can't decide whether to take this information back up country or to hand it over here.'

'Well make up your mind soon. Go and sort it out, but remember Douglas will need to be watched and I don't want this affecting him any more. Get your fucking act together Glen.'

It takes all her control to exit calmly—she doesn't want to be seen storming out of the room.

Glen has no such control. He grabs his lap-top, bag and barges out of the house. It is unusual that he acts like this but it is not the first time. On the few occasions he and Pam have argued Glen drives a few kilometres North to one of the beachside hotels positioned up Dar es Salaam's coastline. Once there he sits and uses the Ocean to calm himself down as one might use the naive of a church.

———◎———

Glen only uses the Sea View hotel as a retreat when he is most desperate. He admits he is confused and is having trouble interpreting the emotions of the past few weeks. He's locked up too many of his personal feelings brought on by Douglas's kidnapping, in order to work on his research. He wants to be sure he's making the right choice now on what to do next. He believes things peaked this afternoon. He showed extreme insensitivity towards Douglas. He can't believe he's failing as a father; it's the one thing he's most proud of.

He drags a plastic chair to the low fence and sits with his feet up. The sharp line of the horizon cuts across a patchy turquoise Indian Ocean. He breathes deeply and tries to relax. It's good to be here, even if it is so close to Dar es Salaam. This spot has proved to be therapeutic before. He might have to pay thousands of dollars to a therapist in Canada to be calmed in the same way that this view makes him feel.

The clouds drift by in a conga-line of cotton wool floats. This is what he's come for, a brief release from **responsibility**. He feels he needs to decide urgently, but realises there could be side effects with either decision. Local inquires may go nowhere. International headlines might spread the word on how lucrative a business this is and turn more people into copycats. Not everyone hears news with a balanced and reasoned response.

The sea laps onto the beach in its own rhythm, one that Glen's heart relates to. It relaxes him with every sweep ashore, at least that's the self suggestion he repeats to himself. He's safe here. The roaring sounds of the waves are fierce, followed by a hypnotic rush of silence.

Glen's plastic chair is positioned under a palm tree, a few yards away from a large Henna tree. Three young local children appear from nowhere and run into the foaming water. Their squeals of delight drift towards him. He smiles. They seem alone, on their way somewhere, or just down for a swim and a wash at the beach. Glen lies back on his chair lifting it onto two legs. He bunches his cloth bag into a makeshift pillow on the trunk and looks up at the blue sky.

Across from him through the leaves of the tree he sees a branch loose and swinging in the breeze. It looks like it has been here a while and is balanced across a spray of thinner branches. It's not that big a branch but it's no twig either. It is a walking stick shaped branch, stripped of leaves except for a few dead at the end, like the flights of a dart. It hovers over a trail of foot prints that the children are making in the sand beneath. It swings like the sword of Damocles above the three unsuspecting boys. How much danger are they in? At what point does one interfere, or does one not? The scene before Glen suddenly becomes a classroom of life with today's subject being, **how and when to interfere for the sake of good**.

Glen is a good twenty feet from the boys. He considers the situation as carefully as he can, allowing his analysis to overrule his concerns. There is a chance the branch could swing free and fall; an extra strong gust of wind might do it. What chance does this branch have of it hitting a fast moving five year old? But then Glen feels a sense of responsibility return to him and he feels annoyed that no passing locals are jumping up giving warnings. Perhaps it's just that no one else has noticed. The children themselves are oblivious to any danger. There's more threat likely from the stray dogs at the end of the beach, or from a large ocean wave catching them off guard.

Glen knows the children do not see the branch, but he does. Why him? The wheels of responsibility and the brakes on common sense screech in his head. He is being driven by the fear of the guilt should something happen. Slowly, he stands and walks over towards the boys.

The breeze stops for a moment and he cups his hands round his eyes for a better look at the now motionless branch. The ocean waves sound louder, the children move up the beach a little, their play now out of range from the tree. Glen relaxes again. This branch may never fall, and it's too high for anyone to remove it. It will remain untouched until it turns to dust or completes its final flight to the ground. Glen strolls back to his comfort zone. The sun cloaks his body. He sits back in his chair, opens his shirt, closes his eyes and breathes deep. His mind drifts back to his research, its significance and the decision he must soon make about handing in evidence.

Glen hears the return of a boy's voice. His decision making process is once again disturbed. There is always something to distract. Why is this so hard? He has a sudden vision of this large branch falling straight onto the head of a child. He stands up quickly to make sure it is not happening. The children are back and are digging a hole in the sand right underneath the loose branch. If it falls straight down now, it will certainly penetrate a skull and cause instant death. He calls a warning, waves his arms and runs towards the boys.

The children think Glen is chasing them away from the Hotel. He stops under the tree and tries to mime a branch falling, pointing up, and then covering his hands over his head. The children gather their sandy flip—flops and wet t shirts and shout to each other in Swahili.

To them Glen is just another frustrated *Mzungu* (European) tourist with hang-ups. No matter, they are out of danger.

Glen is suddenly struck, on the shoulder. A fist size coconut has crashed down and hit him. The beach children crack up with laughter and start slapping each other's hands like miniature basketball stars. Glen is both shocked and bruised. He rubs his shoulder and looks up at some larger coconuts positioned above him. A few inches to the left and it might have struck Glen's head. Glen realises that he's been very lucky, it could have been the branch.

———————◦(◦)◦———————

Glen makes his decision on what to do with the Kawanga evidence as he lies back in his chair with a bruised shoulder. After analysing everything that has just happened he sees some sort of sign for himself. It's no burning bush that has talked to him, but he sees a relevance and guidance where others may not. He rehearses his explanation to Pam. He is going back up country to Crystal's to deliver the information and photo to the police chief there and he will inform Reverend Mosha of his decision. This way he will avoid the media attention of doing things in Dar. His mind is now busy with plans. The ocean roars it's way up the sand towards him, trying to draw his attention. The waves get louder; they are trying harder. Glen settles in his plastic chair having chosen what he considers to be the safest option for his family. He might have just as easily tossed a coin to decide, but he didn't.

On his drive home Glen stops at Professor Michael Graham's house and tells him everything that has happened. He talks about his son Douglas. He mentions what happened at the beach. He talks of the boys, the tree branch and his decision to go back up country. Professor Michael doesn't really understand the inner meaning that Glen is drawing from his beach experiences. Much of it to him seems hopelessly confused.

This is the last time Professor Michael sees Glen alive. The rest of the story is pieced together from accounts from several people.

CHAPTER SIX

THE HUNT

Up-country Crystal's children are petrified. They are looking at a tree-lined dirt road strewn with bodies. Grass roofed huts are burning in the back ground. Three men lie in the dirt in contorted different positions with their throats cut. Pools of blood cover the ground and a single warrior stands, looking up to the heavens. The warrior is semi-naked and covered in the blood of his victims. He cries out to his ancestors in a language the boys do not understand. He thanks the deities for their strength. The boys barely understand the sub-titles.

The two boys run outside, shouting for their mother, upset by the images. They race from the house calling in Swahili.

'Mama, the warrior, he killed them all. He cut, cut, cut them with a sword. They're all dead. The village is saved!' The two boys wave their arms as if brandishing swords and felling villains.

'Switch off that TV. I've told you not to watch these programmes. Don't you ever listen to your mother? No television . . . especially not on school nights.'

'Sorry mama,' the boys run back into the house.

Meantime outside under the Mwaharubaini tree, Crystal is treating her very own warrior's hand. She pours iodine onto Big O's punctured finger. This time he accepts the pain in a controlled manner. Crystal notices the lion's tooth talisman around his neck knowing that Azaad gave it to Big O. She takes a waterproof plaster and binds it tight around the pulsing muscular finger.

After packing up her medical bag, Crystal walks around her yard to inspect Big O's handiwork. He has patched up the gaps in the fence and fixed Crystal's gate so that both sides swing closed with some ease. It also locks firmly from the inside with sisal rope and a bamboo bolt that Big O has fashioned to fit.

'*Mzuri* (Good) I hope this is un-necessary. You have done a good job. Thanks, and thank you for coming Oli sie Tip-tip.' She pronounces his full name in Maasai.

In broken Swahili Big O replies. 'It's better to be safe, than dead!'

'Yes, I'd definitely say so.'

As dusk approaches, the clouds glow pink and the red cloth that Big O wears seems even redder. He sets out all three of his belongings at the vantage spot where he will spend the night. He stands his spear against the tree and moves his head stool so that he can rest his back against the tree trunk. He places his small Samsung mobile into his ear-lob. The house sparrows gather for their nightly party, dancing among the branches and chirping incessantly.

Crystal goes to the house and prepares a flask of tea. She brings it out and places it at the foot of Big O's tree. Crystal's phone rings and as she answers it, she notices that her battery is almost dead so she's forced to talk quickly.

'Yes, this is Doctor Crystal. Oh hello Chief. My phone is about to run out of battery. Yes I understand. I will call you back, yes immediately.'

Big O's phone also rings and the couple laugh at this coincidence of calls. O's ring tone consists of loud grunts, a chorus of Maasai chants supplied by Azaad. He struggles for a moment to ease the device out of his ear. He then talks into it very loudly.

'Yoo-Azaad-bro,' he says as if it's one word, copying the phrase he learned from Azaad. He then continues in Swahili.

'*Nyumbani nu salama tu.*' (House secure.) 'Yes, *Ndio* . . . OK.'

He gives the phone to Crystal and she walks across the garden to find some privacy before speaking.

'Yes . . . he's been great. He has fixed the fence and gate and I'm feeling much safer. Don't worry about me. I will see you at the week-end. Big O will take care of me now.' Crystal taunts Azaad.

'You know, you have to talk to him about where he keeps his cell phone. Yes, well it's bad for the lobes. No . . . not only the ear lobes; the frontal lobes of the brain. You'll have to talk him out of this before the microwaves damage him. No, he's not indestructible. I'll tell you later how a Thorn tree got the better of him. OK bye.'

Crystal then asks Big O if she can use his phone to call back the police chief and he agrees. As Crystal listens to what the police chief is telling her, she turns serious. She nods in agreement with him although she knows he cannot see her nodding. She only has one brief comment during the police chief's eight-minute call. 'Yes I will.' She ends the call and inadvertently puts the phone into her medical bag before walking quickly into the house.

⇒◉⇐

Pam has quietened Douglas several times in the night. She is sleeping beside him in his bed, and when he wakens she comforts him by stroking his hair. The heat of the night is oppressive even with the little air con in the room they've managed to milk from the power grid before it cut off. The house sits in darkness except for a few solar lanterns as power is rationed on the peninsula. Any thought activity Pam has seems to bring rivers of sweat.

It is also too hot for Glen. He brushes his teeth in the dark, being careful not to use Savlon among strewn tubes of toothpaste, or most unpleasant, as he once did, Deep Heat muscle balm. He carries a mattress onto the roof and slings a makeshift mosquito net tent over it. Bats fly like phantoms at the net before swerving at the last second to avoid contact. He doesn't mind this since he knows the bats are picking up mouthfuls of drifting mosquitoes as they pass. They're like military drones protecting him from at least one of his current enemies. Glen closes his eyes and tries to get some sleep, dozing to the rhythmic rush of bat wings.

In the morning, the previous day's drama has left the couple tired and fractious.

'I'm going to go up-country again to give this photo and information about the abductors to the police chief there'

'Why do you have to go in person, Glen?'

Pam uses the word Glen like a swear word. She only uses his Christian name when she wants to be insulting or aggressive in a conversation. She might just as well have said 'why do you have to go in person, you ass!'

'Because I want to be sure I can convince the police to do something. Also to emphasise that although Douglas has identified this man I don't want him involved any more.'

'And you think this is better than turning over your findings here in Dar along with your research?'

'They are two different things, Pam.' Glen swears back. 'My research and its findings have nothing to do with the abduction of Douglas.'

'You would not have had one without the other.'

'No, but some other poor souls will suffer until these killers are found. You can't compare a one-off research consultancy with a spate of ritualistic killing. Too many albinos and their parents have suffered already. It's basic civic duty to report my findings.'

'I hope you know what you are doing. Your judgement on things has not been great as of late.'

'Thanks for your vote of confidence.'

'You know I'm right.'

Pam stands at the sink washing dishes she need not wash. Helen does all the housework and is far better at it. But Pam needs her own distraction. She realises how deeply affected she has been since the night in Dawakubwa. She's also being taken to the brink of her worst fear, losing a child. Her imagination keeps coming up with exaggerated thoughts. This 'almost-bad' experience has left her nervous and uncomfortable, because deep down she doesn't believe the danger has passed.

Pam feels she is witnessing pure evil, it's spreading and she is terrified. She is unable to shake off a flood of worries which keep growing in her. She would do anything to escape this situation. She will only believe it is over when the children appear normal once more and she seriously considers taking leave and getting on a plane to Canada immediately to achieve this. She schemes to take the children to her parents if necessary. If Douglas does not seem himself in the next few days, she will tell Glen that this is her plan.

Glen comes back into the kitchen holding his phone.

'That was Azaad. He's back in Mwanza. He told me that Crystal called him a week ago to say the three men had returned to her village.'

'I knew it,' says Pam, as if to confirm her fears.

'Azaad said he's sent a Maasai guard up to her house to provide security a couple of days ago. But now he can't get in touch with either of them. He's worried. He plans to go to Dawakubwa tomorrow.'

'What did you say to him?'

'I told him that Douglas had confirmed the photo of Joseph Kawanga as one of the men who took him. I said I was planning to come up there myself to give the photo to the police chief. He said if I can also get there tomorrow, we can drive to Dawakubwa together.'

Pam says nothing to Glen about her plans to leave the country. She knows that if she does travel with the children, she will start to worry about Glen being alone here. This silence from Crystal sounds ominous and she knows that Glen must be concerned for her safety.

'Go then. All I ask is that you keep the safety of our children paramount in your mind.'

Glen is a little angered and insulted by Pam's statement. What other priority does she think he has? What a self righteous, condescending thing to say. It's like her UN jargon job has taught her to talk like this.

'All right Pam. I'll try.' Glen swears then says sarcastically. 'Really!'

———◆———

The rainy season has arrived with a vengeance and many of the land lines, including one to the Dawakubwa Clinic are down. The one thing that keeps Azaad positive about the situation is the absence of a negative. He has not heard any news at all from Crystal's clinic. He is sure that if something had happened, that either Big O or someone else would have been in touch with him. He continues to call Crystal's and Big O's mobile but without success.

Finally Azaad calls the district health chief in Mwanza and is given the mobile number of the Dawakubwa Clinic administrator. He immediately calls her and is told that the police chief has taken Crystal to his village, where there is an outbreak of cholera. She has been gone for three days and no one at the clinic has heard from her. There is no power or mobile reception in the police chief's village.

Azaad asks if the administrator has seen anything of a Maasai.

'What does he look like?'

'He's big—he's a Maasai. You'd recognise him if you saw him.'

'No. I can't say I've seen any Maasai.'

Azaad drives his father's Toyota Land Cruiser four by four slowly to the airport to meet Glen's plane. He is not about to tackle wet muddy roads with his motorbike. Before too long he is driving in the same aggressive style as he does his bike. He keeps the petrol guzzler at high revs, in third gear so he can speed past slow lorries on the single-lane road.

At the airport Glen is first off and only carries some hand luggage. Azaad explains the latest news about Crystal's emergency.

'Maybe we shouldn't go up to the clinic so soon,' Glen responds, 'especially if neither Crystal nor the police chief are there. I could use a day or so in Mwanza to talk to the Reverend before we go.'

'I need to go now Glen. I promised Crystal I'd come. I've set everything up with my family. I've borrowed my Dad's car. I even told my folks that Crystal and I are in a relationship. I don't want to go home before they have fully absorbed this news. Besides I've not heard from Big O and I don't know if he has gone with her or whether he's still at her house.'

'Who is this Big O?'

'He's my Maasai friend, the one I told you I lived with for a while.'

'OK, let's go. If it's a serious outbreak of cholera, Crystal might need some help.'

Azaad floors the vehicle's accelerator and overtakes a line of buses. It is not an unusual driving manoeuvre for these roads. Glen buckles up, and begins mumbling Hail Marys and a variety of tribal and ethnic chants he knows that give protection and ward off bad luck. Azaad's challenge today is to remember he's sitting in a four-wheeled vehicle that's wider than the two-wheeler he's used to.

The larger the vehicle, the more loaded with passengers it is, the faster the driver goes with disregard for everything in its path. This could be the first page instruction on the Tanzanian Highway code booklets . . . if observation was the judge. The idea that a public service vehicle or an empty lorry should just creep along safely within a speed limit is rare. There is a belief in strength and weight, or so it's assumed and often it's the impatient passengers who urge drivers on.

On route Azaad tells Glen a little more about his friendship with Big O. He confesses that he's worried about his friend since he knows he keeps his mobile next to his ear, literally. On a long stretch of empty road, Azaad tells Glen about a time when he was walking with Big O through the savannah.

'Big O was taking me to see a circumcision ceremony and told me that we needed to cross a dry riverbed. There was a deep trench to the right of us, completely dusty and dry, about two hundred yards across. All of a sudden some small boys came out of the bush shouting in Maasai to Big O. They were pointing up stream and were jumping up and down. As we looked around all I could see was a wall of water coming down the river. The next thing I knew Big O had a hold of my shirt and was dragging me down the bank. It was a steep ten feet to the river bed, and then we started to run across the soft sand. I don't think I've ever run that fast in my life. I was exhausted half way across. I ran like a sprinter, but my feet kept sliding in the sand so I stumbled everywhere. All the time this water was coming towards us carrying trees and branches and it looked about twice the height of us. Thirty yards from the opposite bank I fell down. I thought I was a goner, thought for sure I would drown. Big O was twenty yard ahead, nearly safe, but he stopped and ran back. With one big grasp he caught hold of my belt strap and lifted me onto my feet. I ran like a child holding his hand to the edge of the river bank. I was wet, because I'd peed myself. Big O nearly did the same laughing. By the time we got to the top of the banking, the river was a hundred yards passed us. We stood there looking across at something the size of the Mara River. It was twelve feet deep and flowing as fast as hell. This river-bed had become full of dirty brown water in a matter of seconds and, if it had been a few yards wider, who knows what would have happened?'

'So Big O saved your life?'

'Yes, but let's get this straight, he's the one that risked my life in the first place.'

'So how was the circumcision ceremony?' Glen asks with academic interest.

Azaad suddenly bursts out laughing at his own thoughts. He can hardly speak, he is laughing so hard.

'We never got there. After we stood watching the river flow by and fill up to its brim, we walked barely fifty yards to find we had ran on to an island! We were stuck there for two days until the water went down. By the time we got to the village, all the young men had been cut and sent home.'

'How did you survive, on the island?'

'That was the easy part. The river was carrying all sort of animals passed us. Big O just did his total Maasai thing. It was like having an East African food buffet on a conveyor belt passing us. Big O trawled the river edge and he came back with two dead goats and a chicken to choose from. Big O even saw a cow float by that he recognised. He knew its name. There were several drowned wild animals also, some gazelle and a zebra, but Maasai never eat wild animals. A large crocodile made a mystery appearance on the second night and even O didn't know where that came from, since it was basically a desert area. He encouraged the creature to go further down-stream with his spear. He collected some wood, rubbed dry branches together and started a fire. He cooked up the goat a treat.'

Azaad looks across at Glen while still driving and adds, 'It was quite romantic, in a survivor sort of a way.'

⸺◉⸺

Crystal arrives back at the Dawakubwa clinic before lunch time. She enters with the police chief and his driver and orders her assistant to bring her children from the administrator's house. Crystal had placed her boys there because the administrator has a son the same age as her oldest and she did not want to leave her children at home alone. She has not spoken to her boys since she left and she's now desperate to see them.

The police chief thanks Crystal for her assistance. With her help they have not only managed to contain the cholera outbreak, but also in the process saved his mother who was one of the first to fall sick.

Crystal suspects that she might never have been called in if the Chief's mother was not taken ill, but that matters little, she did a good job. The rains are always a dangerous time, especially for young children. This year the flooded rivers brought with them an increase threat from villages up stream. Faeces, which are left to dry in the sun on riverbanks, are suddenly washed into the rivers. Since so many people still depend on the river for drinking water, the risk of disease is high, whenever the rivers are high.

Crystal did not have to practice much medicine during this outbreak. Seven years of medical study can be rendered irrelevant when confronted with a single illness on such a large scale; something that can also be so easily prevented. Crystal's job was more a case of separating those infected from those who were not. The distribution of oral rehydration solution helped people to recover. Within three days of Crystal arriving, the situation was under control. Relentlessly giving out the right information at the right time saved the day. If she had not gone, no amount of singing or dancing or sacrifice would have saved this village.

Almost as soon as she left Dawakubwa, Crystal realised that she had taken Big O's mobile phone with her by mistake. She puts both phones onto a socket at the clinic to charge. As soon as she does, both phones begin ringing and registering a number of missed calls, most coming from Azaad. Crystal takes her own phone and calls him back.

'Hello.'

'Where are you?'

'I'm at the clinic.'

'Are you all right?'

'Yes, I've been out at the police chief's village. There was an outbreak of cholera. I'm just this minute back. How are you?'

'I'm good. I'm with Glen, we are just forty minutes from the clinic.'

'You're coming here? You're a day early.'

'Yes, well no reply from my girlfriend causes me concern.'

'You mean its official I'm your girlfriend?'

'Yes I left my parents pondering the cultural consequences.'

'Well done.'

'I've not heard anything from Big O. I couldn't reach him either.'

'Well, sorry that's my fault. I walked off with his phone after I spoke to you last week-end. He's still at the house as far as I know.'

'I see. There's always a simple solution isn't there? Oh wait, Glen is saying not always . . . that it's almost always a complex social anthropological solution. Where shall we meet you?'

'I have a few things to do here at the clinic and my boys are being dropped here, so why don't you come pick us all up. We can go home together. But be warned. It will be the same sleeping conditions as last time.'

'But you're my official girlfriend. You are so cruel.'

'Well, maybe. Why don't you ask Glen if he wants to go out for a run tonight?'

'I will. Hey Glen, are you up for a half marathon when we get to Dawakubwa?'

———— ◉ ————

Azaad drives into the clinic compound like a rally driver crossing the finish line. Crystal is sitting on the steps with her two boys beside her. She is looking a bit gaunt and tired but she seems happy and clearly relieved to see her boys and the two men. They all embrace, chatter like sparrows and waste no time in loading Crystal's travel bag into the car and setting off to her house.

'I didn't tell you that Glen's son identified Joseph Kawanga as one of the men who took him.' Azaad says.

'So that's why you have come. And here's me thinking it was concern over me.'

'Have you heard anything more about his whereabouts?' asks Glen.

'No nothing, no one has mentioned him at the clinic. All three seem to have disappeared.'

'Well, I'm glad the police chief came back with you. I'll go and have a long talk with him tomorrow. I think he'll be pleased to know that he has the backing of the Reverend Mosha on following this case.'

Azaad stops the Land Cruiser at Crystal's gate. It is closed and he sounds the horn. There is no reply so Azaad and Crystal get out of the car to try and open the gate. It is closed firmly. Azaad shouts once more in Maasai to Big O.

'*Ero Supai!* Hey, big man, are you there?' Glen also gets out of the car, but Crystal's boys remain inside. After another rattle of the gate, one side of it slowly opens and Big O steps out with a smile on his face and sleep in his eyes.

'You been sleeping on the job, Big O?' Azaad asks.

'You told me to sleep in the day-time,' Big O replies in Swahili.

'So you've been doing your job all this time, keeping guard?'

'Yes, like you told me.'

Crystal greets Big O then pushes past the men to get to her house. She's desperate for a wash and to settle the boys. She carries her bag and walks through the open side of the gate.

'Can you open the gate properly, and I'll drive in?' Azaad says.

'No.'

'Why?'

"Come see.'

Azaad follows Big O and Glen follows Crystal through the half opened gate. As they march through, Azaad is still questioning Big O.

'Why can't we open the full gate? Come I'll help you.'

'Thieves came while you were away,' says Big O.

Crystal is halfway to the house but stops suddenly when she hears this. Glen continues on because he does not understand what Big O is saying.

'I left him, so you could see.'

As Crystal turns, she drops her bags and screams. In front of her, pinned to the inside of her gate, is the body of a man with a spear through his back. His feet are off the ground and it looks like he has been caught while climbing over. He is slumped but still supported by the spear. It looks like he has been there for days. The flies are already claiming their bounty. Crystal hears the doors of the Land Cruiser open, and she runs quickly to the car to stops her sons from coming through the gate.

Glen also stops and turns when he hears Crystal scream. Azaad sees the same image at the same time and repeats religious chants that he has not spoken since he was a child. The two men move slowly towards the body, Azaad with his hand over his mouth. Big O stands in front of the man stuck there like a biology specimen on a display-board, looking for approval from his employers. His spear has entered the victim high up beside the spine, but it is now positioned below the rib cage. There is a visible tear down the man's back. Glen walks over to examine the corpse and despite the grotesque distortion on the face, he recognises it as Joseph Kawanga.

Glen is mesmerised by what he is witnessing. Birds are singing, the sun is shining, everything seems completely normal-except for the blood drained body of Joseph Kawanga, dangling like a rag doll. Crystal is talking to her two sons through the window of Azaad's car, to keep them stationary. Glen begins to accept that the man he has been trying to find, is now dead.

Glen turns to see Azaad talking intensely to Big O. He sees the Maasai re-enacting his throwing of the spear. All Glen can pick up is an explanation that a Maasai spear would not have been able to do such a thorough job, since it is a much lighter throwing weapon. It is this Dinka spear that is best for close killing conditions, like this. Big O seems to be giving Azaad a killing lesson, and he's obviously proud of his achievement.

When Azaad finishes his conversation with Big O, he approaches Glen.

'We need to go and talk to the police chief and bring him over.'

'This is Joseph Kawanga . . . one of the men who took my son Douglas.'

'Really, are you sure?'

'Yes.'

'Well it seems that three men were here.'

'What do you think will happen to Big O?'

'I don't know, really, but Big O says the men were inside the house, and that they have ransacked it. He thinks they did not take anything because he saw them leave, but he says they seemed to be looking for something.'

'Will he be arrested?'

'If you can identify him as one of those who kidnapped your son I don't think he's in any real trouble, as long as we don't let him boast about this. Big O was officially employed as Crystal's security guard,'

'It's good that Crystal is also on friendly terms with the police chief.'

'Yes for sure. Now, we better go and report this. Big O wants his spear back.'

—◄O►—

After the attack, Juma runs most of the way home. He is exhausted and thirsty when he reaches his village. He needs to tell Kaka what happened at Dawakubwa. Kaka is inside his home with a respected client, so Juma can't interrupt him. He knows he will not be long so he sits to catch his breath. He looks across the compound and catches a glimpse of Nyanzu carrying some washing down towards the river. Although barely eleven Juma sees her shape begin to take on that of a bride.

Inside Kaka's house the healer hears Juma breathing hard outside. He does not expect him back so soon. He recalls something he felt that very morning when he nearly stood on a dead chameleon lying in the bougainvillea outside his door. The chameleon is the fifth creature that the gods created, so it has significance beyond most other animals. Anything dead outside one's door can be a sign and Kaka knows the ability to read these signs is his gift. Kaka tells his client that today may not be a good day to continue with his treatment for penal-dysfunction. At the mention of it not being a good day, the client puts his business back in his trousers and leaves.

Kaka comes out of his house and Juma almost pounces on him with his news.

'They killed Kawanga.'

'Calm down Juma, everything will be all right.' Kaka adjusts his crooked lion-skin headband and carefully puts it straight on his head.

'We went to the house of the *Daktari* (doctor) to see if we could find the photo she took of Joseph. We heard she had left. While we were inside, devils starts to talk to us.'

'Devils?'

'Yes I swear Kaka, devils. We heard voices from every window. We did not no how many there were. Joseph became terrified, and started talking about his curse. Then suddenly John took off running out the door shouting at the devils, shouting that we should all run. I was not really frightened so I called for them to be calm, but John was already climbing over the gate. Joseph followed him and that's when I saw it.'

'A devil?'

'No, a spear! It flew through the air like nothing I have seen before. Only a devil could have thrown such a thing. It went straight through Joseph and nailed him to the gate. He was screaming but tried to keep climbing. John put his hand over the top to help pull him over, not knowing he was stuck. The more they struggled the deeper the spear sliced him. It was like the spear had a mind of its own. By the time I got to him he was dead. Cut from here to here.' Juma runs his fingers from Kaka's lower back up to his shoulder blades.

'I thought it was my time too. I saw this tall Maasai walk towards me with a short sword. All I had was my *rungu* (club). John kept shouting from the other side of the gate. Come Joseph, come Juma. I managed to jump over the gate before the Maasai got to me.'

'A Maasai?'

'Yes . . . I swear. A giant Maasai.'

'Not the Afriti? (a devil)'

'It could have been devils dressed like Maasai, I'm sure he wasn't alone.'

'So where is John now?'

'When I told him that Joseph was dead and that I'd seen a Maasai, he went crazy. He was even more frightened of a Maasai chasing him than a devil. He kept saying we have to hide, we have to hide. He said if we run the Maasai will track us, hunt us down. He refused to come back with me. He has gone into hiding in the village. I came straight back here to tell you.'

'Were you followed?'

'No I don't think so. I was careful in the beginning. I was not scared,' Juma lies. 'I ran here to tell you the news fast.'

Kaka walks back into his house and returns with a small elbow-bone knife. He sits on a three legged stool outside his door. He invites Juma to bring another stool and sit with him. He looks down at his right forearm where there are five small scars lined neatly in a row. It is not often that he does this, but on the previous five occasions, it has worked. He takes his knife and cuts his forearm below the scars to make a sixth. It bleeds and he rubs some soil into it so that the scar heals rough, raised and obvious. He then hands the knife to Juma, who makes a tenth scar on his arm.

'Such bad news'

'Yes.'

'Have you told Joseph's family?'

'No, I came straight here.'

'Will you go there now?'

'Yes, if you want me to.'

'Yes, go. Tell his wife we will help her.'

'The authorities will hear of this.'

'What will they do?'

'I don't know.'

'The truth is a man has been murdered while visiting the doctor who could not save his son. People will talk forever over this. We need to take some action. It may have been Joseph's curse that led us into this, but now we are involved. We need to take steps to protect ourselves. Let's wait until John gets back and then decide what must be done.'

Kaka pours some water over his cut and the knife blade. He then bends and picks up an army ant, squeezing it onto his arm until its pinchers grab both sides of his cut. He breaks off the back of the ant leaving the head as an effective stitch. He does this twice more before Juma leaves to go and inform Mrs Kawanga of her latest loss.

——●《◎》●——

Glen calls Pam. First, he asks how Douglas is feeling and how he's acting.

'He's fine. He told me he had drunk four glasses of coca-cola at school the day he got hysterical—four full glasses that other people had left during a birthday party. I think he's trying to apologise, trying to cover up the fact he lost it. Can a six year old do that, cover up?'

'I'm not sure, but I think in some sort of Darwinian way if six year olds are evolving to do it, Douglas will be among the first.'

'How is it going with you?'

Glen talks rapidly for fifteen minutes. He tells Pam the full story. He is excited and is clearly a little relieved by what has happened.

Pam pictures in her mind the scene at Crystal's gate, and she is gripped with a new wave of fear.

'I'm scared Glen. I don't like how this is unfolding.'

'It's over Pam. There's nothing to worry about. Everything will be all right.'

'How is Crystal taking this?'

'She's fine. She managed to stop her boys from seeing anything at the scene. She's calmer than I am, she's a doctor.'

'What will the police do?'

'Big O and Azaad are with the police chief now. I don't know what they will do but, I've informed them that this was definitely one of the men who took Douglas.'

'And what about the other two?'

'They got away, it seems.'

'God! So you are coming home now?'

'Yes, my work's done here. It's over Pam. I'll go and see the Reverend once more in Mwanza. I'll tell him that I've followed his advice and gone local with the information. It'll soon be out of my hands.'

'How long do you think they'll take to arrest the other two?'

'I reckon they will be a bit slow here but I'm certain that the police chief will follow through. He'll get support from others now that he has a body to show.'

'Come home soon.'

———◦《◉》◦———

John stayed hidden for two days in the hope that he might recover Joseph's body. He crept around the clinic and the hut that is used as a mortuary, but saw no sign of his friend's body. After the arrival of the white man and the police chief, John gave up waiting and walked home.

His first stop, like Juma was to report to Kaka Damu.

This latest account tells Kaka that the white man is back in Dawakubwa. This white skinned man, he is the source of so many of his recent

135

thoughts; he is the one that may have upset the spirits; the source of so much bad luck. Why do things continue to get worse, why are things not getting back to normal? What can he do to change things?

John confirms that Joseph was killed by a Maasai, not devils. These are men, not spirits that Kaka is fighting. Men can be defeated, they are mortal. Their end can be quick.

Kaka knows hundreds of ways to humble a human, make them bow to the spirits, fear his power. He is not afraid of men. Put him in front of any man and he can make them tremble with fear, without even touching them. He thinks over the sequence of events, back to when things started to go wrong. He starts to see it clearly. It's as if the spirits themselves are showing him. He sees the moment when his luck changed, and he sees a plan to make things right. This plan will appease the spirits, and more to the point, will send his white hunter fleeing in fear.

Kaka has made it clear to Joseph Kawanga's wife that she and her family will be taken care of, and that they will conduct a small ceremony to celebrate him joining his son in the spirit world. Arrangements will be made soon.

Kaka sits with Juma and John. With some seriousness, he calls them the Mbili J's (Two J's).

Nyanzu sweeps away some fallen leaves around the baobab roots. She has been instructed to pin an offering to the tree for Joseph.

Only Juma sees the irony in her offering. As she presses a thorn through the item of Joseph's clothing, Juma remembers the image of Joseph pinned on the gate. He looks away for a second. He watches her throw water around the roots chanting the words that Kaka has taught her. He cannot keep his eyes off Nyanzu since Kaka made his offer. When she is finished she leaves the three men alone.

'I have thought about our situation. There seems only one way to make things right; only one way to put fear into the hearts of the men who hunt us. More fear than they put into ours.'

'What have we done wrong Kaka?'

'When you set out to find the sacrifice for Mafabi, you were guided to a place where an offering was placed before you by the spirits. This is the place where I told you to go, is it not? You took that offering without any resistance. You began to bring him here. The moment when things turned bad for us all was the moment you let that offering go.'

'The white boy?' Juma says.

'The white boy.'

'But, the white boy is not albino.'

'What is the difference? When the spirits present you with such an offering, who are we to refuse it? We must find this boy. We must bring him here. We must tell others our work is not yet complete and we must do what we should have done weeks ago. Only then will the spirits calm. Only then can we stop denying the spirits their rightful sacrifice.'

'The white boy?' John says.

'Yes.'

'Then you might need this.'

John produces a small white card taken from a cork board in Crystal's house. It has the words, 'Thanks for everything' hand written in English above the printed name of Glen Chapman. Below is an address in Msasani, and a telephone number.

'There, you see, the spirits are already working in our favour again. Now Juma, our people in Dar es Salaam, we'll need their help. Cheetah and those who live under the Selanda bridge, can you contact them?'

'Yes Kaka.'

'And call a meeting, as many as are faithful, and keep it a secret.'

———⟪⟫———

Big O sits in his jail cell talking to the police chief. He is laughing and joking with the chief. He tells the chief he's not had this amount of luxury in a while, like a European, a soft bed and a roof that doesn't leak. The door of his cell is open and the chief repeats he is welcome to sleep there as long as it is vacant. Big O says he would prefer to leave despite all the comforts. He reminds the police chief that the Maasai word for European translates to mean, '*the people who piss where they sleep*'. Big O stresses that although the cell is comfortable, he doesn't like the indoors very much at all. He doesn't feel safe, inside buildings.

Outside the police station Azaad talks to Glen.

'I will stay over the week-end to see Crystal is settled again. You saw the mess they made of her place.'

'Yes I did. I'm pretty much finished here. I spoke with the chief and told him everything, so I'll get a taxi back to Mwanza and fly back to Dar. Leave you two on your own.'

'Yeah, it seems Big O is off the hook, if you pardon the butcher pun. It's classic isn't it? We writhe around in educated horror at the sight of something like that while he thinks he's just doing his job. You could say he doesn't respect human life, but that's just not true. He's very smart. He faced up to three dangerous men, killers, who might well have killed him, given the chance.'

'You don't have to defend his actions with me.'

'He told me he made animal noises at each of the windows while he was finding out how many there were in the house. Then he said he let the first one go. Killed the second so that the group was split in two different locations, then he scared the third one off.'

'A real warrior.'

'Not so much a warrior as a seasoned survivor. Do you know what he told me? He has told no one else this, including the police chief.'

'What?'

'Keep this to yourself, for the time being at least.'

'I promise.'

'He told me he followed one of the men back to the village where he lives. He told me that it's a two day walk or a one day run for him. He say's there was nothing to keep him here, so he trailed the man. He says that the first thing the man did was visit a witch doctor's house. He watched them talk before he came back here, to wait for us.'

'A witch doctor?'

'He called him a Laibon, but it's much the same thing, no?'

'Why is he not telling the police chief?'

'He does not want to lead the police there. He says they will find it easy enough on their own. He said he just needed to know exactly where any future danger might come from, to know the source. Now he knows the village and the exact house. Does that strike you as weird?'

'I'm an anthropologist, Azaad, you wanna hear weird?'

'Well I've lived here most all my life, but I still can't get use to this sort of creepy, instinct, witchcraft stuff that goes on here all the time.'

'It goes on in the west also, but we have different collective names for it. All these same instincts expressed in slightly different ways.'

'Well, in Islam we have no tolerance for witchcraft. They execute witches in Saudi Arabia, did you know that?'

139

'I'm talking about a tennis player asking for a 'lucky' ball to be returned to him for his next serve, or the sign of the cross that athletes make before competing.'

'Oh, OK . . . blessings and the slightly safer luck-generating, witchcraft things?'

'Yes.'

CHAPTER SEVEN

THE KIDNAPPING

In the taxi on his way back to Mwanza, Glen finds himself wondering what the chances are of there being a mastermind behind the Dawakubwa abduction. He has suspected for some time that the three men were not working alone. They are most likely part of a larger group or cult, and therefore they must have a leader.

As he approaches the town outskirts Glen calls up the Reverend and tells him he would like to meet up with him, if he's free. He is told he is already expected.

'How did you know I was coming?'

'The Lord provides some of us with the capacity to know things that other's do not,' he says, 'I have a mobile phone.' The Reverend bellows laughter at the other end of the line.

'We can meet at the church offices, tomorrow mid-morning,' the Reverend says, 'I will also invite the district police chief to the meeting, since he is a regular church member and he's the one who told me about the goings on in Dawakubwa.'

'Very good! See you tomorrow then?'

'Yes, you did the right thing Glen, going local with the information . . . at the right time too. We'll talk more tomorrow.'

Glen checks once more into the Champion hotel. Within minutes his room is a mess with his papers spread across the bed and his travel clothes on the floor where he stepped out of them. He takes a shower and then tries to call Pam. She does not answer the phone, which he thinks is unusual. He texts her a message saying he is now in Mwanza and has booked in for two nights so he can see the Reverend and put some finishing touches to his research. He'll be home in a couple of day's time. He then plugs his phone in to charge it.

Glen goes down to the hotel bar, which is packed with locals in red shirts. The Mwanza Manchester United football fans are watching their team play live in the English Football league. Glen studies their behaviour as any anthropologist might. 'Rooney Rooney,' chants from the bar in time with chants from a stadium full of people in Manchester, England. Glen is intrigued. International mass hysteria, triggered by one physical action, comes from the right foot of Wayne Rooney. Basic male celebration deemed culturally appropriate to one group . . . adopted instantly by another. Such is the power of empathy on TV, even though these groups have never met each other.

———◦◉◦———

On Toure Drive, Cheetah sits in the back of a three wheeled Bad Bajaji motor scooter which is whining up the coastal road. It is his friend's vehicle, and he uses it to deliver his potions, along with an assortment of recreational drugs, around Dar and Msasani.

They are over-taken by a team of enthusiastic cyclists with helmets and racing bikes pumping around the Peninsula that's become their mini-Europe. Cheetah's phone rings or rather the ring tone lets out a burst of baby's laughter. It repeats the infectious laughter. Cheetah often lets it play to cheer himself up. He begins to talk in his own tribal language, in his own village dialect. The Bad Bajaji driver who also comes from Cheetah's village, hears only one side of the conversation.

'Greetings, Kaka Damu, how are you? Where are you? How are things in the village?'

'Oh, I'm sorry to hear that.'

'Yes, Yes I remember Joseph Kawanga, how can I forget him, he performed my circumcision.'

'OK. What can I do to help?'

Cheetah then asks the Bad Bajaji driver to pull over. The vehicle stops outside the Sea Cliff hotel and Cheetah listens to a full set of instructions from Kaka Damu.

'Yes, I can do this, but how do I get him to you?'

'Yes, I understand. OK, I know. Yes, I'll leave that bit to you.'

After a few more minutes of conversation Cheetah says, 'Yes. Give me two or three days. I will call John when he's on the road.'

'Yes, I understand this will put things right. Leave this to me Kaka.'

Cheetah then turns to the Bad Bajaji driver and tells him to drive down Hailie Salassie and look for the place where Bakhressa sell ice cream. He wants to look at a house there.

<hr />

The Reverend Albert Mosha is dressed in a short-sleeved brown shirt. He is sitting in his church office and introduces Glen to the district police chief Ernest Bigonne. Glen shakes their hands and after the customary Swahili good-mannered greetings, he takes a seat beside Chief Ernie.

'You will be happy to know that the police chief has been in contact with his officers around Dawakubwa and they are putting together a special force to go and apprehend the remaining two men suspected of taking your son from the clinic,' the Reverend says. 'You must keep this information to yourself until things are fully arranged properly.'

'Excellent. Thank you for moving so fast on this.'

'Ah well, we are not there yet. Pole (slowly) pole, catch the piglet.'

'How did you hear about this so quickly?' Glen asks the district police chief.

Chief Ernie replies in good English. 'The senior police officer in Dawakubwa called me and asked for assistance. He has the address from Joseph Kawanga's son's death certificate. I told him to proceed with extreme caution.'

'Tell Mr Glen what else you are planning to do, Ernie,' the Reverend adds.

'I will also send a squad of five para-military officers who have had special training in counter terrorism to help.'

'A counter terrorist squad?' Glen tries not to smile.

'With due respect Mr Chapman, I can see from your perspective that this might seem strange, but when we have requests to help with global problems such as terrorism, we take as much advantage of training opportunities as possible. We have help from some embassies to train our police in these matters and as a result some of our best-equipped men now sit for days idle at airports, while poachers petty criminals and smugglers all over the country go unchallenged and unpunished. It is not our fault that we do not have any terrorists, and we should not be criticised for diverting our man-power as we wish.'

'You see Glen,' continues the Reverend in his sermon voice, 'the entire English speaking world works on the assumption that the rest of us talk about the same subjects as they do, in the same detail, but only in different languages. Nothing could be further from the truth. There are thousands of languages in this world, and even within the same language there are millions of topics and multi-millions of minute details that fascinate us. In other words there are priorities here that are beyond the comprehension of most English speakers.'

'I understand this Reverend, better than most people. I welcome any help available to apprehend these men. Bring out the airport security detail, the air-force, the King's guards, a gang of Hells Angels and all the secret military you have if it will help catch these men.'

'Good, we agree.'

'There is something else you should know. I think there is a leader of this group. He is likely to be a Shaman with substantial power in the community. I'm hoping that you can capture him also, not just his henchmen.'

'How do you know it's a man?'

'I don't Sir. You're right I should not assume such things. But there has to be a mastermind behind these events and unless we stop them, this will continue.'

'They will be stopped, I assure you. If there is any 'evidence' of wrong doing, they will be stopped,' the Chief says.

'When do you think that the police will make their move?'

'It will take another two days for our para-military police to get here from the airport at Arusha. They are waiting on a fuel truck we are sending them from Dar. That's the best we can do at the moment, in terms of urgent response. There is no rush anyway—these criminals will be dealt with. They have nowhere to go. Have no doubt, their days are numbered.'

'I hope so.' Glen says.

'One more thing Glen,' the Reverend says. 'Since we first spoke I have had meetings with some government officials. There is much renewed interest in solving this problem and several ministers are now deeply involved. They have come forward with a proposal to hold a referendum asking people to report any suspects who may have committed any atrocities. They are also taking measures to bring albino families to shelters where they can be better protected. There is even one suggestion that all albinos should be given mobile phones to report any suspicious behaviour.'

'Mobile phones?' Glen says, quietly to himself.

'What did you say?'

'Oh nothing really. I was thinking if this was Republican America there might be a suggestion that we give out hand-guns to albinos, that would be seen as offering protection, but mobile phones?'

'Don't mock us. We are unique, Glen. We do things our own way here.'

'I understand.'

The Reverend leans over his desk and places a bare arm next to Glen's showing the difference in colour.

'Different, see?' He speaks then laughs out loud.

'I'm surprised that you bring colour into this Reverend. There are black leaders in North America who have worked for years to convincing everyone that black American's are the same as white Americans, that the colour of their skin did not matter.'

The Reverend laughs out even louder. 'They are right. They are the same.' he says. 'They are all Americans, black, white, yellow, green, I hear no difference what so ever in their rhetoric. Americans are my favourites among the chosen peoples. You're from Canada you should know them well. We on the other hand are simple Africans. Surely **you** can recognise the differences I'm talking about?'

'I'm sorry Reverend, I do not mean to offend.'

'We may all be built the same, but it is our **differences** we use to get what we want.' The Reverend says this in a more serious tone.

Glen decides not to take this conversation further. He smiles and thanks both men once more.

'I will leave this all in your capable hands, gentlemen. I will go back to Dar es Salaam and finish my research project. Reverend, I will make sure that you're sent a copy as soon as it's finished. I wish you all the success in apprehending these men Chief.'

Both men stand to say good bye to Glen.

'Go home to your family Glen. You have done the right thing by giving the local police the chance to solve this. Your family are now safe from the superstitious monsters that conduct these crimes.'

'Touch wood.' Glen says as he taps the Reverend's desk.

—————◦‹‹◦››‹—————

Helen is ironing one of Pam's dresses. She is listening to a local radio station that is conducting a phone-in sponsored by a local NGO (Non Government Organisation) to draw awareness to the situation of albino children. This type of call-in programme is unique, and Helen likes what they are saying, although she's shocked at some of the responses of listeners. If you are educated enough to call into such a programme, Helen thinks, you should be educated enough to know what is fact and what is fiction. She was curious to hear how many men blamed the women's family for producing an albino child.

Helen's father was Maasai and educated in a Christian school in Nairobi. Her mother came from a Maasai village in Tanzania near Magadi on the border with Kenya. Her parents lived apart for most of their life. Helen's mother was uneducated and far more fearing of the unusual events in her daughter's life. It was her father who was responsible for educating

Helen and later in helping her cope with the birth of her own albino boy Emanuel. He managed to help her find work through his church connections and a European family took her on as a maid. Her brief marriage to a Kikuyu boyfriend did not last and when her father died suddenly Helen moved to Tanzania with the European family. In Dar es Salaam she has managed to find continual work as a house-help and she's been given support for her boy, his condition and his education. She's now been working for the Chapmans for two years.

She sprays the white dress with starch so the cotton will be firm and smart. Pam likes her cotton clothes to be starched, because they look neat and they are much more comfortable than anything made of synthetic materials. Helen is alone in the house with the two Chapman children. While the Chapmans are watching TV, Helen's son Emanuel is outside playing a game with bottle tops and feathers in the dirt, near to the front gate.

When finished her ironing, she takes the pile of neatly folded clothes into Pam's changing room. As she is putting the clothes away, she sees a children's book on the floor. She thinks about leaving it there, but this is definitely Pam's side of the house, not Glens, so she picks it up to tidy it a way. The book is an illustrated story of two children, one white girl and the other Maasai.

Helen, out of curiosity, reads the first few pages. She reads English easily and speaks the words aloud to herself.

"*'Linda compares her daily activities to those of a Maasai.'* Helen flips a page or two. *'I walk home to a block of flats. If I were a Maasai would have no neighbours who were strangers.'* again she flips. *'We have to wait for Daddy to get home before we eat. If I were a Maasai, Daddy would be eating with all the other men. I set out for school with my new white trainers. If I were a Maasai, I'd run in my bare feet.'*"

Helen reads through the book, emphasising the underscored text, *'If I were a Maasai.* She finds the comparisons amusing but far short of the truth she knows. Although she understands the *Wazungu* attempt to familiarise their children with the ways of the Maasai, she remembers the hardships and the poverty of her father's clan when she made visits to her mother and grandmother. Sure, there was pride and tradition, but there was also lots of petty bickering among cow shit and insects. She was never happy during these visits. The smell and the deafening sound of flies inside the *Boma* (house). The smell alone was hard to deal with. She remembers asking her Grandmother what she would like to have if she could have anything in the world. Her grandmother thought for a moment, and then said she would like to have a can of 'Doom' insect spray. It was the one product in the whole world she'd seen used and was impressed with, for its fly-killing power. Helen remembers the endless hours of work as a girl, the chores fetching wood, water and cow dung for the walls of the house. Then there was also the fiasco of her marriage and how her Kikuyu husband was never really accepted and how he disappeared as soon as she gave birth to her albino son Emanuel. All this would make an interesting children's book. She is pleased to work for the Chapmans. She has learned a lot about *Mzungus*, but she thinks they have a lot to learn about Maasai.

Helen turns to the last page of the book to see if it covers the teenage years and puberty. It does not. Helen continues her stream of thought. *If I were a Maasai,* she thinks, *I'd have my clitoris cut off and my genitalia mutilated in a dangerous outdated ceremony for no reason other than our ancestors did it.* Helen closes the book but continues to talk. '*If I were a Maasai* . . . **I am a Maasai!**' Helen slaps the book onto a shelf.

Helen goes outside the house where she finds the guard holding an African pigmy hedgehog. He has found two babies abandoned by their mother in the garden. He holds one in the palm of his hand and watches the other stumble around his feet. Helen knows instinctively that this will bring the Chapman children away from the TV. She calls out.

'Douglas, Gail, come. Come see these baby animals.'

She walks over to the house and repeats her call, in through the open window.

The two children run out from the house together. The security guard bends down to show them the hedgehog he is holding in his hands. He passes it on to Douglas. He is wary of the spikes. The hedgehog uncurls in his hand and looks at Douglas. It is very cute. Helen laughs because Gail is too afraid to hold the hedgehog.

'Where is Emanuel?' Helen asks the guard.

'He was here a moment ago. He was waving a thousand shilling note he found in the empty washing machine. I told him to give it to you.'

'That boy, he'll claim it's his. He thinks he is born a lucky boy.'

Helen walks over to a pile of bottle tops with feathers stuck in the top. Next to this arrangement of toys, is another discarded bottle of sun-cream, the spray on kind. It is almost empty.

'Can we feed the hedgehogs some ice cream?' Douglas shouts as the Ice Cream cart plays 'O sole mio' plays outside their gate.

———⇒«()»⇐———

On his walk back to the Champion hotel, Glen thinks about the last thing the Reverend said to him; that we use our differences, to get what we want. He thinks about this in the context of his research. He would not be here today if his son had not been abducted all those weeks ago. A chill comes over him at that moment. He knows the driving force behind his enquires was the threat to his own child. Someone messing with his family is what made this assignment different from any others. When he reaches his room at the Champion he sees his phone flashing. He sees he has had seven missed calls from Pam. He immediately calls her.

'Hello, have you been trying to reach me.'

'Oh God. Glen, a terrible thing has happened.'

'What's wrong! Are the children OK?

'Yes, our children are OK but Helen's son Emanuel is missing.'

'How do you mean missing?'

'He's gone. No one can find him! Everyone's been looking for hours.'

'You know Emanuel, Pam, he can be very naughty. Maybe he's just hiding. Give him time and he's likely to show up.'

'Glen, Helen is beside herself with worry. He went outside and bought an ice cream, the Bakhressa seller confirms this, but then he never returned to the house. It's so unusual. He doesn't normally go off on his own. Glen come home I'm afraid. What if this is something to do with these same men that took Douglas.'

'Pam what are you saying?'

'Glen, think it through. You tell me one of the men who took Douglas has been killed, a few days later our house-girl's albino son disappears under strange circumstances. What do you think the odds are for this to be pure coincidence?'

'Oh God, have you informed the police?'

'Yes of course and the UN security also. I think you should get here as soon as possible. The police are going to come by soon, and I don't want to be left dealing with them on my own.'

'Pam do you realise if you are right and these incidents are connected they will likely bring the boy back here.'

'In what state Glen?'

'Alive, if they have not butchered him in front of the parents.'

'Oh God. How can you be sure?'

'I'm not . . . but the authorities in Dar are far harder to avoid, than up here in their home territory.

'Let the authorities there deal with it. Glen, I want you here.'

'Pam, we know where this village is. The police are planning to raid it. I can help them.'

'How can you help?'

'I'm the only one here who can recognise Emanuel.'

'Glen, he's an albino boy they'll recognise him. What if this is just the start. What if they come back here in numbers for Douglas?'

Glen shudders at this thought. 'Pam, do what you have to do to feel safe. Move the kids out to a Hotel, or go stay with friends. Take Helen and Thomas with you. I have to go back to Shinyanga and help put an end to this once and for all.'

'Glen, the police are here. I'll call you back. Don't do anything until we talk again. Promise me. This is all so terrible.'

Pam hangs up and Glen feels frustrated and alone in his hotel room. He immediately calls Azaad.

'Hi Azaad are you still in Dawakubwa? Yes, I'm OK. Something has come up. Is Big O still with you? Good. Listen. Our house-girl in Dar es Salaam . . . her albino son has gone missing. Yes, Pam thinks it's too much of a coincidence, don't you think so too? I suspect he's been taken by folk connected to those who came to Dawakubwa. I know these cults well. They would have not survived for thousands of years if they did not have the capacity to adapt things to suit themselves. In the end they believe that everything that happens is the will of the spirits. They are unwavering on this and they could be planning a ceremony of some sort to ward off more bad luck following Joseph Kawanga's death. The police are on their way but they may not get there in time. I want to come back there now. It's a full moon later this week and I'm guessing they may want to take advantage of an auspicious night like that. Yes, I know. But doesn't Big O know exactly where to go? I thought of that. We can go together, yeah remember I like running. OK see you tomorrow. Keep your eyes on Crystal and her children; who knows what this cult's real plans are?'

———⇒⊪⊂———

(HOURS EARLIER)

Cheetah makes potions for everything, from putting people to sleep, to keeping them awake. He has ointment to keep a penis erect and jelly to keep a woman moist. Among the many potions and soap stone carvings, Cheetah's personal pharmacy contains a whole assortment of local herbs for his equally varied set of clients.

For his assignment from Kaka, Cheetah chooses to use a technique he saw in a movie. While watching an old Turner Classic Movie on TV he'd seen Sherlock Holmes in black and white and learned that chloroform on a rag is a very effective way to subdue a person quickly. He now obtains this chloroform substance easily in exchange for some bottles of raw Aloe Vera at a local pharmacy.

Cheetah can't believe his luck. In broad daylight, on the second day he sits in the *Bad Bajaji* (three wheeled scooter) in front of Glen Chapman's house, he see a young white boy with a Baseball cap come out the gate and head for the Ice Cream man. From a distance he thinks this is the white boy he has been asked to abduct. He knows the risk with such a kidnapping and he may only have one chance to succeed. He cannot refuse Kaka Damu's demands and the price promised in herbal supplies is good. He checks one more time the address is right, the chance to grab him is now too opportune to miss.

Cheetah guides the *Bad Bajaji* driver to move closer as the boy buys the ice cream. As the child walks back to the house, they wait until the Ice cream seller's back is turned. Cheetah pounces and places the rag over the boy's mouth quickly and without any witnesses. The Bad Bajaji takes off while the boy is being pulled into the back. They round the corner onto Hailie Salassie so quickly that the boy almost slips from their grasp. He is covered in sun cream.

153

Cheetah realises straight away that the boy is not *Mzungu*, the word that Kaka used in describing their prey. But, now it seems they have an even bigger prize, an albino boy. The spirits of **chance** are good. There will be little interest in the disappearance of this boy. Cheetah knows that some sort of sacrificial offering to the ancestors is needed, and this could be the easiest solution. This boy is not European-white, he is albino African-white, but it does not matter. This will be less risky. He instructs the Bad Bajaji driver to take him to the deserted and vacant apartment towers on Toure Drive.

As darkness falls, they carry the boy to an empty room on the first floor. They dress him to make him look like a young girl. They put the boy into a Muslim girl's school uniform with a long dress and white headscarf that covers his face. Then they wait for a lorry to arrive.

On the sound of a loud horn, Cheetah lifts the drugged boy downstairs, and into the cabin of the lorry. He gives the Somali driver an envelope of cash, and a plastic bag full of Khat (a chewable leaf that gives off a powerful stimulant). This will keep the driver awake at the wheel for as many days as it takes to drop off the child at Kaka's village. He will then head on with his shipment of salt to the Great Lakes. Cheetah also gives the driver a flask of liquid to keep the child docile and drowsy. The driver is told only that the child is a sick albino girl and is to be delivered home as quickly as possible. The lorry driver understands he has to keep administering the medicine till they get there.

Cheetah has to move quickly. Once his delivery is made, Kaka will know what to do. He's done his job well. Cheetah cannot be connected to any missing *Mzungu* boy. Kaka will be grateful.

——————◎——————

'Hello. Glen, the police have just left. They have taken statements from everyone. I've also given the diplomatic police more details and told them to contact you for the location up country. The Dar police have been good. They even sent around a trained women officer to help comfort Helen. They have sent out messages to all the suburbs around Dar and they are beginning to set up road blocks. After I told them this could be related to albino abductions in Shinyanga, they said by this time tomorrow they will have nationwide roadblocks with police looking for Helen's boy. I gave them a photo you took of him with our children.'

'Good, this sounds positive. I will call the Reverend and perhaps we can have the District police chief here speed things up also. I've already talked to Azaad, so he is staying at Dawakubwa to look after Crystal and her children. This seems to be all coming together. This is good.'

'Glen, what chances are there for Emanuel. I can't stand the thought that he'll become the latest victim in these atrocities.'

'I don't know Pam. If it's a cult, they may think this is serving some purpose for them all, but I don't know what. If there is a head of the cult he may feel he has to take things into his own hands, which means if he's still up country there's a chance. If they are as fanatical and delusional as they seem, the boy could be taken alive to some sort of ceremonial ritual. On the other hand if I'm wrong and it's a gang of hardened members of the albino body-parts trade carrying it out, the child might already be dead. They will do the killing in secret not in public. I'm hoping Helen's boy still has a chance because this group seem to believe in ancestral spirits, more so than the mighty dollar. They will have to do something to make him special. They are crafty and cautious and they could also be using this as a decoy, so keep your eyes on Douglas and Gail all the time.'

'A fucking decoy? That's all I need to hear. It's all so weird and cruel Glen. I have a pick-up truck full of guards at the gate. The security company are embarrassed that this happened on their watch. These guys are all ex-military and itching to find someone to blame. They have already hassled the poor ice cream man for information.'

'Time is of the essence, Pam. There is a full moon coming and weird as this can sound, it could be a significant part of their plans. Although I have no proof that this will make a difference, I need to go back to Dawkubwa.'

'Glen, please take care. Go with the police if you have to. Helen is in shock. She's chanting all sort of Christian songs to help make things right.'

'I'm not surprised. Yes I'll try and go along with the police, but I have to get to this village as soon as possible. Let's hope in the meantime the police roadblocks find Helen's boy. This could be good Pam. We are fighting back in numbers. Not just for albino children, but for all children who are abducted and abused.'

'It's always the fucking global cause for you, Glen. Take care of yourself. It's you that I'm concerned about.'

⸻ ❖ ⸻

Juma receives a text that his special delivery is on its way. It will take a little longer on the road than usual, but it will still arrive for the full moon.

Nyanzu is already preparing the site for the ceremony. She knows little of what will take place, but she senses this is an important occasion for Kaka. He has asked her to prepare for the chicken dance, and to take another group of young girls and boys to rehearse a few more of the traditional dances from the surrounding countryside. When Nyanzu asks what costumes the children should wear, she is told to use ox-fat and grease along with lots of white ash. Also they should mark their skins with water through the white ash and make traditional designs, like in the old days. When Nyanzu asks what the traditional designs are, Kaka becomes angry.

'Use your imagination,' he tells her. 'Mix the paste and paint it on anyway you like. Zebra stripes, bamboo rings, use bottle tops, hair combs or whatever you can find to mark your body. Be creative, boys can do their own, girls can do their own, as long as you remember to rehearse the dances. Don't forget your long sleeved dress and a young chicken.'

Juma is in charge of the music. He assembles the local six-man drumming group, and three other musicians with makeshift tambourines and finger pianos. One of the older men plays a long carved wooden xylophone. It takes three men to set up the instrument. No rehearsal is needed for the band. Music is in their genes. They are well experienced in playing such gigs, despite only getting together once or twice a year, because they play the same set of songs.

John knows the local veterinarian service driver and talks him into borrowing the institute's Land Rover. The Somali lorry driver is unlikely to know the neighbourhoods in this part of the country. That's why a Somali was chosen for this task. John is assigned to meet the Somali driver at a pre-arranged turn-off from the *barabara,* the main road. He will tell the driver he needn't come onto the rough roads and that he'll take the sick child the remaining distance to her parents, somewhere in the bush.

At the pre-arranged place where the village dirt road branches off from the major dirt highway, John, sits and waits. He is lucky he doesn't have to wait too long. When the lorry driver stops, John opens the passenger cabin door to see a young albino child fast asleep in the seat.

John groans on seeing the child as an albino. He reels, at the consequences this latest screw-up abduction will cause. He walks away from the lorry to chant some helpful protective spells. He is only brought back to the lorry by the driver calling on him to be quick.

'This child doesn't have anything infectious, does she? She has been asleep all through the journey.'

John knows that the driver has no idea what fate lies in store for this child. The driver starts shouting that he's been told only to deliver a sick child back to this spot. His eyes are red and he seems to be running out of patience. John takes his mobile phone and calls Cheetah.

After a moment of conversation, Cheetah tells John the boy came from the very house they were watching, he's the right age, from the right address and the spirits made the whole thing easy.

157

'Stop complaining . . . you know this is a better solution for things than taking a *Mzungu* child! Listen John, if that boy is with you now; if he has managed to get through police roadblocks then he is definitely the one chosen by the spirits. Listen to me. You must take him to Kaka now. He will understand. I'm certain, this is what he needs.'

John lifts the child from the lorry into the back of the Land Rover. The lorry driver takes another handful of Khat and wipes the pink tears from his staring eyes. What is this all about, he thinks. I will never understand these people. Job done, let's move on.

*

Glen now knows every bend, every bump, and the best places to get out for a pee on the road to Dawakubwa. When the taxi finally reaches Crystal's house, he feels like he's been commuting this road for months, which he has.

Azaad's vehicle is parked inside the gate of Crystal's house and the pool of blood has been cleared up. There is however a rough white-line silhouette of a body painted on the gate where Joseph Kawanga was once impaled. Glen shakes his head in remembrance.

'Who did this?' he asks.

'Lieutenant Colombo was here.' Azaad jokes. 'The police chief has been sorting out the case details because he is expecting a visit from Mwanza senior police people any time now.' says Azaad.

'I know. They will come in the next day or two, with a squad of anti-terrorist police.'

'Anti-terrorist police, are you kidding me, why?' Azaad looks worried at the mention of anti-terror police.

'Practice, I expect. They are taking it very seriously in Mwanza and want to back up the local police here when they make the arrests.'

'Al-humdilallah! (Thanks to Allah.)

'Yeah!'

'So what are you going to do?'

'I'd like to go to the village, as soon as possible. I have to do everything in my power to see if I can rescue Helen's son.'

'Why don't you take my car? I'll be OK here with Crystal.'

'I thought about that. I think its best to go on foot so as not to arouse any suspicion. With everyone carrying mobile phones these days, they could be told that strangers were on the road. I think that's what will happen when the police arrive. They will not have the advantage of surprise. That's one thing we'll have if you let me borrow something.'

'What's that?'

'Big O, of course! He can take us to where he saw the man talking to the Laibon. He knows the way, I know the boy, so together we could definitely make a surprise visit. I brought my running shoes especially.'

Crystal comes out of the house and greets Glen and Azaad. Glen sits on the step and takes off his sandals. He then looks through his bag for his running shoes.

'Welcome back to the crime-scene Glen! I heard you were coming.'

'Hi Crystal, do you think I'm right; that they are likely to bring the boy alive back here.'

'Nothing would surprise me with this lot. I guess its better to check them out than to ignore the prospect of the boy being there.'

'I agree, I need to press on immediately, things are becoming interesting, coming to a head.'

'What small very white feet you have.'

'Don't let's go there Crystal. I'm sure Azaad has much bigger feet than me. Talking of big have you seen Big O?'

'He's inside. I've just been sowing a rip in his robe. He's always catching it on the thorn bushes. He's really quite clumsy. I've already sown up three tears.'

'I need him to take me to Joseph Kawanga's village. He knows the way.'

'Oh, Glen why don't you let the police handle this?'

'There's not enough time.'

'Big O has no weapons. The police took his spear and sword.'

'We won't need weapons I expect. Armed police will be coming soon with plenty of weapons. I need to at least try and find Emanuel. Tonight the moon is almost full. It will be bright in the sky from sunset, besides there is nothing I can do here sitting around waiting.'

'What will you do if you see him, kidnap him back? They will chase you Glen, these are dangerous desperate men.'

'Please, just tell the police chief that we have gone ahead, and to come as soon as he can.'

Big O appears at the door of Crystal's house. He is standing tall adjusting his robe. He nods recognition of Glen and says in Maasai to Azaad that Glen has very small feet.

'Have you asked Big O if he'll take you?'

'No I haven't. Azaad, can you help?'

Azaad takes Big O into the garden and explains the situation. He tells him he need only guide Glen back to the village where he trailed one of the men who robbed Crystal's house.

'They did not rob Crystal. I prevented them from robbing her.'

'Yes, but you know who I mean?'

Big O then voices some concern that he does not have his weapons and says he cannot go into the bush without them.

'I thought so,' says Azaad and he in turn relays this message to Glen.

Glen rummages in his bag and produces a Swiss Army Knife from his side pocket. He shows it to Big O. He then throws it to him and tells him he can keep it.

Big O likes it immediately because it is red and he knows once in the bush he can make quite a few weapons using this knife.

'Oh, and tell Big O that the albino child I want to save is part Maasai.'

Azaad does this and Big O agrees to take Glen to the Bantu Laibon's house.

—◦◦◦◦—

It is late afternoon when John arrives back in the village in the Veterinarian Institute Land Rover. It's the day Kaka has planned his ceremony. People are used to seeing animals being carried in the back of the Land Rover so little attention is given to a wrapped up bundle that is quickly pulled into Kaka's compound and then put into his house.

Juma has successfully circulated word of the traditional gathering and he is surprised at how big the response has been. The surrounding areas have had some bad luck recently. There have also been arguments between neighbouring families over land. The dispute has become bitter and a quarrel over fishing rights has also erupted after some people up stream installed a new wicker dam to trap fish.

The locals are certainly ready for a Kaka special and want to know what the occasion is. Juma tells them it's long over due and will chase away all the bad luck and return things to normal. Kaka has heard this from the ancestral spirits. After this full moon everything will be all right. The celebration will contain some special magic to appease the spirits. It will be one of Kaka most elaborate feasts and ceremonies for years.

Usually Kaka's good luck rituals are never as popular as his coming of age gatherings or one of his local fertility night dances, but he still expects a large crowd this time. The people who are not on his invitation list are those not likely to attend anyway—all the school teachers, government employees, all those with salaried jobs and those who go to a church or a mosque. He does not have much influence over them on such occasions.

The musicians are first to set up their instruments and have already started to drink beer. Nyanzu has organised the troupe of dancers who have oiled up their bodies and now smear themselves in ash. They take wet fingers through the white substance and draw lines and squiggles on their skin. Although Nyanzu is the youngest, she knows her responsibilities and she is one of the best dancers. A group of young men are also set to perform and have told Juma that they have included a routine that they saw on TV from China. They will do a new set of tumbles and acrobatics still dressed in local costumes, with sticks and bells attached to their legs.

Kaka Damu takes a walk around his territory. He has been told that everything is under control. He remembers the ceremonies that his *Baba* (Father) used to conduct here, where the whole village attended. It was almost compulsory to be there for these festivities. His father was knick-named *Mfalme Kinyonga* (King Chameleon) on account of his communicative powers with the animal and spirit kingdom. These ceremonies would also be organised on auspicious days, like this, usually in celebration of a good harvest or the onset of rain. It was only on occasion when the village was threatened by diseases like small pox that ritual sacrifices were needed. Some ceremonies, he remembers his father telling him, involved the scaring of faces and the bodies of young children to ward off further outbreaks of small pox. Elaborate patterns were designed on the faces and the belly of girls. These practices are less in demand now, but there are still a few who survive the era of smallpox, that come and ask him for scaring on their children's faces. People are easily convinced that these things work, and despite things changing in other parts of the country, nothing much has changed here.

The most pain Kaka remembers, amongst the scaring and the circumcision ceremonies of the past, is the pain of having his lower teeth pulled out by his father, to prevent him starving with lockjaw. He never suffered from the illness, but his teeth were pulled out as a precaution, in case he needed to be fed soup through a straw. They were bashing at his front tooth with a rock and a stick for a while before it popped out. He also remembers his circumcision ceremony, walking for days around relative's houses, not sleeping, trying to stay awake, knowing that the more tired he got, the more trance-like he would be when they cut him. He stood there with his arms locked high on a stick braced across his shoulders. The men approached him and pulled his foreskin towards them, all the way over his penis and then cut it off, with a sharpened European butter knife. He was fourteen at the time. He had stood through it all, never flinching or showing any sign of pain.

Tonight, he has decided he will not make a big exhibition of the cut. He accepts that many no longer want to see what goes on, despite their willingness to accept what happens behind closed doors to release the power of the sacrifice. If all his commands are obeyed and John does his job, the boy will be delivered, and this will be a sign in itself that the spirits are backing him. If he is told the boy is not available he will have to accept that as well. Everything that is, is the will of the spirits. He knows he can make a show around anything, even food and drink. He will be subtle; he will let the entertainment lead the night. He will, without hesitation, obey his traditions, because he must . . . because he has been chosen and is ordained by the spirits.

CHAPTER EIGHT

THE SACRIFICE

Glen grabs his small runner's backpack and puts a few essentials inside. He packs a hand towel, a clean T-shirt, toothbrush, some groundnuts and a bottle of water. He then sets off at a fair running pace with Big O. He knows he can run for ten kilometres like this and at first Big O struggles to keep up. O doesn't really understand why Glen is running so fast when they have so far to go. Big O stops several times to bend over and catch his breath. Glen jogs on the spot to maintain his tempo, like a boxer on a training run, displaying his fitness with athletic machismo. He is keen to reach this village, to see if his reason and instincts are guiding him properly towards Helen's son.

After fifteen miles it is Glen who is struggling for breath, and Big O is jogging at a pace far more suitable for the distance. At twenty miles Glen turns his water bottle upside down to show Big O he has ran out of water and is now exhausted. They stop under the shade of a tree and Big O gestures for Glen to sit for a while. He takes the empty bottle and goes off in search of water. To the best of Glen's knowledge, the Maasai has not drunk anything on his way here. Aside from initially loosing his breath, he has hardly broken sweat.

Fifteen minutes later Big O comes back with a bottle of water, a gourd of milk, what looks like a long wooden stick and a small succulent plant. Big O gives the water to Glen then begins to sharpen his new wooden spear with his new Swiss army knife. He stops Glen from picking up the plant and indicates the leaves are dangerous to touch. He pretends to rub the leaves on the point of the spear, and mimes unconsciousness and death if touched. Glen understands that open hands and a stare into the sky, is a mime to indicate death. Without actually coating the spear tip, he puts the plant carefully into Glen's backpack.

Glen is impressed. His partner has armed himself with a deadly weapon after only a fifteen-minute forage in the bush. He guesses that Big O must have come across another pastoralist and traded or borrowed the milk gourd. The spear looks dangerous enough without any poison. He is pleased that Big O will now feel confident to face any foe, but Glen doesn't want any more deaths.

Glen is also grateful for the brief rest. As the sun begins to drop, he sees the full moon rising. He stands quickly when the thinks he hears the sound of drums in the distance. He realises they must be near and that they must move on quickly now.

A line of dancers come out from the space between two huts. They are in a straight line one behind the other. Nyanzu is in the lead, jumping forward on two feet, legs apart, rippling her stomach and hips in time to the drum beats. One, two, three jumps forward, followed by another frenzy of hip movements. One, two, three, jumps forward until all the girls are lined up dancing in the open. The drums provide a solid background of beat, accentuated by cow bells and whistles. The noise from the dancer's feet adds to the rhythmic sound, as does the individual high pitched screams from women at the side. The group's bodies are patterned in black and white strips, and each has a monkey-skin short skirt.

The crowd begins to thicken around the edge of Kaka's compound. Bats which usually inhabit the rooftops and trees at sunset are frightened off. Kaka is dressed in his finest contemporary witch doctor's outfit. He has a set of Kudu horns strapped upside down on his head. He has a goatskin draped over his shoulders and a large necklace made from ambatch (cork). He wears the short leopard skin skirt of his father. On his ankles are small bells and his shoes are white plastic, made

165

in Taiwan. Kaka walks through the crowd, welcoming people. The drumming is so loud his conversations are kept to a short greeting and handshakes. He also has a huge hippo tooth round his neck which he holds and rubs regularly like a Genie's lantern.

In the centre of the compound, the girls are joined by a line of boys who hop on one leg till they are alongside the girls. They face each other and continue dancing. The drums go silent except for one drummer who leaves the group and move forward beside the dancers. The dancers stop. The man with a small drum creeps along behind the dancers, changing the beat. The girls turn their back on the boys and pick up on the new beat. All the drums follow. The boys' steps forward, thrusting in rhythm into the back of their female partners.

Juma looks on from the crowd. There is Nyanza at the front, the youngest and one of the best dancers. Even before she has reached puberty, every muscle that is used for conception and childbirth is being trained here tonight. Juma takes in all her movements. He casts his eyes over the other girls. He can tell from their movements those whose bodies will soon be fertile, those who have already experienced a man and those who will likely be picked first by the next generation of young men in the village. This year's crop of fertile wombs seems as good as any he has ever seen. A woman's facial beauty means little to Juma. There is so little chance to look at it for any length of time. The condition and control of her body is everything, at least at this age.

John has not told Kaka about the albino semi-conscious boy he is now preparing in Kaka house except that for the fact that the *dhabihu* (sacrifice) has arrived. John feels conflicted and confused. He had expected the *mzungu* child they had originally abducted in Dawakubwa, in mistake for an albino. Now he has an albino child that has been mistaken for the *mzungu*. The spirits work in mysterious ways. He covers the drugged boy in goat fat and ash. He smears the white paste all over the boy's body, including his hair. He has a job to do and he believes it is best that he continues his part of it rather than risk any disruption or cancellation of events at this late stage. Kaka is in charge it is his festival. In half an hour this will be Kaka's problem to face, and his decision on what to do next.

Big O stops Glen as they approach the village. The drums are now very loud. They move deeper into the moon shadows, and Big O takes the milk gourd, and wipes his finger around the inside. There is a dark charcoal ring inside the neck of the gourd where the Maasai usually put a fire-stick to smoke and keep the milk longer. Big O covers Glen's face with the charcoal dust, like a marine commando, to make his white skin less obvious.

As they reach the perimeter of the Laibon's compound, Big O takes Glen to the place where he saw the two men talk and points to the house. There is no fence, but one side of the compound has an unfinished cement wall with small square holes. Big O thinks they will be able to get a better view if they move along behind it. Glen follows until they have a spot which is central to observing all the activities.

The drums go silent for a moment, and Glen hears the volume of voices increase, spurring them on. He is surprised by the size of the crowd. This is not some dying cult performing a set of dances purely for entertainment. It looks as serious and organised as a prom night in North America, except coming of age teenager mingle with parents and children in celebration of puberty. People are getting together and talking. There are oil lamps and torches placed around in strategic places. A few seem intoxicated, but the ratio of drunken men to women seems about equal.

The drums begin once more and this time Glen hears a more sinister beat. He is amazed how a drumbeat can alter the mood of a gathering. The crowd respond and crush in closer into the circle. One minute it is a happy dance beat, the next it the slow thump of a struggling heartbeat. Then the Shaman makes his grand entrance.

Glen stands on some concrete blocks to get a better look. He sees the Shaman parading around in a circle, and Glen thinks he is magnificent. He wears the large horns turned upside down on his head like a devil. He is walking like an animal to the slow beat of the drum. As he walks in a circle around the crowd, men fall on their face in front of him. As soon as they do, a large wooden bowl is placed on their back and two of the male dancers step forward with pounding sticks, hammering the bowl in time to the drum. It's part of the act, possibly an offering to the ancestors for good harvests.

Women also step in front of the Shaman who takes his stick and a small knife to lift and part their clothes sensuously. He traces lines on their skin, across their breasts and stomach. He does not cut anyone, but in some cases their bodies are exposed. At some time in the past, Glen thinks these women would have been naked. They are likely seeking help with fertility, or they are re-living a time when they were fertile. Older women come forward first, then with encouragement from the crowd, younger women also step forward. The Shaman takes off his goatskin cloak, puts it on the ground and offers it to one young woman to lie on. As she does, her eyes roll back in her head, looking away from the Shaman, perhaps feeling the effect of a strong hallucinogenic drug, perhaps a self induced trance. The Shaman straddles the woman and squats down on top of her. The crowd roars approval and he rises up and down to their calls.

Glen knows this is not a performance for tourists. Everyone here is doing their bit to satisfy some inner need for security and reproductive prowess according to their beliefs. Nothing looks staged and neither does it look like it's all an elaborate distraction from the daily grind of village life. It looks like it is all happening spontaneously to address some basic spiritual purpose felt by all. It may be a performance to change a community's luck, but it also seems cruder than that. It is a display of power by those that feel they have it . . . towards those that feel they need it.

The crowd packs itself around the open central space, so that the back of the Laibon's house is deserted. Big O taps Glen on the shoulder and points to an open gap where a window is not yet fitted. He gestures a route they can take to get to this window without being seen. Glen reluctantly steps down from the wall and follows him.

Big O carefully peers into the room and sees a young girl changing into a long sleeved dress that seems a size too small for her. He realises she is one of the lead dancers he saw out front earlier. She is wiping the colouring from her face. He looks around further. There is a chicken in a basket near the door. On the floor, on a matt in the corner, lies a boy asleep, covered in white ash. Big O signals Glen over and points at the boy in the far corner of the room.

Glen also peeks through the window and sees the boy. He quickly drops his head back down; his heart is racing. He takes a second look. He can't quite make out the boys face, but he is almost certain that it's Emanuel, Helen's boy. He needs to get closer to be sure. He hears the drum beat change and the crowd roar louder. The beat turns back into a dancing mood out front. Glen takes another quick peep inside. He sees the girl take the chicken from the basket, put it onto her head and then walk out the door. The boy is alone.

As soon as the girl leaves, Glen stands and leans into the room. He indicates to Big O that he wants to climb in through the window. Big O stops him and then with some reluctance, steps through the window first. He then helps Glen into the room. The crowd outside are once more shouting along with the drum rhythm. There are loud prolonged screeches from women. Glen checks to see if it is Emanuel, but at this stage he doesn't care. He knows this is an albino boy in grave danger, in need of rescue. He checks to see if the boy is breathing and then sees the freckled shapes of giant African lakes on Emanuel's back and feels relieved it's him. The boy is breathing but drowsy and not able to waken up.

Glen continues to examine the boy for any wounds or injuries. Since the thought had occurred to him when he saw the boy was covered in a blanket. He's relieved to see he still has all his limbs! His timing has been perfect. He lifts the boy from the matt and carries him over nearer to the window. He places the boy on the floor and takes off his back pack. He pulls out his spare T-shirt and in the moonlight, wipes the ash from the boys face. By now Glen's eyes have adjusted to the dark room, and he sees a set of sharp knives laid out on a rush matt, one cutlass size and two smaller pointed blades with bone handles. It is then that Glen's phone rings.

To the ring-tone of The Killers, 'This is your Life,' Glen scrambles to find his phone and switch it to silent. He reads the screen and sees it is Azaad who is calling, so he listens and talks very quietly.

Azaad tells Glen the police have arrived in numbers in Dawakubwa. They have no intention of going any further until dawn, so they are resting in two groups at the clinic and at the police chief's house for the night. Azaad asks if Glen has reached the village.

Glen whispers that he has just found the boy alive but drugged and that they will now attempt to rescue him. He tells Azaad to try to convince the police to come as quickly as possible, that he and Big O will search for a place on the outskirts of the village to safely hide with the boy. He asks if Azaad can help explain this plan to Big O if he puts him on the phone. He stresses that if this crowd find the boy is missing they could begin to hunt them down easily with the numbers of people here.

'In a few moments a large crowd are going to be very disappointed Azaadji. I'm thinking on my feet with this, and I need you to explain all this to Big O, since I can't.'

Glen then gives Big O the phone.

Big O takes the phone and for a moment the reception is interrupted. He stands up from his crouched position, and walks around the room trying to get a better reception. He hates enclosed spaces. He starts to talk loudly to Azaad in Swahili. Glen signals him to keep his voice down as the drums change beat once more. Big O does not understand that a single finger held across the lips means for him to be silent. Big O moves over to the open window and sticks his head out. As Glen tries to lift the boy once more from the floor, he sees movement to the left of Big O, out of sight of the Maasai. The moon shadow moves closer to Big O as Glen sees the silhouette of a man with a *rungu* as it comes swinging towards the base of Big O's skull. With a chilling crack, the Maasai slumps heavily forwards over the window ledge.

Glen stands in shock and his first instinct is to rush over to grab a knife before moving towards the window where Big O lies. The door behind

Glen suddenly bursts open. A girl with a dead chicken walks in followed by the Shaman. A man appears at the window, standing guard over Big O's body. The drumming begins to speed up again. As if in slow motion, the girl walks over to the sleeping boy. Behind her the Shaman stares at Glen, then at the Maasai and Juma in the window. Both men in the house stand rooted to the spot staring over their ancestry at each other, each holding a knife. They both believe, more than anything else in the world at this moment, that each is in danger from the other.

Kaka Damu is high on adrenaline and calculates in a few seconds what the situation means to him. He sees before him a white man with a blackened face and an albino with a white ashen face on the floor. He realises instantly that this is the white man who has hunted and plagued his thoughts. He believes that he must have come here to rescue his son. Why then has he replaced his son with an albino child sacrifice? Is he offering us this sacrifice? He sees the fallen Maasai and realises that Juma has taken care of at least one of the devils from Dawakubwa. Could there be more? Kaka steps more aggressively into the centre of his room. This is his house; these are his people outside, how many and who exactly are these devils he is facing? Who is this child who has been delivered to him?

Glen backs up to the window and turns for a moment to check Big O's condition. He keeps his eyes on Kaka and feels Big O's neck for a pulse. He feels no heartbeat, there is no movement at all; his friend is slumped over the window ledge like a sack of maize in a red cloth bag. Glen is gripped in a mix of fear and sheer outrage. Big O has fallen in an instant, as most warriors do, because he was feared. Glen needs to use his intelligence to get through the next few moments.

The girl is watching Glen's every move, witnessing every act that is unfolding. The Shaman shouts in Swahili and Juma climbs in through the window with his *rungu* at the ready. This startles Glen even more; he does not know what to do. He's trapped and he doesn't think his white skin will save him. The girl moves in front of him and looks into his face.

Kaka Damu begins to chant and crouch. He suddenly points his knife towards the white man and keeps it pointing at him.

Glen looks down and sees a pointed spike in the girl's hand. She places it against his chest. Realising what she is about to do, Glen collapses on the floor holding his chest before she has a chance to stab him.

Nyanzu steps back in shock. She knows she has not used the spike, but the white man has collapsed anyway. What power Kaka has. Even while he is lying there, the white man's eyes are looking at her and his head is shaking sideways in some sort of signal to her, yet she does not move. Why, she thinks, is he closing and opening one eye? Nyanzu hears Juma's voice, talking to Kaka; he is saying 'Haraka sana' (be quick, it is time.) The crowd is now chanting impatiently out side.

Kaka's mind is swarming with options. He walks over to the window and takes Juma's *rungu*. He walks back to the obviously feigning white man and raises the club. He swings it hard and deliberate against the top part of Glen's head. Glen's skull cracks inward like a crushed peanut shell on impact. *'Never more, invade my thoughts,'* Kaka says in his tribal language.

Kaka drops the *rungu* with a victory scream, and almost before it hits the ground he grabs his sharpest cutlass and starts hacking off the foot of the white man just above the ankle. Four strong blows do it.

Nyanzu has never seen Kaka like this. He seems crazed and overjoyed at what has happened. *It ends here.* He chants. Everything has happened so quickly that the white man's heart has not stop beating. Blood is spraying everywhere as Kaka wrenches off the foot using a small sharp knife to cut through the flesh. Nyanza gathers the blanket and covers the boy once more, a boy that Kaka now ignores.

Kaka takes the white skinned foot and wraps it in a T-shirt he finds on the floor. *'Kuan tafauti gain?'* (what's the difference?) He says to himself. He marches outside to loud cheers and holds up his wrapped up trophy to the heavens. He does not show off the flesh. He doesn't need to; it has been done to appease the spirits, not this crowd. It has been an appropriate sacrifice. The spirits know him better than any person; they would not have delivered this man to him, if this were not right. The fact he holds this bloody offering proves he is still in harmony with them. He dances around the crowd. The shape of the foot can clearly be seen. Some people walk away and leave the ritual, but some push forward trying to touch the bundle that Kaka carries. Kaka only teases them. He smells the package as if it is a fresh fruit offering. Blood covers the front of his body and is dripping from this sacrificial limb. The drums become louder. This is the climax of the evening. This is the moment reserved for a final full onslaught of sound. People kneel in prayer and satisfaction. As Kaka dances past a few of his most devout follows he lifts the T shirt and shows off the white toes.

———◉———

Two hours after Azaad's call, Kaka's village is full of white starch—uniformed policemen. Around twenty police officers lead by the district police chief arrive in four vehicles. A heavily armed paramilitary unit, all six dressed in black, pull up last in a black Humvee. It is the paramilitary officers who perform a systematic search of the village and find two bodies, one of a Maasai hanging over a window ledge, alongside the mutilated body of a white man they suspect is Glen Chapman. They also find two children in the same house; a young albino boy being looked after by a girl near to where the bodies lie. The boy has been drugged but is now slowly regaining consciousness. It is confirmed that he is the albino boy Emanuel, kidnapped in Dar es Salaam some days ago.

Police gather as many witnesses to the celebration ritual as they can find. Some are still lying around in Kaka's compound, either drunk or drugged. Police find Juma sleeping along side a group of musicians. The police take over Kaka's compound, erect a tent and begin to question people about the night's events. The police chief thanks the paramilitary unit for their help and dismisses them so they can return to Kilimanjaro Airport. 'Drive slowly,' he tells their leader,' three quarters of the cost of this operation has been spent on the fuel to get you here in that Humvee.'

The district police chief calls Reverend Mosha, and informs him of Glen Chapman's death. He's asks the Reverend's help in informing the Chapman family. The police chief then calls his superiors in Dar es Salaam and tells them what has happened. He warns them to be prepared for questions about a white man's death when this story gets out. He assures them he will do his best to find out who is responsible and bring them to justice. No, he doesn't think he needs any help from Dar es Salaam.

As the investigation continues through the morning, the police hold onto Juma as their main suspect, but they want to question Kaka Damu who is nowhere to be found. The police also hold two groups of dancers plus the musicians and a few other people known to be associated with the healer. Everyone denies any knowledge or involvement in either murder, of the white man or the Maasai. But the police chief knows that by detaining this large a group, he will be able to apply extra pressure on relatives to disclose the whereabouts of Kaka. He is hoping that by holding this many people the infamous witch doctor will either hand himself in or be located before too long.

———◈———

Helen awakens Pam early in the morning. She tells her excitedly she has just received a message from the police who have told her that her son is alive and well. He is to be escorted back to Dar es Salaam later in the day. Helen is elated. She and Pam hug for a long time after she delivers this news. They sit together with tears streaming down their face without speaking.

Pam is also very relieved. She has had nightmares and difficulty in sleeping all through the night. She has found it hard to shake off a feeling of complete dread. After Helen leaves, she immediately searches for her cell phone and calls Glen to tell him the good news. The phone rings but there is no answer.

———◈———

In a makeshift morgue room in Kaka Damu's village, a phone rings in the clenched fist of a dead Maasai. It goes on unanswered until a policeman hears it and finds it. The policeman wrestles it from the fingers of the victim and looks at the sleek flat screen of the phone. Before it stops ringing he places it in his back pocket, under his uniform. He then sees a lion-tooth talisman around the neck of the victim. He tugs this off too and with his boots, kicks a hole in the ground to bury it. There is nothing more unwanted than a failed talisman.

——⸱◉⸱——

By late afternoon, Kinyonga, the father of Kaka Damu comes to speak to the police who have taken over his son's house. He sits with the district police chief on a heavy wooden chair and makes an impassioned plea for his son's innocence. He asks the police why they are so keen to question his son. He denies any knowledge of the abduction of any albino children. He tells the chief that the findings of two bodies, a Maasai and a white man are complete mysteries to him. The Maasai may have killed the white man. Why either of them should be in his son's house he doesn't know. They were not invited guests, they may well have been thieves.

The old healer stresses to the police chief that this type of cultural festival is a regular occurrence in his village and not illegal. Twice or three times a year they are organised by his son, as they have been by him and his forefathers for hundreds of years. He pleads with the police to let the dancers and the musician go. There is work to be done around the village and they do not have the manpower or the idle time, to sit around like folks from the big towns.

The police chief assures the old healer that everyone will be released as soon as Kaka Damu comes to him and answers a few questions. It is up to him to help his son through this. If he knows where Kaka is he should go and bring him in. The police chief says that he will not leave the village until they have talked to Kaka Damu. The chief also adds that there is another of Kaka's accomplices they want to talk to, a man named John.

175

⋙⟨⊙⟩⋘

Early morning on the day after Glen has been so brutally killed, Pam still does not know of his death. She prepares a breakfast for the children. Everyone is excited and happy because of Helen's news that Emanuel is safe. The children are dispatched to school and Pam's goes off to work.

She is in her office when a senior delegation of the diplomatic police, arrive along with a member of Reverend Mosha's church. From her desk she can see the two men talking to her secretary. At first Pam believes their visit is in connection with the finding of Helen's boy. A sudden spike of nausea hits her when she sees her secretary grasp her mouth with her hand. Slowly a wave of dread creeps over her while she continues to see faces with solemn expressions. This is not a good news visit she thinks as her secretary runs crying to the Head of the UN's office. Pam watches this in silence through the glass wall in her room as if she is watching a reality show on TV. Pam's boss and the other two men come towards her door. She wants to bar them but they enter her office. At the words, 'we are so sorry Mrs Chapman!' grief strikes its first blow deep in the pit of Pam's stomach. She does not hear the finish of the sentence although the words 'death of your husband,' linger in her mind like an echo. She does not cry, but she asks the police a series of specific questions, as if she too has rehearsed control of this moment in her head. The police seem surprised at Pam's reaction to the news. The Reverend's delegate holds out a hand of comfort which is ignored. The head of the UN office summons another female colleague to sit close beside Pam.

Pam asks to be told the exact circumstances of Glen's death, she asks for all the details and despite being hesitant, the police officer obliges her. She then asks the policeman whether anyone has been arrested either in connection with Glen's death or the earlier abduction of Helen's son in Dar es Salaam. She is told that the police are currently in the village where Glen was found and they expect progress on both of these matters soon.

'He was a hero Ms Chapman. Without your husband's help the young boy may never have been found alive.'

'Are the people who killed Glen in custody?'

'Not the main suspect, but we are closing in on him quickly.'

Pam is intense in thought. She wills herself to keep focused. She thanks the policeman and the churchman for their time. They awkwardly and somewhat apologetically leave her office. They say they will keep her informed. At this moment Pam trusts no-one. She rushes out of her room and into another empty office of her colleague. She closes the door and sits down. She needs to get a hold of both her children and get them out of this place. The news and the full consequences of Glen's death have no time to sink in properly. Pam believes an assault on her family is taking place and that it could be continuing. Her children may be in grave danger. Another abduction may be planned or in progress. Pam denies herself any grief at this moment, out of fear for her children.

Pam runs through a range of possibilities in her head. These men have not all been arrested. If Glen is gone, it might only be a matter of time before others come for her or her children. It is not the speed at which bad things happen here that is frightening her. Pam is terrified by the slowness that surrounds her, the pleasantry and the apathy towards action. Everything that's working for good, at this moment, is too slow for her. The slowness of thought, the slowness of any of the authorities to put a stop to this type of insanity, eats away at her core. The morning had started so positively with news of Helen's son. It seemed like a lucky day. Pam thinks how swiftly things can change.

⇒»《◉》«⇐

Azaad cannot forget that unfortunate moment he was on the phone to Big O. The sudden silence when his speech and his life ended. He blames himself. If only he hadn't made the call. If only Glen had not answered. If only he had not heard the whole soundtrack of Glen's death that followed.

When the local police chief tells Azaad what happened, he puts all the gruesome details together in his head. He can only guess at how horrible it must have been for Glen. His newfound friend Glen had been butchered in the manner of a typical albino killing. The one consolation being that the quick action of both his friends had saved the young kidnapped albino boy Emanuel.

Azaad makes arrangements for Big O's body to be brought back to the Dawakubwa clinic. Once there, Crystal examines Big O's injuries and tells Azaad the cause of death. A blow to the back of his neck snapped Big O's vertebrae. He must have become instantly paralysed and as a consolation Crystal tells Azaad his death would have been painless.

Crystal insists that once Azaad has taken care of Big O's funeral arrangements, they should both take a trip to Dar es Salaam to see Pam. They still have Glen's research notes and his belongings and Crystal thinks it is important for them to see Pam. It's also important that Glen's work be passed on and finished.

Azaad informs the relatives and family of Big O. He offers to purchase a plot of ground near Mwanza as a burial site for his friend. Big O's family remind Azaad that Big O was not a Laibon and therefore should not be buried in the ground. The family request that Big O's body is sent back to them so they can give it the traditional send off it deserves. His body will be laid out in the open plains to be consumed by wild animals. It is a time honoured burial procedure. Digging up the earth's soil to bury a Maasai who was not a Laibon, would be tantamount to cursing the land.

In the few days that follow the two deaths the police continue to camp out in Kaka's compound. They are inundated with people demanding time to discuss local wrong doings. There are reports of fishing disputes, unresolved arguments over land, violent clashes between neighbours and some domestic violence. The villagers have never seen so many police in the one place, and so they insist the police take notes of all their complaints. Several relentless villagers are beaten with thin branches, chased away by police for talking about minor grievances. They shout back that it takes the death of a white man to see any police at all in their village.

After a week, Kaka's father makes a return visit to see Juma, who has been kept in detention. Shortly after this visit Juma confesses to the killing of both the Maasai and the white man. He tells he the police that he was officially acting as the guard for Kaka's compound and that he caught two intruders and defended himself. He did not know that one was a white man. After all the man's face was painted black. Juma denies any knowledge of the abduction of an albino boy earlier in Dar es Salaam. He also has no knowledge of any previous albino killings. When questioned further about Emmanuel, Juma says that the police need to speak to John. That he did not kidnap this boy; he did not order the kidnapping of this boy. That he knows nothing about this boy.

Police believe that the wily old healer Kinyonga has briefed Juma well. Juma seems no longer frightened of the police, but he's frightened of the Damu family. They think it's unlikely he will be sent to prison if he keeps to this story of being a night guard. After all . . . is this not the story the Maasai told the police in Dawakubwa. Is this not the same reason that the Maasai was let go after killing Joseph?

Juma has also been told that Nyanzu is safe and being looked after by Kaka's father until such time as Juma is free. His confidence grows when later that same afternoon Kaka Damu walks into his compound and gives himself up to the police.

Kaka is questioned until dark and then kept locked up and guarded until morning. He denies any wrong doing. He is simply serving his community. He just wants to be left in peace. On the question of the missing white right foot of one of the victims, Kaka suggests that maybe one of his guard dogs gnawed it off. The police chief informs Kaka with disdain, that several witnesses saw him display the foot. He also tells Kaka they don't need any Western scientific tools to tell if a limb was hacked off, rather than bitten off by dogs.

Kaka says no more. As the police pack up camp, there is a mini demonstration against the removal of the village Shaman by Kaka's father and local followers. The police bundle Juma and Kaka into a vehicle. Both Kaka Damu and Juma are then taken to prison in Mwanza. The search for the man called John continues.

━━◅◦▻━━

After the news of Glen's death spreads in Dar es Salaam, her colleagues and friends immediately rush to Pam's side. They follow her everywhere. They are aware that she is terrified to be left alone. It's as if they are on a suicide watch. They know she will not take her own life, but she is so desperate to keep company, they take turns at staying with her to make her feel secure. Her boss assures her that she is not in any danger, and assigns his top security officer to put a special protection team around Pam, Helen and their children. He also signs into effect six weeks of compassionate leave, to be taken immediately if she wants to.

Pam, at last, lets her emotions out. It comes after she picks up her children and takes them home and is faced with the challenge of telling them. Surrounded by a few close UN friends, she also calls Glen's parents in Canada. She makes sure in advance that Glen's father is with his mother to give each other support. At first she tells them there has been an accident during one of Glen's assignments. Then as the conversation progresses this untruth eats at her. She breaks down while she is talking and tells them the full story.

Glen's parents encourage her to come home. They, like every sensitive experienced parent also delay their own grief, so that they can sound strong for Pam. She weeps uncontrollably on the phone to them in the face of their strength. They don't really understand why Pam and Glen wanted to go to Africa in the first place. They have always said that Glen should have stayed home in Canada and found a real job to support his family.

━━◅◦▻━━

While the main Chapman house is shrouded in sadness and mourning, the servant's quarters in the compound is a place of muted celebration. Helen is overjoyed as her boy is returned to her. She hears his side of the story for the first time. It doesn't contain many details. He remembers only playing in the outside wash room and finding a crumpled bank note in the Chapman's washing machine. Then he sprayed himself with Douglas's sun-cream and ran out to buy an ice cream. He says a

180

man grabbed him then put a cloth across his mouth while it was still full of ice cream. It made the ice cream taste funny and he struggled for a moment, then he says he forgets everything that happened after that. There are a few strange faces in his long dream. He remembers bumping his head inside a lorry and waking up very hungry. There was a young girl who gave him water to drink. She also gave him a blanket to cover himself with after he woke up.

The police had questioned Emanuel for a whole day before returning him. Nearly all of their questions were about what happened in Glen's final moments in that room. Questions, that still remained unanswered. Emanuel cannot remember anything. He felt ill and weak for a long time after hearing the news of Glen. The police told him that Bwana Glen Chapman had saved his life.

Azaad and Crystal arrive at Pam's house a few days before she plans to take Glen's body back to Canada for burial. There are more emotional scenes before they enter the house. Crystal meets Helen for the first time. They speak at length in Swahili. Crystal is as emotional that Emanuel has been saved, as she is at the loss of Glen.

Crystal asks Pam how her children are coping with the news.

'They are affected more by the sight of me crying, than they are with talk of Glen. I think it will hit them at the funeral in Canada. I've been slowly trying to prepare them for that.'

'We have brought all his belongings, his notes and his lap-top with his research. What will happen with all this now?' Azaad asks.

'Thanks. I've been assured, by the Canadian High Commission that they will complete Glen's research and publish it. I've also been told, by Reverend Mosha, that the government is giving priority to the albino killings. Apparently it has nothing to do with Glen's death, there seems to be a genuine effort to root these practices out, they realise how much damage its doing to the country's image overseas.'

'It'll become a priority in a country whose main natural resource is **'priorities**.' Crystal says.

'I think some development doors are also being rattled by donors. It's only by tying all this albino stuff into ongoing activities aimed at other minorities that this will gain any further financial support.'

'I see.' says Azaad. 'I think that's where Glen's research may help.'

'I'm sorry about your Maasai friend.' Pam says.

'Yes, thanks. What a way to go.'

'Did you go to the funeral?'

'He arranged it and he paid for all Big O's relatives to attend,' says Crystal.

'Yes, they were all very curious to hear what happened and how Big O died. He had a big reputation in his clan. It's funny as soon as they all heard he was killed indoors they all nodded as if they understood. Big O hated to be indoors. It's the only place they believed that someone could take any advantage of him. Indoors, for Big O, was only a place to sleep at the worst of times. I said as much at his funeral.'

'The open sky was his roof and the savannah his living room. I was at the funeral. I heard Azaad say it, and corny as it sounds . . . it's true.' Crystal says. 'They put him out to be eaten by the hyenas, can you believe that?'

'It's their way Crystal you have to respect it. It's doing no one any harm.' Azaad chimes in defensively.

'I'm all for local culture, when its harmless and entertaining but it all seemed too brutal.' Crystal turns to Pam for support. 'I left the funeral with people all standing around waiting to watch a loved one being torn to pieces.'

'They didn't watch!' snaps Azaad.

Pam's eyes well with tears, 'This is all a bit too much reality for me,' she says.

'Sorry, Pam,' says Crystal.

'Very sorry,' says Azaad

'Do you have any information on how the police are getting on with their investigation?' Pam asks, struggling to gain control.

'It was Glen's wish to let them handle things up country with the Douglas kidnapping thing although I don't expect they'll be left to handle his murder enquiry on their own.' Azaad says.

'The main suspects are a local Shaman and one of his henchmen, the ones suspected of taking both Douglas and Emanuel, both are under arrest. There is one suspect that has not been found.' Crystal says.

'One, still out there?' Pam swallows hard.

'Yes, one of the men suspected of involvement with taking Emanuel. The other two have spoken of him but no one can find him.' Crystal says.

Pam moves uncomfortably at this news. She gets up and excuses herself to go and look into the children's bedroom. They are both asleep. She walks over to them to check the windows are locked tight. The sensation to flee immediately is controlled once more. She feels there will be no rest until she can put enough space between herself and those she fears. She just has to get through the night. The plane will take her away from all this tomorrow. She'll be home in a day or so. Pam returns to the living room.

'What will you do now?' Crystal asks.

'We go back to Canada tomorrow. I will then consider my options. I've been employed for so long, I'm not worried about getting work immediately. I can choose wherever I want to go. But, I'll miss . . . '

Pam does not finish her sentence. She is once more consumed by grief. She has to breathe slowly for as long as it takes to recover her composure. Glen's sudden departure tumbles through her mind, stirring up emotional gaps when she's forced to think of her future plans.

Crystal moves closer and Pam buries her head into Crystal's neck and sobs.

Azaad stands looking helplessly at his feet.

'When will you come back?'

'I don't know, for the trial of Glen's killers definitely. Maybe not before.'

Pam flies home to Montreal with Glen's body and their children. Pam's parents have helped Glen's parents to arrange the funeral. Despite having lived overseas for several years, the Chapmans still have large numbers of friends in Montreal, as many as they do anywhere else.

At the funeral a group of Inuit elders, who Glen lived with, come to pay their respects. They are dressed in their traditional costumes and sing a traditional burial song. They speak a serious of prayers in their own language. The congregation, most of who are from a Christian background, accept this contribution. Pam is keen, for her own sake as much as for her family and their friends, not to brand all ethnic cultures with barbaric superstitious beliefs. She knows that most cultures have had them, but have out-grown them. She refuses several invitations to speak to the media in Canada.

A spokesperson for the Canadian High Commission in Dar es Salaam tells reporters that Glen's death was related to the abductions and killing of albinos. He points once more to the fact that recently over thirty albinos, mostly children have been killed as a result of superstitious beliefs and profiteering from the trafficking of their body parts. He describes this as near to serial killings as you can find. There may be more than one killer involved, but they all need to be hunted with the same vigour as any set of serial killings demands. The press want more details of Glen's murder. The spokesman declines to give details except to say that the investigation is ongoing. 'We will answer no more questions on this until such time as Glen Chapman's killers and those involved in this trade are brought to justice.' The spokesman adds, 'I can say however is that it is our intention to complete and publish Glen Chapman's research, and we have asked Professor Michael Graham to help with this.'

Chapter Nine

The Aftermath

Shortly after the imprisonment of his son, Kaka Damu's father Kinyonga, takes a trip, for only the third time in his life, to Mwanza. On arrival, he speaks to the police chief. He maintains his argument that his son has done nothing wrong and there is no proof linking him to either of the killings. Despite long talks with the police and city officials, he cannot find anyone in local government to believe his side of the story. He stresses Kaka is a respected healer with far more people thanking him for their recovery than there are people complaining or disappointed with his help. He says he can bring sworn statements from some police officers saying that Kaka has helped them in the past and that he is a respectable distributor of good luck.

When confronted with the opinion that Kaka is an ignorant criminal suspected of conducting several human sacrifices, and that there are countless complaints from albinos and their families, Kaka's father simply shrugs. He asks the police to look at the overall good performed by his son in the community, as opposed to the complaints of *zero* people who are cursed at birth and have a life of no value.

When he visits Kaka in jail, they speak in their own dialect so the guards do not understand what is being said. Kaka tells his father that some guards are afraid of him. That he is being treated well but despite his weeks in prison the police are still searching for John in connection with the abduction of the albino boy from Dar es Salaam.

'Don't worry son, John is smart. He will remain invisible as long as needed. I don't like seeing you here like this.'

'I know, father.'

'When is this trial set for?'

'I don't know. Some guards say the police have very little evidence to show that I have broken the law.'

'Yes, I have already spoken to Juma. He is sticking to his story that he was guarding your house and that he fought with both intruders. It does not matter what they say, we are allowed to protect ourselves from thieves that enter our house. They know there are few police where we are, and we take care of things ourselves.'

'I've never seen so many police as I did in our village that night. Some were dressed like black devils with guns.'

'I've told Juma that he must continue to protect you. His one condition is that you honour your word to keep the girl Nyanzu for his release, if there is any time in prison for him.'

'The girl Nyanzu saw everything.'

'She told me.'

' Where is she now?'

'She is staying with me, at my house.'

'Has she said anything to the police?'

'They have spoken to her already but they want to speak to her again. She told me what she has told the police. She cannot read or write so they want to record her statement. They have sent for a recording machine to do this.'

'She's the one who killed the white man father, with her spike into his heart.'

'She told me that she didn't kill him. That he just fell down pretending to be stabbed.'

'Pretending?'

'Yes, the police say there was no sign of any stab wound in the heart. The white man's skull was crushed.'

'Father I can't remember much of the moment. I was angry and overjoyed at what the ancestral spirits had brought me. They provided me with the very source of our bad luck, there in my own home. I thought he was dead. I was keen to fulfil my own prophecy, that a special sacrifice was needed.'

'I understand son. I have been in this position myself.'

'So what shall we do about Nyanzu?'

'Leave her to me.'

——➤◉◄——

The Canadian High Commission publishes Glen's research, posthumously in English. It is full of rambling colourful references to tribal cultures and their differences. He also discusses briefly the integration of tribal values into Tanzania's modern society; the single party state that frowned on tribal differences after independence and the transition to a multi-party system in 1995. The early census data across the country does not give any breakdown of the one hundred and twenty main ethnic groups. Even the latest census does not include tribal information nor display any numbers of people in each group. Yet the march of progress has left some people behind. Almost half of all women still cannot read or write. Between the cracks in education there are still pockets of real poverty. Around the country in isolated communities, it is the tribal traditions and loyalties that hold the communities together. In these places there is a distinct lack of sustained or significant assistance from the central government. Within these pockets of poverty, the local attitude towards children who have some disability or born with albinism, differs greatly.

Glen makes the point that it is almost impossible to target educational efforts to change behaviour in these pockets without knowing the numbers and how widespread these discriminatory attitudes and superstitious attitudes are.

The communication links that hold the country together are based on the National language. However Glen suggests that because village loyalties and nepotism are rife, any national efforts to deal with grass roots superstitions against albinos are limited. Local efforts led by concerned local leaders are also necessary.

People defend the practices which separate them as much as they embrace a common interest in progress. For example, in national communication efforts it is largely the converted that hear, understand and pass on a message of human rights. It is not enough to run radio adverts, print brochures or make speeches from pulpits against witch doctors or local faith healers. Outlawing a tribal institution can simply strengthen a tribal attitude against distant unwanted authority. There is also a danger that publicity on the issue can stimulate even more interest and support in certain places coming from outside. Habits that are performed by a tiny minority can be strengthened when they link themselves to others in widespread networks.

Glen repeats his suggestion that it is those who are educated within each of the tribal groups who are best placed to assist in a transition from barbaric practices to cultural preservation and community enriching behaviour. There is nothing ground-breaking about this statement. However he goes on to stress the importance of creativity and how every positive effort needs to be supported and publicised. He sights several examples of this already happening. There are many key individuals using creativity to lead the way and change things. There are those out there who know the cultural specifics of how to effectively retire, and remove outdated practices, if they are brave enough and motivated enough to take action. Each geographic area is unique, not just because of its tribal features but because of its unique rate of absorption of modern influences among its traditions.

Ironically Glen sees the remoteness of these groups as strength and being one of the main reasons that some of their practices have not become even more widespread or international. They want to keep it to themselves because they do not want to be exploited by foreigners. They are doing it for profit, yes, but it is also their belief system, one that ignores the consequences. It is a belief system that for the sake of albinos, needs to change

Glen also warns against looking at these events purely from an anthropological perspective. Glen lists a number of psycho-social problems that are experienced by people in every culture. That these mental problems can lead to people being used without their knowledge or understanding. The iodine deficient villager who is exploited to do things no one else would do. Gullible uneducated people can often be guilty of initiating proceedings without any empathy for victims. These unstable mental conditions can be caused by abuse of drugs or alcohol or simply as the result of deficiencies in diet. In many cases these conditions can reduce a person's capacity to know right from wrong or to feel any social responsibility at all. Glen points out there are little data on the extent of such conditions in villages in Tanzania. And the drug treatments available for such conditions in the West are almost non-existent.

It is this last part of Glen's research that is left unfinished, and yet, the Canadian's are keen to move things forward; they publish it anyway.

In all of his interviews and research Glen found no evidence of their being any international influence on the demand for human body parts as charms or medicine. Given the extent of other illegal international trade in the country; in animals, animal parts and gemstones, this is a relief. There is a lot of documentation on concerns for the trade in ivory that Glen references, along with the effect on the rhino population that comes from a fascination with rhino horn scarabs for daggers in the Middle East. Glen also mentions the Far Eastern superstitions in China, that powdered rhino horn is an aphrodisiac . . . a myth which remains unchallenged, by perhaps the most successful socialist government communication apparatus that has every been created, that of the People's Republic.

Some people at the Canadian High Commission had feared that the illegal trade in ivory and other goods could easily expand to accommodate a new demand in human organs and that albinos might suffer even more if this ever happens. It would be relatively easy to exploit a country like Tanzania where there is a disproportionate number of albinos living. However aside from a couple of reports of cross border trade between witch doctors in Kenya, Uganda and Burundi, this problem has been so far contained.

———=《⊙》=———

Pam decides not to return to Tanzania with her children. She stops working for the United Nations soon after her compassionate leave ends. She starts her own business in Montreal using her knowledge and contacts in East Africa. She begins the importation of raw Shea butter as a product to be distributed throughout the substantial skin cream market.

She comes to this decision quickly when she sees her children respond to the safe home environment in Canada. She feels that if she moves again with a new UN assignment she might have difficulty in providing the sort of mental security they need, on her own, especially if she is out working. She prefers at this moment in time to stay in Montreal, raising her children there.

Pam believes she's handled the media frenzy that followed Glen's death with some restraint and dignity. She has been careful not to criticise Africa or blame Tanzanians for the death of her husband. She is too intelligent and diplomatic for that. She does however stress that when it comes to the albino population, a serious cult of neglect and exclusion exists in the country, saying that many middle class are in denial that there is a problem.

'In a country with so many social issues to deal with,' she repeats in one interview, 'every politician can find an excuse for not doing something about an issue they perceive as small or less important, by listing all the major problems that are taking up their time; preventing them taking action. With serious water problems, poor electricity supply and lack of higher educational opportunities, the middle and upper classes are suffering what could be called 'inconveniences'. While albino's in rural areas are often living in fear for their lives.'

Pam refers to statistics that Glen gathered for his research about teenagers. Less than six percent of the population attend secondary school. Women especially are isolated from information with less than thirty percent having access to any media at all. In some extreme cases women are denied their basic rights to be mothers by men who choose to abandon or neglect a child who is disabled or in their eyes less than perfect at birth.

Quoting Professor Graham, Pam points out that democracy should not be seen as a tool to keep small minorities in isolation. Democracy has become the most popular form of international government, because it basically allows a country to self-correct, to move away from entrenched beliefs and dictatorships and if necessary change it's mind on outdated beliefs. It changes direction each time new leaders are elected and social improvements can then be made. This is a facet of democracy that few African countries have taken advantage of. The law states that criminals must not be left unpunished. This does not mean that someone who steals a mobile phone should be beaten to death by a mob, or that a sacrificial murderer should go free. The law must apply equally and yet it cannot if it is not represented or enforced equally. Ignorance of the law is no excuse for the mass of the population, but ignorance means just what it says . . . and **ignoring** law-breakers, by those up the ladder of law enforcement, is also no excuse either.

———◦◉◦———

Professor Michael Graham becomes a changed man by the tragic death of Glen and all these events. He feels he can no longer sit out his retirement in peace and quiet. The albino professor takes more interest in the plight of Tanzania's albinos when he hears of the abduction of Helen's son from his very neighbourhood. He offers Helen and her two boys a place in his compound after Pam leaves for Canada. The gifted, handsome and philanthropic professor employs Helen and gives her a home in his vacant servant's quarters.

Despite initially not having a security guard the professor tells Helen that she will be safe within his compound. Helen however takes her own precautions and hangs charms and relics around his garden fence. She buys these from a stall near the Selander Bridge.

'The more ignorance people have, the more it can be used against them! No one will dare harm us here.' Helen tells the professor.

Along with this collection of charms and protective symbols around the perimeter of the house, the professor employs a sturdy Somali guard for the first time. He also has an Internet connection installed inside his home.

Over the next ten months he and Pam talk regularly on Skype. He also lets Helen talk to Pam and for Emanuel and Thomas to talk to Douglas and Gail. Both families communicate to each other regularly on Facebook also. They post photos and talk to each other in conversations modelled on the exploits of the rich and famous. The children, like millions of others, have begun to bring themselves up as mini celebrities. They copy the format of the newscasts, to bring each other up to date. They make visits into adventures for themselves and let their imaginations list their accomplishments. They copy much of what they see and enjoy on TV shows, movies and music to each other regularly.

Professor Graham sees this evolution unfold before his eyes in his study. Academic knowledge, once distributed only by the educational institutions, is now an open vault for anyone who understands the languages of the Internet.

Douglas has taken up ice-skating and although he's happiest playing ice hockey, Pam encourages him to take part in dance and figure skating also. As children brought up in warm climates, when they are dressed in winter clothes and sliding on sledges in snow, they find it strange and exciting. However Pam tells the professor that any physical activity also reminds them of being chased by their father. It makes them remember the intense heat, the sun-cream and the pool at their home in Dar es Salaam.

'How are the wheels of justice turning in Tanzania?' Pam enquires of the professor.

'The wheels are turning slowly, but I believe it is because they want to get this one right. There is a lot of pressure on the police from the judiciary to provide evidence, because they know that they have an international reputation to maintain in terms of the International Criminal Courts here and their conduct.'

'So what have you been doing meantime?'

The professor tells Pam that he is now fed automatically any information that is published or posted on the Internet, about the abduction or killings of albinos anywhere. He has set up a facility on an existing albino website he calls the **'Triple A'—Albino Ambulance Appeal.** In the case of any reported incident concerning albinos he can find a donor who will send a small amount of money immediately to be administered to help victims or families. Timing and the proper dispersal of money can make all the difference to families living in fear. Slowly the number of subscribers who answer this emergency call is growing.

But Professor Graham tells Pam he takes a more cautious view of using modern information technology for 'development'. He sees development budgets being used-up providing bureaucrats and decision makers with laptops, and taking them to meetings in five star hotels, while there are still villages without water-pumps. He tells Pam he has written a lengthy piece on his favourite subject, democracy and education in Africa, to be published in the Guardian newspaper magazine. At the beginning of the article the professor for the first time makes specific reference to the fact that he is an albino.

The article contains illustrations, photos and graphs to make the professor's point. Time and again there are photos of starving pastoral children. The only way to tell the date of these photos is through the identity of the celebrity who is standing next to the starving children. If it is Danny Kaye or Audrey Hepburn it's from the last century. If it is Angelina Jolie or Ewan McGregor it's more recent.

The articles final paragraph talks of the digital gap between industrial communities and those in rural areas without power. How those who are currently on line are inadvertently being used to design the world's future. A future of jobs forever looking at screens; forever higher in degrees of sophistication, but screens never the less. The professor sees these TV and computer screens as no different from the old tools of industry, the looms in Dickensian Britain, the factory floors of post war growth. It's just the latest industrial herding of people into jobs; but herding none the less. What of the rest of us Professor Graham asks? What about those here in Africa who do not have electricity? When is the starting line going to be modified sensibly for children here? When is it going to include the basics of clean water, electricity, health services and education for every child? Especially when the cost of this provision seems to be reducing itself every year proportionally to profits from the world's financial services.

Pam understands that because the article is to be syndicated internationally there may be backslapping and congratulatory comments coming to the professor from all over the development network. As it does whenever an insightful story has been published. People will be pleased that one of their own has broken through the marital affair headlines of footballers, and told it like it is. Pleased that some of the issues they themselves have been dealing with, are highlighted in such a high profile article.

But Pam also knows that this article will make no difference what-so-ever to the grass roots development worker. The confusion that currently exists over information and its usefulness has all but paralysed every sector of development. When information does not bring about action it is merely people talking to themselves. And to Pam there seems a lot of that.

———◉———

Pam's new import business offers grass roots support to African growers and makers of shea butter. Sponsoring change in someone's mind is like sponsoring financial change in there bank account. A series of small individual loans of money is much better than gifting out large sums. Shea butter is pressed from seeds of the *Lulu* tree and is harvested mostly by women. Pam then sells the raw product to a variety of Health outlets across Canada. The butter is in demand as a skin care product. Pam's publicity materials talk of the healing properties when it's mixed in with a variety of oils.

One day she catches her advertising agency using the words 'Miracle Cure' and she reacts aggressively. She stops the advertisers from releasing the campaign, and halts the production line until she can sort out this issue of claiming its something it is not. She stresses that the shea butter has certain time-tested qualities that help dry skin. It does not protect the skin from the sun, it is no help whatsoever for albinos wishing to cure their condition or protect them selves from sunlight. In fact it is dangerous, since it heats the skin disproportionately in sunlight.

This type of product publicity is something that Pam takes very seriously. Sometimes she feels there is no difference in the exaggerated claims of advertisers and those of Shaman in East Africa. Both are equally exploitative of the gullibility of the consumer to believe them.

Pam loses some business with her modification of the product's publicity but overall it's a success and her exchanges with the professor are soon translated into a new funding initiative in Tanzania. Pam becomes the sponsor of a hostel, specifically for albino children, near the Dawakubwa Clinic. The hostel is supervised by Dr Crystal Mpira.

———◉———

After ten months in custody Kaka Damu, is still being held without trial. The district police chief Ernest Bigonne, visits the Reverend

Albert Mosha and briefs him on the next set of proceedings with regard to the trial.

The Reverend is grateful for the information but he is not too happy to hear some of the news. 'Why are things moving so slowly, Ernie?'

'We still have no physical evidence to charge this man with murder Reverend. He has no prior conviction. There is no record of complaints, no photos from the night in question, nothing we collected from the scene. All we have is a set of very bleary-eye-witness accounts. Half the people say they saw him carry out a baby, the other half a dead chicken, many did not see anything. No proof that Kaka Damu himself was directly responsible for the death of Glen Chapman or the Maasai. No proof that he ordered the killing or that he had any connection with the initial abduction of the Chapman boy and the albino boy from Dar. No one is talking about this as a ritual sacrifice at all; everyone is saying it was a traditional dance festival. There is no concrete evidence against him.'

'This man has built a concrete house out of the profits of witchcraft, what do you mean there is no concrete evidence?' The Reverend probes his friend further.

'I'm fairly confident we can convict his accomplice Juma, and we are still looking for the other one named John. But we need something more to keep Kaka Damu locked up.'

The Reverend in desperation then sites the laws of international terrorism. 'You must keep this man locked up,' he tells the chief, 'if he is not a terrorist suspect, directing a campaign against our minority albino population, then, I don't know what terrorism is!'

'This man Juma, has confessed to both the killings,' says the police chief, 'but we suspect that Kaka is the actual killer of Glen Chapman because I was told by a young girl witness. She disappeared before we had time to record her testimony. The abducted albino boy was too drugged to remember anything that night.'

—————◉—————

As more months pass with little progress on the Kaka Damu case, the Reverend writes a long email to Pam Chapman and her children and he offers to assist her in anyway she thinks might be helpful. Pam in return sends the Reverend a copy of Glen's research that has now been translated into Kiswahili.

After reading the long awaited Swahili version, the Reverend is inspired by one statement that Glen has written about creativity, and decides to try and assist the police further. He calls into his office one of his flock that he knows comes from the same district as Kaka Damu. He reads aloud to this man Gilbert in Swahili, 'that it is up to the educated members of each community to be creative in trying to put an end to these barbaric practices while maintaining a record of each cultural activity for the sake of history'. The Reverend follows this reading by asking parishioner Gilbert if he might be willing to help bring to justice Kaka Damu.

'What can I do, Reverend?'

'You heard the story of how this white man was murdered near your village?'

'Yes, it shocked many people. My parents told me about it.'

'I want you to see if anyone around your village could be encouraged to help the police.'

'By doing what, exactly?'

'You can start some enquires around your community, to see if there are any people willing to step forward and testify against Kaka Damu.'

'His family are powerful in that area. Although he is in prison his father is still very respected.'

'I would like you to find some Christian people who may have recently converted. Talk to them. Assure them of the strength of the Lord. Tell them they will be protected against any witchcraft. Tell them they should fear only the wrath of God if they remain silent.'

'What will I do if I find someone?'

'Let me know immediately. We shall put them into the Jehovah's Witness protection programme.' The Reverend laughs aloud. Gilbert doesn't get the joke, but he laughs also.

'If this is a fight between a satanic Shaman's power and the great Almighty, there is only one winner.' The Reverend says, still laughing.

'Do you have anyone in mind that I should speak to?'

'There is someone the police chief spoke of. Someone who is mentioned in the police reports, but since then she has not been seen. She apparently witnessed the whole thing. She is Kaka Damu's assistant, a young girl called Nyanzu. Find her for a start, if you can.'

<hr />

Nyanzu has been kept out of sight doing her chores in the compound of Kaka Damu's father since Kaka's arrest. She must be controlled and protected, since she is key to Juma maintaining his confession of the two killings.

She feels lucky to have been taken in by Kaka's father, luck that she believes could be the result of saving the albino boy back at Kaka's ceremony. She remembers being terrified by the sight of a white man and a dead Maasai. She will never forget the fear on the face of the white man when he was pretending to be spiked. There was such a commotion that followed the white man's death she decided to stay with the albino boy. She saw the fear in his eyes also when he woke up, because he was painted up and he did not know where he was. She saw him become calm and thankful, when she spoke to him.

When the police arrived she helped them to clean the boy up. She told the police her story. She did not tell them she saw Kaka hit the white man. She told them she did not see Juma hit the Maasai or the white man. She knew that Kaka would be pleased with her.

Kaka Damu's father summons Nyanzu from her chores. He takes her for a rare walk along the riverside. With such an investment in this girl, he believes there is only one course of action available to him, which will benefit everyone.

'Are you happy with what Kaka Damu has done for you?

'Yes.'

'Do you know that Kaka has promised you to the man Juma?'

'No.'

'Yes, he has promised Juma, that you will be married to him after your circumcision and when he is released from prison. Is this what you want?'

Nyanzu does not reply. She has accepted the words circumcision and marriage as being something that is inevitable in her life, but she is too young to know what the consequences or demands of these may be. She sees Juma simply as an old man. She has been surrounded by old men for a long time, taking their instructions, obeying their wives. She feels an affinity to Kaka. He has always been kind to her. She feels a kinship with him, but this man Juma she is not sure about. This is too much to think about just now.

Kaka's father senses some reluctance in the girl. He needs her to think carefully of the responsibilities he has put to her. He steps forward and grabs her, physically pushing her to the ground. He bends down and rips the dress from her. He grabs her arm as she slides and kicks back away from him in fear.

'Do you know what it's like when a man takes you for a wife?' he says. She shakes her head in terror. He grabs her foot and lifts her half off the ground. He grabs her firmly between her legs and says, 'Do you know what it's like to be cut, so that you feel nothing in these parts here?' The girl is on the point of hysterics. Kaka's father then squats down beside her and changes his tone.

'There is something that you can do for us that will give you a good future; something that will give you control over your own life; something that could help you become a priestess in the ways of our clan.'

Nyanzu responds to his tone rather than his words. She cannot think this fast, she cannot take in or understand his words.

'I'd like you to visit Juma in prison. I will explain everything later. All you will need is your little chicken spike.'

Nyanzu stands up and picks up her tattered dress, she does not cover herself, it is the dress she is more concerned with rather than her naked body. She is still shaking from the assault. She stands tall and looks at Kaka's father. She detects she is no longer in danger. She turns and walks back towards his home. After a few steps she takes a skip then begins running, fast, all the way.

Kaka's father congratulates himself. He has not lost his talent to bully someone into submission; to put so much fear in them they will listen and do, whatever he says. It is a gift, and his whole family has it.

———— ⊂◍⊃ ————

By the time the parishioner Gilbert visits his parent's home, his village has become famous all over Tanzania. In Msasani in the bars, it is known as 'Albino-ville' after a Hollywood horror movie. Insensitive humour is not confined to one race. It's also locally known as the village where the albino killers live; the village that practices witchcraft and human sacrifice; the village where a white man was battered then chopped up.

Gilbert sees little difference in the place where he first ran around as a child. He is educated and interested enough to follow the news and local events. He reads the local district newspapers with their full columns of problems and crimes. He reads of the number of road deaths, the political scandals and the mob justice that often dominates the main headlines. He reads when there's an outbreak of cholera or malaria and other killer diseases. He reads of the terrible conditions in schools, and of pupils without job opportunities. If you believe the newspapers, he thinks, this place is a hell.

Gilbert sees nothing but laughing children whenever he visits home. He sees them being inventive and happy. He remembers his own childhood full of wonderful memories. He had no shoes at a time when it did not matter. He never once felt hungry. He never once needed to see a witch doctor or any other kind of doctor. His parents were strict but they brought him up well. His father was Christian and monogamous, despite being surrounded by other Christian men in his village with several wives.

Gilbert also travelled briefly to England, where he stayed and prayed in a suburban church he visited for six weeks. He remembers speaking to children in the church there. They seemed educated, but seemed to complain all the time. At least that's what he remembers most, English children arguing with authority all the time, over being in church, over football teams or TV shows to watch. A good bamboo stick would have sorted them out. They even competed over different brands of shoes and clothes, feeling better off as the result of wearing a certain label. He also remembers the church-going parents who referred to him as an African and how sorry they were he'd have to return to such poverty after experiencing the luxuries of England.

Gilbert enjoyed pointing out that he and his fellow villages were all living quite well. Life was poor but less complicated. He could not agree with the assumption people made that everyone in the world was aspiring to the sort of life people lived in Middle England. Many even said that going to Africa was like going back in history. In Gilbert's mind there was no question about the date of the Lord's calendar. His village was living in the 21st Century as much as anyone in England

and in a part of Africa that had been inhabited longer than England. In fact it had 'preserved' some things much longer than England and had shown human survival skills despite its problems. He felt he lived like the majority of the people on the planet, still enjoying the values of a rural life.

Gilbert also has experience with the Christian visitors who have made occasional trips to his church in Mwanza. Few, he believes, ever came to Africa to do some good, and not left without some good being done to them. He often thinks that when he's finished teaching in Mwanza that it's his village he wants to retire to.

Gilbert remembers Kaka Damu as an arrogant boy. Kaka did not attend school, but he was influential in and around the school. When Gilbert first attended school many children were from families that had recently arrived in the village, who had been persecuted elsewhere and who had only recently settled. Some came from around Lake Victoria. He remembers that Kaka Damu's family were at the centre of organising traditional dances and ceremonies to welcome them, some of which Gilbert attended.

Gilbert's priority is to follow the Reverend's advice and seek out Nyanzu. But first he feels he has to meet Kaka's father, despite the knowledge he may lock horns with him on superstition, beliefs and the recent behaviour of his son.

'Greetings *mwalimu* (teacher) Gilbert. What brings you to my home?'

'I mean you no disrespect, but I come to talk about the shame that your son has brought to our village.'

'Shame? What shame? Can you see any shame here? Point it out *Mwalimu*, teach me what this shame is.'

'Have you not heard what people are saying about this village?'

'Who is saying these things? People who don't live here? I have no ears for what they say.'

'But you should have.'

'Why? Have you spoken to the people who live here, do you see any changes yourself, from when you were a boy?'

'Yes there are changes.'

'Where? What?'

'There is now a church and a new school nearby.'

'These are physical things. There are also trees that are higher, more houses and more children. These are things that make no difference to me.'

'These physical things have also brought new ideas, new beliefs.'

'Show me the relevance of these beliefs . . . to worship something distant that is not here? So much of what you believe, is just make-believe. The singing in a church is like the grunts of a hippo; the laughs of a hyena, these are background noises to the real workings of our village.'

'I would like to talk to the girl Nyanzu.'

'She is not here.'

'Where is she?'

'She has left to visit Kaka Damu in prison and has not yet returned.'

'Did she go to Mwanza alone?'

'No, she travelled with Kaka's wife and son.'

'Can you tell me, swearing on your ancestor's spirits if you have conducted any sacrifices involving albinos?'

'You ask me to swear on my ancestor's spirits, but you do not believe in the power of our ancestors.'

'But I know that you do.'

'What then is truth, if I tell you something you accept to be true from my belief . . . that you then hold not to be true from your own belief?'

'Please answer my question. Have you ever killed any albino's or used their body parts in ritual practices? Tell me your truth.'

'I have done nothing the ancestors have not instructed me to do.'

Lack of progress with the prosecution of Kaka Damu spreads another wave of fear through families with albino children. Those who live near Kaka's village are frightened of a backlash from locals deprived of their healer and who believe that Kaka should be released. Also affected by the increased publicity surrounding this case are the many albinos who have managed to make a life for themselves in towns and cities despite all their previous difficulties. They do not like the slow pace of justice or the possibility that Kaka Damu will be released.

One solution put forward by the authorities, to calm the fears of families with albino children is to expand the provision of safe houses and special hostels that offer protection for those affected. Crystal already rents a vacant home in Dawakubwa and now runs it as a hostel. She has set things up with the substantial grant of money she received from Pam Chapman. They've decided that the space in the hostel will only be offered to families for a limited time for protection or for convalescence from any frightening experience they may have suffered. They are keen to avoid the creation of a hostel where families simply come to dump their newborn albino children, never to have contact with them again. Pam had suggested the hostel be named the 'Chapman Shelter for Albino Family Support.' But both Crystal and Azaad were against such a name and suggested it change simply to 'The Chapman Shelter', Dawakubwa.' Azaad pointed out in an email to Pam, that the last thing they wanted was a name that might draw attention to those who living there and make the building a target. He jokingly suggested it might be better to call it the 'Chapman Hostel for Violent Criminals and Retired Soldiers', to keep prowling opportunistic witch doctors away.

Azaad procured beds and furniture and when it opened there were two families with six children who moved in immediately. One family has an albino girl, and two older black brothers. The other family, with twin albino children, have been back and forth to Dawakubwa before. It is a mother Crystal already knows with her boy and girl twins and two older black siblings. The Chapman Hostel functions quietly and without any publicity.

———»«»«———

One morning ten months after his arrest Juma is found dead in prison. The official cause of death is listed as a snakebite but there are suspicious circumstances and several rumours surrounding his demise. He is found in a bougainvillea lined exercise yard with a dead snake in his hand. Beside him is a poisoned arrow from a Maasai bow. There is a small puncture mark on his chest. Inside his cell guards find the markings and ritual symbols of a shaman carved into the wall. A small broken neck chain is found under his bed. The seeds from a Henna tree are found on his window ledge. A dead chameleon is discovered in the corner of his cell, the water in his toilet bucket is black and there is also a discarded bottle of sun-cream under his mattress.

All of this is enough for a wave of paranoid superstition to wash over the prison and the investigation that follows. For weeks after Juma's death no one goes near the spot where he died and his cell is not cleaned.

Juma is buried without any autopsy or ceremony in an unmarked animist graveyard, four miles from the prison.

CHAPTER TEN

THE TRIAL AND JUSTICE OF SORTS!

One year after Glen's death, Kaka Damu is still being held in prison in Mwanza. On three occasions he has been brought before a judge and detained until a further set of enquires can be concluded. Evidence of any links with a serious crime against the Shaman remain weak, and with the main suspect now dead, the State's prosecutors know they may have to release Kaka soon. Political and religious pressure to keep the man in prison is all that seems to be holding up his release.

Kaka's assistant John has never been caught although prison guards suggest to police after Juma's death that a man resembling John's description may have visited Kaka twice in prison. Police are continuing to search for him.

———◆———

Meanwhile a day in the life of the Chapman Hostel consists of a pre-dawn journey, by the black boys, to the village water pump. The river is much nearer, but Crystal insists that everyone staying at the hostel use only clean water from the pump. The river is fine to wash in, but not to drink from. Two large yellow plastic containers, originally sold with cooking oil, are used to carry the water. The boys go with their mother to the pump and they complain bitterly. This is girl's work and they don't like it. The mother carries a bucket of clothes for washing and she stresses that it is still too dangerous for their albino brothers and sister to be doing this task. Also Crystal has told them the sun is bad for them, and besides the girl does plenty of work inside the hostel. This situation will not last for long. The boys carry the two ten litre containers back with enough water for eight people for a day.

Back at the house, the building is shaped like a two car garage, divided into compartments. It has four small size rooms on one side and one large living area on the other. It has metal window frames and a tin roof and it's more secure than its cosier mud-walled, thatched-roof neighbours.

The albino twins open the windows at first light and begin to sweep the floor. They use hand brooms, made from long grasses they have bunched and tied themselves. They crouch and sweep very effectively, collecting the dust without raising it into the air from the cement floor. The house still smells as if the concrete was laid recently. It's common for the dampness to persist for several months within such a structure if the wrong sand has been used in the concrete mix. There is mould growing up the white painted concrete walls.

The heavy new furniture brought by Azaad is left unused. The current occupants prefer to sit on floor mats in the main room and all the chairs have been stacked on top of each other to cater for easier cleaning. There is a single dining table with six old upright chairs, also rarely used. The families prefer eating on the ground.

These residents have lived here for almost three months now since the hostel opened. Three other women came separately for shelter, but two left immediately after seeing the albino children and the other one left after three weeks.

There is provision for three meals a day. Breakfast is a maize-meal porridge followed by bananas and a sugary milky tea. Lunch contains a vegetable and meat dish, either chicken or goat and the evening meal is usually beans and *ugali* (ground corn paste). It's all cooked on a charcoal burner in a space allocated at the back for a proper kitchen that is not yet constructed. There is no electricity. It is the abundance and the variety of food that is the main attraction for the mothers who came here. Pam's grant allows for meat every day and the home visit of a schoolteacher for the children, so they can keep with up their education.

Crystal drops in on the families once a week, and she employs help from the clinic administrator to run the hostel. The only health concern Crystal has for the families, is the extra weight that they all seem to be putting on. She scolds the mothers and complains that they are eating too much, too often and there is also too little exercise for the children.

'You know that it is safe to go out around here in the day time.' Crystal tells the two mothers.

'Yes, we let the two brothers go out, but we do not let the special ones out in the daylight,' says the mother of the twins.

'Why?'

'We do not feel they are safe outside. Some women in the village still talk about Kaka Damu. His people live around here also. Word has spread that albino children are here. Kaka Damu is going to be released soon they say.'

'When did you hear this?'

'They talk of this all the time. They shout things at us. Say that we are not welcome here. Especially these abused women who came here to stay, they have also been telling stories of us. How we live so well in here.'

'I thought they would know better. How is the schooling going for the children?'

'They are doing well. The teacher is very good. The twins are now learning English.'

'Mwalimu teaches them English?'

'Yes. He says he got a letter from Mistress Pam in Canada asking him to teach English.'

'I wonder why she is asking for this.'

'Mwalimu thinks she is trying to raise money to bring the special ones to Canada for a visit.'

—∞◎∞—

On Gilbert's return to Mwanza, he attends a Sunday morning service conducted by his friend the Reverend. He stays behind to talk afterwards. He tells him that he's had no success in finding the girl Nyanzu. That he cannot find anyone even interested in talking about Kaka Damu, never mind giving evidence against him.

'But you tried?'

'Yes, I even spoke to Kaka Damu's father.'

'So, how is it in your village . . . the village of the damned?' The Reverend laughs.

'It is much as it always was.'

'You like the place?'

'Yes, it's my home.'

'Will you ever go back there to live?'

'My parents are still there, and yes I want to live out my retirement there. It's better for me than here in the city. That's what I'm saving for.'

'So people are not bothered by all these stories of the witch doctor Kaka Damu?'

'They are too busy with their lives to be bothered. They're like people everywhere. In Nottingham where I visited, here were plenty murders there but most people just carried on.'

'No one is troubled by this?'

'They certainly don't trouble his father, and I can't blame them. I bet there are people here in Mwanza who are far worse criminals, right under our noses, but we don't have people gathering to hunt them down. We must be careful not to become vigilantes Reverend?'

'What a pity. I heard they are likely to release Kaka Damu soon.'

'Then it must be God's will.'

'That sounds very fatalist for a good Christian, Mr Gilbert.'

'Why do you say that Reverend?'

'Ah, why indeed! Whenever I read, 'Thy will be done,' I think the good Lord gave us the responsibility to *apply* His will, rather than just accepting everything that happens *as* his will.'

Azaad invites Crystal to come to Mwanza to meet his parents and stay with him. She leaves her two boys with the clinic administrator and travels to the city for the week-end. When she arrives in town, Azaad speaks on her mobile to the taxi driver and gives him directions to his home. His mother and father are out at evening *Jamat Khana* (Mosque) when Crystal reaches his house.

In a street full of large houses, the taxi turns into Azaad's arched gate. Behind a tall plain painted wall, the taxi drives up a tree lined pathway to reveal a two storied mansion with a pillared entrance like the White House. At the front door Crystal steps out to be met by Azaad.

'Wow. I didn't realise you were inviting me to meet the Obamas.'

'It's not **that** big.'

'What was the name of Hilary Clinton's book? It takes a village?'

'Meaning?'

'Well you could certainly fit a village in here,' Crystal says.

'Its just something my father built . . . to fit the Bill Clinton you might say.' Azaad laughs as he murders his punch line, and continues. 'The Obama and the O fatha are both at the Mosque right now. Come in, and make yourself at home . . . in my village.'

'Are you sure they are all right with this?'

'Sure. It's like some people said you would never see a black American family in the White House. Welcome to my house. Actually, that's unfair. My folks are ahead in the multi-culture race-relations game. They've a lot of black friends along with some wayward inter-racial relatives too.'

Azaad turns to argue with the taxi driver, once he's told the fare. He barters the man down by a third.

'It always doubles . . . if they drive past that gate.'

'You mean the arch de triumph!' Crystal teases Azaad.

Inside the front door a servant, in a white tunic, greets Crystal and takes her bags. The house has large windows with drape curtains and little leather belts to hold them open. The hallway has a grey marble floor. In the large living room the furniture is heavy, with rows of couches set in a square. There is a large low coffee table in the middle with piles of books and magazines. All the cushions have square corners as if they have been made from mattress foam and there is a large gold chandelier in the centre of the high ceiling.

'Am I sleeping in the Lincoln bedroom?' Crystal asks.

'No, it's closed for renovation.'

'So, which couch is mine?'

'We need to talk about that.'

'Talk, as in negotiate?'

'Yes, I mean no. I've already told my folks that . . .' Azaad stops abruptly.

'That what?

'That . . . '

'Come on Azaad.'

'That I intend to ask you to marry me, and that we will be sleeping together and . . . God, I've really screwed this up already haven't I?'

Crystal sits down on one of the couches. Azaad sits on the one facing her, ten feet away.

'I guess you have. I can keep this all a secret if you like . . . until you actually ask me first Azaad.'

'Sorry. It's all gone wrong. I should have given you your own bedroom then brought this up later. I just couldn't stand the thought of us not sleeping in the same room after all this time apart.'

'All this time apart or all this time we've been together?'

'I know. I was talking with my parents and I got very angry and emotional with them. I'm nearly thirty and I'm asking permission to have a girl in my bedroom?'

'What did they say?'

'They had no idea just how serious I was, about you.'

'That's interesting. I had no idea either.'

'Come on Crystal you know how I feel about you. What do you say?'

'You mean about the marriage proposal I think I just heard, somewhere in that apology?'

'Yes.'

'I have some questions Azaad.'

'Questions?'

'Yes, some things I need to know.'

'Like what?'

'Are you polygamous or monogamous in your religion?'

'We're mono . . . mostly.'

'Because I don't think I could deal with the polygamous younger wife in a few years time, thing.'

'I've no plans for a younger wife in a few years. One's enough.'

'Good. And how do you see this working? Are you thinking of coming to Dawakubwa and living there or do you see us in your boyhood bedroom for the rest of our lives?'

'Stop it Crystal. I want to get my own place, our own place. And I think there could be work for you here in Mwanza either in the main hospital or at the Aga Khan clinic.'

Crystal stands and walks over to Azaad. She stands in front of him as he remains seated and she puts her hands on his shoulders.

'OK. One last question Azaad. Are you homosexual or straight, or even a little bi-sexual?'

Azaad stands and puts his arms around Crystal. Their foreheads touch and he looks into her eyes.

'What do you think Crystal?'

'I'm not sure, with all these stories about you and the Big O.'

'Do, I take that as a yes?'

'Mm, maybe yes, for tonight. Call it a trial run.' Crystal kisses Azaad long and passionately.

That evening Crystal and Azaad eat with his parents in their large dining room. Azaad introduces Crystal formally as his fiancé and his parents, seemingly prepared, are very pleasant in their conversations with her. The dinner talk is kept restricted to local affairs rather than any plans for their future. Pleasant things and a little politics is discussed in Kiswahili and other topics such as Crystal's work are discussed in English.

After dinner, Azaad's mother asks Crystal how many children she has, Azaad is furious. He scolds his mother in Guajarati, a language Crystal does not understand.

'I have two boys Mrs Velji. And Azaad will be my third husband. If things don't work out, in my tribe, I can still take several more husbands.'

Azaad tells his mother in Guajarati that Crystal has a wicked sense of humour.

'Surely.' Azaad's mother says, answering both of them with one English word.

That night in Azaad's oversized Zanzibar bed, Crystal and Azaad consummate their trial agreement. Crystal screams louder than usual in her love-making. Azaad is caught unexpectedly by the volume of her gasps. He takes a fit of laughter and rolls off her. Crystal continues to pant and whimper lying on her back. She stops and also laughs. She rolls over and whispers to Azaad that she has never heard the echoes of her orgasm before. She wants to make the most of the experience.

'You mean this is your first echo chamber rumpy?' he says.

'Yes' she says loudly, 'My first big room with walls, high ceiling and pillars. Listen.' she says, and begins her groaning again. 'It's like doing it with another couple in the room.'

———— ◦◉◦ ————

The Reverend Mosha is pleased at what the government have done recently in their over-all efforts to protect albinos from discrimination. The situation has been discussed seriously in the Bunge (Parliament) and not skipped or 'Bungee-jumped' as the Reverend calls it. The courts have restated they will severely punish, under the law, anyone convicted of crimes against albinos. There are now several more hostels around the country that aid and assist families with albino children. Also a referendum has been conducted to ask people to come forward and report any suspicious behaviour of people suspected of witchcraft or albino abductions. This effort has been coordinated well, despite some fears that people would simply come forward and name their enemies in land disputes or other people that they don't like so police can arrest them.

As the months without any prosecution of the high profile suspect Kaka Damu mount up, the Reverend becomes frustrated that he may be released soon. Meanwhile more albinos are being herded, in his mind, into shelters and incarcerated for their own protection. Where is the real justice in this he thinks. The Reverend decides it's time to make another attempt at finding evidence against Kaka Damu, in and around his village. Once more he calls on his friend Gilbert to help. Gilbert however is not keen to help this time and it is the Reverend in this case who has to be creative to convince him to help.

'There is something more that I want you to do for me Gilbert.'

'What can I do, that has not already been done?'

'Tell me, have you ever met or spoken to anyone who is albino?'

'Not really.'

'I would like you to help me. I am considering starting a small shelter here inside the church, but I need to know more about how the other hostels are being run.'

'Is there a need for such a safe house here in this part of Mwanza?'

'That's exactly what I want you to find out Gilbert. I have arranged a visit for you, at your convenience, to a hostel at Dawakubwa. There is a Doctor Crystal Mpira there. I've heard it is one of the smaller but better run shelter for albinos. She will show you how the hostel operates. It is funded by the widow of the white man who was killed in your village.'

'When can I possibly go? I have work to do here?'

'There is a public holiday the weekend after next. Go then?'

'I suppose . . . '

'Excellent. I will arrange everything.'

———— ◉ ————

Crystal is informed of Gilbert's visit as she finishes packing up her house to move to Mwanza. She has secured a medical officer post at the Central Maternity hospital. It will be a far more time consuming job, with fifteen to twenty births a week. She will live with Azaad and she knows the schooling opportunities for her boys will be better.

Crystal has agreed with Pam that she will maintain in a supervisory role with the Chapman Hostel. She will seek a new caretaker but will continue visits at least once a month to see how things are going.

On the day that Gilbert arrives, Crystal meets him at the Dawakubwa clinic then invites him to stay overnight at her place, rather than the hostel. She takes him to her house and offers tea. She tells him the full story of the hostel. She talks of the initial visit of Glen Chapman, his interviews with albinos and the local faith healers. She asks Gilbert if he has read Glen's research.

'Only a few paragraphs.'

'I will send you a full copy of his research. It's tragic really that we have his killer in jail and he is going to be released. People here are terrified of this man Kaka Damu.'

Crystal takes Gilbert outside and shows him the gate to which Joseph Kawanga was impaled by the Maasai and his spear. She tells him of her own fears at the time for her children as well as those twins now safe in the hostel.

'This man does not just generate fear among his followers. It is also ordinary people that have fear of going against him. Even some police officers are reluctant to have anything to do with him. People feel that it's better to leave things as they are, and not disturb these traditional charlatans, even if there are those in the community who suffer. What men like Kaka Damu say about albinos and disabled children is vile. He will say that albinos are ghost of humans, that if you bury them they will disappear when in actual fact it is people like him who dig up their bodies to use their bones in their potions. You don't have to be outraged to feel passionate about this. People need to shake themselves out of their indifference. Don't you think?'

Gilbert has rarely spoken to such an articulate woman before. He is impressed. He does not answer her question. Crystal then insists that he sees the hostel.

When Crystal introduces Gilbert to the two families, they are immediately suspicious of his motives for being there. They can tell where he comes from, by the subtle sounds in his accent, and they are worried. They are not used to someone coming into the hostel just to hang out and speak with them. Gilbert talks to the children and he is surprised when Crystal encourages them to talk in English.

Gilbert speaks to their teacher when he arrives and asks how well they are doing in his classes. He has many questions for the teacher about their learning potential. Gilbert is overwhelmed by how absolutely normal these children are.

Gilbert stays for the whole day at the hostel and talks for hours, especially to the twins and the two black brothers of the albino girl. Before he leaves he takes the albino children aside and asks them individually some questions.

First he asks the twins their names.

'I'm Kunwa,' says the twin boy, 'but Mama Crystal calls me Justice.'

'I'm Doto,' says the twin girl, 'but they call me Hope.'

Then the third answers 'I'm Amina.'

'If you could have anything in the world, what would you like to have . . . to make your life better?'

Two of the children jump up and down, in childish anticipation of their own thoughts. After a moment or so, Amina requests a white doll with long hair so she can weave it into plats. Justice asks for a machine that has games on it. Hope, the twin girl is silent and does not answer.

'What would you like most in the world, Hope?' Gilbert asks her directly.

'She won't tell you', says her twin brother, 'she wants to go home to our village'.

'Why don't you go home?'

Hope speaks out. 'My mother is afraid, but I'm not. I'm not a chicken to be sacrificed, or to be kept in a pen. I'm a human being. I want to go home and live like before in my village. I want to go back to my school and play with my friends.'

In the evening Gilbert walks back to Crystal's to spend the night. He relaxes in the empty room she has offered him. He still has his schoolteacher's talent for taking notes and he fills an exercise book of his observations. He is moved by his experience in the hostel and adds more notes. If people could only interact with these children, he writes, the more the myths surrounding them would disappear.

Gilbert talks to Crystal after dinner about the future for the families at the hostel. She accepts there's need at certain times for such a hostel, but she sees the habits of the mothers and the comfort level they have grown into . . . as a real problem in them ever moving on.

'They have living conditions which are better than what they have at home. Their work is simply to keep the place clean. They have a good diet, but they also have limitations in what they can do. They don't have much interaction with other people and the children especially are being brought up in isolation. It's not good enough.'

'But isn't it the same for all those who are born with disabilities, they also need help from the state.'

'Yes, but help to the disabled is aimed at increasing their choices in life not limiting them. Albinos have only two choices in the matter. To stay here, or to go home and face the people who have run them out of their village, off their land, for being born with a skin condition.'

'It will be safer back in villages once people change their attitudes.'

'Exactly Gilbert! That's what I'm saying. But how long will that take? Tell me who is working on that problem. We should be giving them all the support they need. Not creating refugees out of people with a dermatology problem, if you forgive this expression.'

That night Crystal wakes Gilbert at about midnight. It is a full moon and she does not want to waken her boys. Gilbert is startled, but after dressing quietly he follows Crystal. She takes his hand and leads him out her house and through a few deserted lanes past the clinic.

'There is something I want to show you.' She whispers.

'Where?'

'By the river.'

After a ten minute walk Crystal signals for Gilbert to slow down and be quiet and to follow closely behind her. She creeps though a thicket of succulent marsh plants. There is a clearing ahead and she opens the reeds to show Gilbert a muddy beach that runs in a gentle slope into the river.

'The twins told me that they come here once a month on a full moon.'

Gilbert looks over Crystal's shoulder and sees five children playing at the water's edge. They are splashing each other but are otherwise quiet. They are naked except for a set of school-issue white shorts. A mother is sitting watching them and breastfeeding her two year old boy in her lap. In the moon-light the water shimmers like silver and the wet children all look the same colour. They swim out a little, and turn back. One turns over stones with a stick looking for fresh water crabs. There are a few distant hippo roars from down stream that go unnoticed.

Out of another clearing, the second mother arrives and startles them. She brings a kettle full of milk tea and six metal cups. They relax and resume their play. No one sees either Crystal or Gilbert sitting in the bushes watching the group.

Back at the house Gilbert says nothing about this encounter. Crystal asks him if he will return to Mwanza in the morning.

'No, there is somewhere else I want to visit, before I go back.'

——————➤◆◆◆◆————

In Tanzania's Town courts, things are conducted different compared to the neighbouring Commonwealth countries. There is little pageantry or ceremony to the judge's entrance. Here the early independent government outlawed any type of tribal dress in its law courts, including the English-tribal High Court Judge's wig and robe.

Here in Mwanza the judge wears a Nyerere suit and within these walls, it is the laws of the land that provide the criteria for a judgement of conduct, not the beliefs of individual tribal traditions as to what is right and what is wrong. Here there are laws that are understood and that are strong because they are also internationally accepted. People are taught to respect the law, because these laws have become the basis of a national identity and pride.

A few hundred miles to the East in Arusha, the United Nation's International Criminal Court also sits regularly to prosecute crimes against humanity. The most notorious criminals on the African continent have appeared here, but the list is long of those who have yet to appear before it. The commitment and the resources needed to enforce the law are regularly sighted as part of the continent's failure. There are those who have so far escaped prosecution from the genocide in Rwanda; the massacres in Congo; the blatant abuse of power in Zimbabwe, Sudan and Kenya. Leaders kept in power by ancient loyalties rather than an adherence to international laws.

Ignorance of the law is no excuse for citizens in Tanzania, the same as in every country. Freedom and justice within the law, is at the core of the country's political agenda as it is with every member state of the United Nations. But judges can be like doctors who spend years studying their trade then find themselves swamped with patients with minor preventable illnesses. It is rare that either a doctor or a judge is called on to apply all the professional knowledge they have learned. It is rare but finally there is a chance for the judge in Mwanza to apply all his understanding of the law and to administer justice to a man called Kaka Damu.

The judge takes his seat in a courthouse where the fans strain to keep the temperature down. The public gallery, lined with dark African wood, is full. In the dock is Kaka Damu on trial for a series of crimes against the people, including the murder of Glen Chapman.

Here the prosecution has no surveillance tapes, no wiretaps, no written confessions and no forensic samples to be called into evidence in the trial. Most evidence will be hear-say, made all the more convincing if two or more people hear and say the same thing.

Today is the day of reckoning for Kaka Damu. He has been brought to trial in a last ditch attempt to convict him. He and his supporters are expecting him to be released immediately after the jury deliberate. He knows how weak the prosecution's case against him is. He believes no one dare come forward to condemn him and there is no disputing the fact that his security guard Juma confessed to the killing of Glen Chapman and the Maasai in Kaka's home, before his death.

Kaka's lawyer has schooled him in his conduct for the courtroom. He is not to make any outrageous or aggressive statements against albinos in public. He needs to stay focused and appear humble in court. He knows there is a country-wide interest in the case and there is a lot of hostility towards him from the political and educated elite. His lawyer also knows that Kaka's accusers need to follow the letter of the law or else they themselves can be accused of bending rules and beliefs to suit their will. He has been told that the People have a new witness but at present this witness's identity is being kept secret for his or her own safety. And as often happens on the actual day of a trial, no one has yet appeared in the courtroom.

Professor Graham informed Pam on her Facebook link that the trial was eminent. She now sits in the front row of the public gallery along with the Reverend Mosha, looking down at the back of the head of the man she believes killed her husband. She has flown thirteen thousand kilometres to see justice done. Azaad and Crystal are sitting at the back of the room and they acknowledge Pam with a wave.

Kaka's head is shaved and he is shackled in chains that are almost too heavy to lift. He is confident within himself, but he is uncomfortable in this environment. His lawyer's guidance has made him aware he can be judged on his demeanour as much as his words. He has never been in such a room, so packed with richly dressed people before. It takes all his concentration not to turn and stare everyone in the eye.

Pam holds a white bag with a red cross on the side in her lap. She turns to ask the Reverend why he insisted that she bring this bag from Canada and that she should display it in court.

'Why the medical kit?'

'I'll tell you later.'

'It's so crowded in here, who is supposed to see it?'

'Kaka Damu, be patient Pam.'

When proceedings begin, it does not take long for the prosecution to give an elaborate description of the recent environment in which albino children, albino adults, albino parents, albino grandparents, albino citizens, their caregivers and their families are living in. This situation has not always existed here in Tanzania he states. The tangible atmosphere of fear, the geographic hostility shown to this group is relatively new and can no longer be tolerated. At the core of this unacceptable situation is a dangerous and unusual prejudice, promoted by people like Kaka Damu. He and his like exploit the ignorance and prejudices of uneducated people; they are essentially at the centre of the supply and demand for human body parts as charms and medicine. People like Kaka Damu have inflicted indescribable atrocities on those brothers and sisters among us we call albino. The prosecution at this stage does not mention Glen Chapman.

'However,' the prosecutor goes on, 'people gathered here today are not only going to convict Kaka on crimes against humanity, despite there being many similarities to the cases that are heard in Arusha. The prosecution wants to prove today, beyond doubt that Kaka Damu was personally responsible for the death of an albino infant and that he is also closely linked to the murder of the Canadian researcher Glen Chapman. I will then ask you, the jury, for a guilty verdict and for the death penalty. This is the only verdict that can come out of these proceedings and the only way to ensure justice and a message to people like Kaka Damu is delivered.'

Almost on cue with this statement, Gilbert arrives at the back of the court with a village midwife at his side. They push forward and take two seats on the empty witness bench. Kaka turns his head to look at the midwife and stares. She clasps tightly to a crucifix she is holding in her hand and she looks away from the Shaman. Kaka recognises Gilbert and then stares menacingly towards him. Gilbert Wananchi stares confidently back.

———— ›‹◊›‹ ————

Gilbert discovered the midwife at his local village church, by chance . . . by luck, he would later say. She had become a recent convert to Christianity, prompted in part by the treatment of the albino child she had helped to deliver. It was by coincidence that the subject of 'a mother's choice to have and to keep a child', came up during a baptism. Someone in the congregation began talking about albinos. Gilbert overheard a woman say it should also be the mother's choice **no matter what** the father said or what physical condition the child was in. Gilbert was amazed to hear the mid-wife suddenly tell the story of her experience and appear to implicate Kaka Damu in the child's death and disposal.

This conversation was like an answer to his prayers. The midwife gave Gilbert details of the family she worked for and even described to him the exact location where she buried the umbilical chord and the afterbirth of the child.

Gilbert passed on this information to the Reverend who in turn approached the prosecutor to charge Kaka Damu with the infant's death along with pursuing the charge against him for killing Glen Chapman. The Reverend spent days talking to the midwife and assuring her that the evil spells of witch doctors like Kaka were no match for the powers of the Lord Jesus Christ. He assured her he would stand by her if she came to testify in court.

When the Reverend heard that Pam was coming from Canada, he asked her specifically to bring a medical bag with a large red cross on it, to bring the bag into the courtroom and to keep it in plain sight. If the defendant chose to stare at people around the courtroom he wanted that logo of the cross to be visible.

⟫◉⟪

The defence lawyer stands and makes a short half hearted statement about Kaka Damu being a respected member of his community. That he has no previous convictions for any crimes. That his client has been kept in custody for a ridiculous length of time, for over a year; that the prosecutor's case is weak and that the defendant should be set free that very afternoon.

The prosecution tells the court that they have simply taken the time needed to be thorough in their investigation. There is new evidence implicating Kaka Damu in the brutal murder of an albino child. That there are strong suspicions this practice has been going on for some years and was indeed the type of sacrifice that was interrupted by the Canadian researcher Glen Chapman, and which caused his death at the hands of the defendant Damu and his henchmen. The prosecutor goes on to state that not all albino deaths are related to the practice of sacrificial offering, but in this case there is a witness and strong evidence to support the Prosecution's case.

When Kaka Damu is finally brought to the stand for questioning, he looks confused and frightened. There is a brief swearing in ceremony which seems senseless to him. Kaka is asked to promise, 'To tell the truth, the whole truth and nothing but the truth, so help me . . . God.'

He stares at the midwife and he recognises her. She does not look back at him. He also sees one white woman in the front row of the public balcony and he stares at her. She stares right back unflinching into his eyes. He notices a white medical bag in her lap, with a large red cross on it.

The Reverend's advice to the Prosecutor is to keep questioning Kaka Damu on the disappearance of the albino child, and to suggest to him that modern science can help the court identify the buried umbilical cord of a child and determine that the child was in fact albino. Kaka Damu is asked to either produce the albino child he took from the midwife or admit that he and his gang killed the child. In the Reverend's scheme, it is modern science that will scare the Shaman into a confession. They can only hint they have proof that the child was an albino and that it was alive when Kaka Damu took it, but they know Kaka will need to *make up* a story about where the child is now. They suspect Kaka will have limitations when faced with covering the truth. The Reverend is being creative. He is in fact desperate, he knows that the umbilical cord has long disappeared but he thinks these theatrics are needed to unsettle Kaka and secure justice. The Prosecutor looks up to the gallery and mentions modern forensic kits as he approaches Kaka with his last question.

'Where is the albino child you took charge of from this mid-wife on April 17th 2009?'

In the end, none of the Reverend's theatrics is necessary. Once the prosecutor asks Kaka where the albino child is, it's as if he can't lie. Kaka forgets his lawyer's advice and rants threats at the midwife. He cannot accept that this stupid woman's talk will convict him, will keep him in prison and could lead to his execution. He calls the prosecutors monkeys and showers curses on them. He says he cannot believe he is being denied his freedom because of the death of '*zero zeros*'. (worthless albinos) He admits openly to killing the child and just stops short of actually describing how he did it. He boasts how thankful his customers were. He goes on about this happening every day somewhere in the country; that it is necessary in these parts to cull the albino population regularly, that only the strong are wanted and only the strong survive.

This out-burst is enough to convict Kaka Damu. The jury find him guilty within an hour. The judge then sentences Kaka Damu, in a most dramatic fashion, to be taken to a place of solitude and to be hanged by the neck until he is dead. The sentence is to be carried out as soon as possible but definitely within one lunar month.

———✦———

After the verdict Azaad and Crystal meet Pam outside the courthouse. There are hugs and relief that this phase of the proceeding is over and justice has prevailed, if not fully in the case of Glen. History will forever tie Glen's death with that of a killer of albino children. Pam gives the medical kit to Crystal. They seem surprised that the verdict and sentencing has come so swiftly. Pam wishes the newly engaged couple all the best in the future. The Reverend Mosha is seen as the hero of the moment, but he heaps praise on Gilbert Wananchi as the man whom the Lord guided to do his work. The Reverend offers to marry Azaad and Crystal at his church if Azaad is willing to convert to Christianity.

As people leave the trial, many notice the presence of three vultures sitting on the roof of the courthouse. Several comments are made as to the significance of this. How many J's were there, someone asks? More meaningful interpretations are given to a random occurrence, another local superstition is fuelled; a fertile crop of rumours spread and the phenomenon known as Apophenia takes on a little more life in Tanzania. Another twist to the story is in the making.

———✦———

People who live under the Selander Bridge now say that Kaka Damu took nearly fifteen minutes to die. That when the rope was cut both his body and the rope turned into a snake and slithered away.

According to the prison guards however, they pulled a hood over his head in the cell before walking him to the gallows, so that he could not stare at anyone and give them the evil eye. Some guards put bees wax in their ears so that they could not hear any curses that he might utter. Although his body twitched for a long time, like one of the thousands of chickens he had sacrificed, witnesses believe that sixty seconds after he dropped from the gallows Kaka Damu was dead. One last realisation may have occurred to him before he dropped, as a null hypothesis message from his ancestors; that there was in fact no connection between killing an albino child and reaping the rewards of good luck. In fact it was quite the opposite outcome; there was a most definite cause and effect between killing another human being and the punishment society imposes for such a crime.

Kaka's body was buried near Juma along with the rope and all the other content of his prison cell. His grave was then cemented over within a day of the burial, so no one could dig up his body parts and sell them as charms.

Kaka Damu's father heard of the execution after it took place. He was not allowed to collect any remains of his son, nor was he permitted to erect any gravestone or remembrance to him. He did however make a trip to the baobab tree near Kaka's compound and stick Kaka's lion headband to the tree with a thorn. This was all that the tree spirits demanded and it was enough for him.

Gilbert escorted the midwife back to his village and on the way he visited the Chapman hostel at Dawakubwa. The midwife was impressed by what she saw at the hostel and has since agreed to help with Crystal's work there. She plans to take up residence near the Dawakubwa clinic. Crystal believes that she is still too fearful to return to Kaka's home village.

————— ⊶◉⊷ —————

Near the Selanda bridge in Dar es Salaam, there is a young priestess, who is rumoured to be the daughter of Kaka Damu. She arrived some time back with a man called John to live and work beside his friend Cheetah. The three of them provide services and more, to a host of workers, street vendors, builders and beggars in the city. However there is a difference in the rhetoric of this priestess. She tells people she has had good luck because she saved the live of an albino child. She promotes the adoration of albinos for their uniqueness and the good luck they seem to have provided her. Whenever potions or advice is needed this young woman Nyanzu delivers powerful medicine, not from the bones of sacrifices but from the herbs and spices so readily available along the coast. She has been known to cure Aids and to put curses on men who assault women. It is believed she can make men bald or infertile with a touch. Some people have seen her walk down Toure Drive in the evening with a flock of bats following her. If she touches your car the engine stops. And if you touch her, your arms will grow hairy. She can kill a tree by spitting on it. She has the stare of a snake and if you look into her eyes you will go blind.

In Dar she has the potential to be very influential but she risks both the wrath as well as the support of people who believe in her powers to cure illness . . . as a healer if she succeeds and as a witch if she does not.

———◉———

There is a brief silence. After ten weeks the Professor has finished his series of talks. There is an outbreak of movement in the lecture hall. Some students at the back begin to talk and stretch their arms. The Professor sees some raise their hands. He realises he has concluded today's talk early so he answers a few questions.

'What happened to the albino twins?' a girl asks.

'In Dawakubwa the albino twins, Hope and Justice are still living in their protective hostel. The others have moved back home, but the time is not quite right for the family of the twins. Out of the sunlight, and playing in the full moonlight the twins go to the river for a few nights every month. No one knows they are there. It is still safer that way for the time being. I've seen this all for myself.'

'Have you ever spoken to Nyanzu?'

'Yes, I have collected this story on good account from all those involved'.

'Does she have any potions to help pass exams?'

After some laughter the Professor resumes.

'If she does, it's not likely to involve albino children. I want you to understand from this talk that Glen Chapman died in exactly the same manner as so many albino children have suffered over the past few years in Tanzania.'

'Being an albino from another country, I always considered my condition fairly unique. I realise that it's not so unique to be born albino here. I expected to see strength in numbers that you might find with sizable minorities anywhere in society. But because of gaps in both education and opportunity, like many other minorities, albinos have very little political clout.'

'Let me say that any albino death causes outrage in the albino community, it causes frustration in the law enforcement agencies, it causes indignation and horror among politicians and the general public. Yet, I've not met anyone with the confidence to declare it will not happen again.'

'But what can we do?'

'If you just want to get on with your life then carry on, study and survive any way you can. But if you take up any job with social responsibility and if you love your country, do not ignore some of the research methods and studies that exist to help you see what your country consists of. Aside from its beautiful landscape, its friendly and fun loving people there are a host of social injustices that can only be corrected if you understand their cause. These studies are freely available to those who want them. The Government, the UN and many other institutions compile these for public use as well as for themselves. They help you form a more accurate personal opinion, they are more revealing than a politician's promises; a journalists sound-bite and far more comprehensive than a novelist's imagination.'

Tanzania has come a long way very quickly. We have more qualified people than ever before. Surely it's only a matter of time before this practice dies out?

'Yes, Tanzania is changing and will soon have a population of some sixty million people . . . twice as many as when most of today's leaders were teenagers. It is you, the young, who are discovering what social issues really need to be tackled . . . at a rate never before discovered. We have not had such a wealth of scientific and cultural information impacting on such numbers of youth at the same time. Beliefs that once seemed sacred and local are now seen to be less unique and powerful when compared to the multitude of other beliefs out there. It is this ability to compare that make this generation unique.'

*'Things will only begin to change for the better if you become an informed part of that change. We need take action if we do not want to double the problems along with the population. Among all the choices and comparisons you face . . . be sure **not** to make the mistake of putting your faith into random events that are **unrelated**, and try to understand better those that are **related**. Do not believe in a connection when there is none. (I.e. that good luck comes from the possession of albino bones) and try and understand some of the real causes and effects that you are surrounded by. (i.e. that the lack of clean water causes illness and death. That a lecturer has a limitation on how long he can talk and spread the word.)'*

' I will not answer any more questions today. But you can if you want contact me on-line'.

Professor Michael Graham then takes the drum and hits it twice to mark the end of his series of talks. The students stand and there is a round of appreciative applause. When the Professor tells the group it is the drum used on the fatal night that Glen Chapman died there is a shiver of discomfort among his audience. He lifts his dark glasses along with his wide brimmed hat and leaves the lecture hall. The challenge of another bright sunny day awaits his attention.

THE END

Lightning Source UK Ltd.
Milton Keynes UK
UKOW051222290612

195207UK00003B/59/P